PRAISE FOR VICTOR

The Secret Witness

"A red-hot suspenser aimed at readers for whom a single serial killer just isn't enough."

—*Kirkus Reviews*

An Unreliable Truth

"A straight-A legal thriller with a final scene as satisfying as it is disturbing."

—*Kirkus Reviews*

A Killer's Wife

An Amazon Best Book of the Month: Mystery, Thriller & Suspense

"*A Killer's Wife* is a high-stakes legal thriller loaded with intense courtroom drama, compelling characters, and surprising twists that will keep you turning the pages at breakneck speed."

—T. R. Ragan, *New York Times* bestselling author

"Exquisitely paced and skillfully crafted, *A Killer's Wife* delivers a wicked psychological suspense wrapped around a hypnotic legal thriller. One cleverly designed twist after another kept me saying, 'I did not see that coming.'"

—Steven Konkoly, *Wall Street Journal* bestselling author

"A gripping thriller that doesn't let up for a single page. Surprising twists with a hero you care about. I read the whole book in one sitting!"
—Chad Zunker, bestselling author of *An Equal Justice*

THE
DECEIVING
LOOK

OTHER TITLES BY VICTOR METHOS

Shepard & Gray Series

The Secret Witness

The Grave Singer

Desert Plains Series

A Killer's Wife

Crimson Lake Road

An Unreliable Truth

Neon Lawyer Series

The Neon Lawyer

Mercy

Other Titles

The Hallows

The Shotgun Lawyer

A Gambler's Jury

An Invisible Client

THE
DECEIVING
LOOK

VICTOR METHOS

Text copyright © 2024 by Victor Methos
All rights reserved.

Published by Thomas & Mercer, Seattle

www.apub.com

Amazon, the Amazon logo, and Thomas & Mercer are trademarks of Amazon.com, Inc., or its affiliates.

ISBN-13: 9781662516245 (paperback)
ISBN-13: 9781662516238 (digital)

Cover design by Faceout Studio, Molly von Borstel
Cover image: © At World's Edge, © AndreyUG, © Realstock / Shutterstock; © Marcos Appelt / ArcAngel

Printed in the United States of America

The heart of another is a dark forest, always, no matter how close it has been to one's own.

—*Willa Cather*

1

Solomon Shepard stood under the morgue's dim yellow light, his pulse echoing as he approached the cold gurney.

Beneath a gray sheet, a lifeless body was hidden, with only dainty painted toenails and an intrusive toe tag in sight. The air was thick, carrying a nauseating mix of damp latex and bleach.

The soft tingle of a bell sent chills down Solomon's spine. In the eighteenth and nineteenth centuries, coroners would tie bells to the cadavers' ankles to prevent accidental burial of the living, and the sound made Solomon wonder what might be lurking in the shadows.

The morgue was far colder than even the icy weather outside, and Solomon exhaled heavily, watching as his breath formed a ghostly mist in the air.

The sound of another bell echoed through the silence.

Solomon knew he was alone down here, but the sound made him turn anyway, his heart pounding even faster as he tried to identify the source of the noise. At this time of night, everyone had gone home, and Solomon had snuck down to the morgue, his heart racing with anticipation.

The door to the morgue had been open, and he'd overheard several ME's assistants joking that there was no reason to lock it. No one wanted to go into a morgue, and no one ever came out.

Solomon looked over to the bodies lined up against the walls, all covered in gray sheets.

Tomorrow, there would be a final check of their information, and then they would be stored in the fridge: a giant metal box with shelves. The body Solomon had come down here for was one of these.

He could have revealed each face beneath the sheets, but fear stopped him. He didn't want to see her changed by death without preparing himself.

Solomon fixed his eyes on the gray sheet that covered the body before him. He could tell it was large even without looking underneath, and the stench of death was suffocating. He forced himself to approach the gurney and read the name and cause of death on the tag: Nicolas Williams, dead from a self-inflicted shotgun wound to the face. Solomon was grateful he hadn't pulled back the sheet first.

Moving on to the next body, he noticed it was slimmer, almost delicate. The tag read Bethany Castle, a young woman who had been murdered three days ago. The details of her death were gruesome—twelve stab wounds on her torso while almost decapitated—and Solomon wondered if it was a domestic murder. Most young women who were murdered were killed by their husbands or boyfriends in their own homes.

Another bell echoed in the morgue. Solomon's head whipped around. The room seemed darker, the smell more pungent, a mix of formaldehyde and bleach that threatened to make him gag. The ringing came again, closer to the door.

He wanted to know what was making the sound, but the draw to the bodies was too much. He had to see her with his own eyes.

He moved across the room to the two bodies lined up against the far wall. One of the gray sheets had a faint wet stain along the chest in the shape of a Y. Solomon checked the tag: Stephen Brown, who had died in a hit-and-run, suffering skull fractures and internal bleeding.

His heart pounding, Solomon turned to the last body, feeling the air grow thinner so that it was hard to breathe. He inhaled deeply and pulled back the sheet, only there was no one there.

A hand grabbed his shoulder, and he spun around. He was met with a pale, cracking corpse with dirty-blonde hair highlighted pink and falling out in clumps. The mouth opened, and blood flowed over the lips.

Solomon jolted awake and screamed.

"Son of a biscuit!" the Uber driver shouted, nearly losing control of the car.

The tires screeched as Solomon flew against the door, his cane tangled in his legs. The sedan came to a sudden stop, and the driver sat motionless, breathing heavily. His fingers were wrapped tightly over the steering wheel, and his chest was heaving.

Solomon struggled to find his voice, his heart still racing. Finally, he managed to say, "Sorry."

The driver took two deep breaths and replied calmly, "If you could not fall asleep the rest of the ride, that'd be great."

The car pulled up to the main gate of his home, out in the middle of nowhere, the nearest neighbors miles away. The first time he'd been here, he was immediately struck by the wild and rugged landscape. The sprawling estate was surrounded by thickets of untamed grass and patches of dense shrubbery that seemed to encroach from all angles. The darkness tonight was made even more ominous by the bare, shadowy trees looming over the property.

"You live way out here in this giant house by yourself?"

Solomon gazed up at the silhouette of the house. "It's better I'm alone. Thanks for the ride."

As the car pulled away, Solomon was left in the eerie silence. On quiet summer nights, he often kept his bedroom window open so he could listen to the soothing sound of the water as it flowed through the rocky bed of a nearby stream. But now, as the winter had taken hold, the stream was silenced, its gentle flow replaced by a frozen expanse.

The darkness seemed to surround him like a living thing, and he felt an icy finger run down his spine at what might be lurking beyond his sight.

As he punched in the code to his gate and went inside, he couldn't shake the image of the corpse he had seen, and felt a shudder run through him.

2

Billie Gray woke to the sound of footsteps outside her bedroom.

She glanced at the alarm clock and saw that it was just past 3:00 a.m. Her grandmother always called this time "the devil's hour," claiming that ghosts and demons were stronger then. Billie found her grandmother's folklore amusing, but she wondered if there are things in the world that are older than people, and that haven't left.

She reached for the Glock 9 mm that lay on her nightstand, a weapon she had never kept there until earlier this year. Her ex, Dax, had become increasingly obsessed and harassing, forcing her to take out a stalking injunction against him. But the day after the injunction had been granted, she received over one hundred texts, Facebook messages, and voice mails from him. As a law enforcement officer, she knew that there came a point in every stalking case when the law was powerless. When the stalker no longer feared incarceration, it became a waiting game.

Billie let her eyes adjust to the darkness before she got out of bed. She looked down at herself and realized she was wearing only underwear and an oversize T-shirt. She couldn't have looked less intimidating if she tried. She slipped on a pair of jeans that was lying on the floor and picked up her 9 mm.

Deputy Aaron Watkins stuffed a sandwich slathered in chocolate-hazelnut spread into his mouth, chewing loudly. His partner, Dave Garcia, watched him with a mixture of disgust and amazement.

"What?" Aaron asked through a mouthful of food.

"Did your girlfriend make that for you?" Dave asked, nodding toward the sandwich.

"No, I made it myself. Why?"

"It's like something a child would eat when their parents aren't home," Dave said.

"You're just jealous that I don't have to worry about maintaining a girlish figure like you and I still get the ladies," Aaron said, patting his ample belly.

"Whatever." Dave flexed his muscular biceps. "That's what two hours a day at the gym will do. You know you're welcome to join me."

"Waste of time," Aaron said dismissively. "We go when we go, and two hours a day jumping around won't change that."

Dave smirked, a sly glint in his eyes. "When you're clutching your chest at fifty, I'll remember this chat," he said.

Aaron was staring out the windshield at the sheriff's house, where they had been assigned to keep watch throughout the night. The sheriff's ex had threatened to kill her and then himself, and the department wasn't taking any chances.

"This is what you get when you have a woman in charge," Aaron said.

"I don't know, Billie's not so bad. Gets things done like her old man did."

"She's an ice queen, and one day it's going to bite her in the ass." He licked his fingers. "Hey, why don't women need to wear a watch?"

"Why?"

"Because the stove has a clock."

Dave shook his head with a chuckle but looked back out at the house. He listened to his partner chew for a moment before asking, "What are we going to do if this guy actually shows up?"

"We'll ask him to leave," Aaron said, smacking his lips.

"He's insane. He's not going to listen to us."

"He will. At least the first time."

"And what if he comes armed and looking for more than just a talk?"

"Well, that's why I . . ." Aaron trailed off, his attention suddenly drawn to something outside the windshield. "What was that?"

"What'd you see?" Dave asked, leaning forward to look.

"I think I saw someone moving inside the house," Aaron said, his hand sliding to his holster.

Billie glanced out into the hallway, which was dark and quiet. She opened the flashlight function on her phone and shone it down the corridor.

Keeping most of her body hidden behind the doorframe, she peeked around the other side of the hallway and saw nothing. She then stepped out, her bare feet sinking into the soft rug that covered the wood floor. As she made her way down the hall, she flipped off the safety of her weapon.

The kitchen smelled like lime-scented cleaner, but it was still a bit musty. She flicked on the light and saw a half-empty glass of wine on the counter. She didn't remember leaving it out, but the sleeping pills she had been taking lately were affecting her in strange ways when mixed with alcohol.

She crossed the kitchen and entered the living room. The blinds were rattling softly from a breeze, and she realized that the window was open. She must have left it open; the alarm was supposed to turn on once everything was secure, which meant that her alarm had been off all night. "Stupid," she muttered to herself.

She closed the window and returned to the kitchen. After placing her weapon on the dining table, she poured the remaining wine from the glass down the drain and rinsed it off. She stared at her reflection in the smooth surface of the glass. The pink strands of hair that mixed with her blonde stood out more than anything else. Her face looked twisted and malformed, a grotesque mirror of what she felt on the inside.

A knock on her door made her heart jump into her throat. "Who is it?" she yelled.

"Sheriff? It's me, Aaron Watkins," a muffled voice said from behind the front door.

She went to the door and saw one of her deputies standing there with chocolate smeared on either side of his mouth.

"I saw someone moving around and thought I would check on you."

"I'm all right, thank you," she replied. "I guess I left a window open and the rattle of the blinds woke me up."

He raised an eyebrow. "You don't remember leaving it open?"

"No, I'm usually careful to check these things," she said. "But I must have been distracted."

She didn't want to tell him about the pills and alcohol because she didn't want anyone to know about her struggles with insomnia.

Most of her thoughts at night were consumed by two men in her life—one who had said he never wanted to see her again, and the other who had threatened to kill her because she refused to see him.

I sure know how to pick 'em.

"Mind if I have a look around, Sheriff?" Aaron asked, gesturing toward the house. Billie glanced behind him and saw another of her deputies parked in a cruiser across the street.

"No, really, it's fine," she said, feeling a bit annoyed. "I hate that you two have to spend the night sitting out there anyway."

"Better safe than sorry," he replied. "How would it look if you got attacked and I was sitting right out there."

Billie watched his face, and his words didn't match his eyes or expression. There was something almost gleeful about it. He knew she was frightened and he enjoyed it.

Billie sighed, but she knew he was right. The district attorney, Roger Lynch, had insisted that she have a unit assigned to protect her. She suspected that it had more to do with how bad the optics would be if something happened to her on Roger's watch than with actual concern for her safety.

"I can protect myself, Aaron, thanks," she said. "But if it means that much to you, go ahead." She opened the door all the way so that he could come inside.

Watkins nodded and started to wander through the house, flipping on lights as he went. Billie went into the kitchen, trying to shake off the unease that had settled over her. She didn't like having someone else in her house, even if it was one of her own deputies.

"You want some coffee?" Billie said, going to her coffee maker on the counter.

"I'll take a cup if you're making it," Aaron replied.

Billie mumbled to herself, "Sure, won't be going back to sleep anyway."

She sat at the kitchen table and let Aaron finish poking around the house. She knew that no one was there because Dax would wait until she was isolated and alone before making a move.

Aaron came back into the kitchen, his thumbs tucked into his utility belt. "All clear," he said. He picked up his cup of coffee and took a sip. "Good coffee. Thanks."

Billie was about to ask him to sit when the small radio on his shoulder crackled to life. "422," a voice said.

Aaron pressed the call button. "422, copy," he responded.

"We have a 10-98 and deputies are requesting backup," the voice said.

"Backup for a suicide?" Aaron asked.

"Roger that."

Billie took a sip of her coffee as she listened. The only reasons someone would request backup at a suicide were if more than a suicide was suspected or if the suicide was someone who would receive media attention. A celebrity or politician. Something where every move the police made would be scrutinized. Within the department, they called these cases "red carpets" because, before computers took over, clerks would organize the documents in any cases that got media attention into red folders.

"Where is that?" Billie said.

"Dispatch, what's the location of the 10-98?" Aaron said into the radio.

"I'm showing 15214 Redondo," the voice on the radio replied. "The victim has been identified as Dennis Yang."

Billie's stomach tightened when she heard the name. She had known Mayor Yang for years, and the thought of him being the victim of a suicide was shocking.

"Dispatch, come again," Aaron said. "Sounds like you said Dennis Yang. You're not talking about Mayor Yang, are you?"

"Affirmative, that is Mayor Yang's address," the voice on the radio replied.

Billie quickly finished her coffee, hoping to ward off the effects of the sleeping pills that still coursed through her system. "I need you to drive me down there," she said to Aaron. "I need to see this for myself."

3

Billie pulled up to Dennis Yang's sprawling property in the early hours of the morning, her sleek black suit feeling too formal. As a woman in law enforcement and the county sheriff, she was always hyperaware of how she was perceived by her colleagues. She had to navigate the treacherous political waters of her job with care. Female officers looked to her for guidance on how to handle unwanted advances from male colleagues, and she was keenly aware of the constant scrutiny she faced from her subordinates, who were quick to label her as "too emotional" at the slightest provocation. But Billie knew that emotions are an inescapable part of the human experience, and trying to deny or suppress them was a fool's errand. She thought back to who had told her that, and it saddened her to think about him.

The SIS unit's black SUV was already parked outside Yang's house, and a young man in the driver's seat was scribbling notes on a tablet. Uniformed officers were milling about, questioning groggy neighbors dressed in luxurious silk gowns and pajamas.

Dave Garcia parked the cruiser with Billie in the back seat, and she stepped out.

The front door of Yang's house was open, and her detectives and the SIS unit had already begun their investigation.

As she strode in, she caught a few discreet glances from the deputies, their smirks swiftly followed by hushed whispers exchanged among them. Although she loathed the perception of being under protection, she understood her vulnerability. If she were to stubbornly refuse assistance, she might be caught off guard.

Billie made her way over to a deputy standing near the home, Mazie Heaton, a relatively recent hire who had graduated from POST only a few months ago. Mazie appeared in her standard beige-and-brown sheriff's department uniform, her vibrant red hair cut into a spiky and sharp style. The uniform hung from her petite frame, a stark contrast to the boldness of her hair. As she walked, the spiky tips seemed to sway with each step, adding an extra bit of flair to her already confident demeanor. Her arms and wrists bore tattoos, a look Billie sported when she was younger, though now she tended to cover them up with long sleeves.

Billie's mind wandered to her excursion to Florida last year for a law enforcement conference, where she had planned to relax on the beach and read, and then have fun going out and enjoying the nightlife. In reality, she had holed up in her hotel room and watched true crime shows on TV.

A friend of hers who was also at the conference, a lieutenant with the Miami-Dade Police Department, had told her to come by the police academy to watch the graduation ceremony of the year's class. Insisting that she needed to mingle more and spend less time watching documentaries in a hotel room.

Feeling a pinch of loneliness, Billie attended the local police academy graduation, where she had watched Mazie Heaton walk across the stage to receive her certification. One of the captains had smacked Mazie's rear end as she passed. Without missing a beat, Mazie spun around and punched him in the face.

Despite her best efforts to remain composed, Billie had burst out laughing.

Clearly, Mazie wouldn't be becoming an officer in Florida. So, Billie made her a deal: come to Utah and become a deputy for me, and we'll pay for your moving expenses. Mazie took the chance and moved out six months ago.

Mazie saw her and left the detectives she was speaking with.

"I didn't know you were coming down," Mazie said as they walked across the lawn leading to the home.

Billie studied her, finding none of the judgment that frequently clouded the gazes of other deputies. Mazie, unlike them, didn't perceive accepting protection in the face of death threats as a sign of weakness. "I just happened to be in the neighborhood."

"Have you heard who it is?"

"I did."

"I knew the mayor. I mean, I met him a couple times."

"Trust me, Mazie, every female employee of the county met him a couple times. He made a point to get to know only the women. Before he decided not to run again, I think he had something like five harassment suits against him."

Several neighbors had gathered around, milling about in curiosity, but the media outlets hadn't yet picked up on it, so there was no police tape around the house. A small trick Billie had instituted to have the department save on police tape. That, and seemingly a hundred other little things, allowed her to stretch the department budget enough to have some surplus and be able to hire more deputies. Like Mazie.

They entered the grand front door of the sprawling mansion, and the air inside was thick with the scent of expensive furniture polish and lingering cigar smoke. A forensic tech greeted them with a box of plastic booties and gloves, which they quickly donned before going on.

The ceilings towered high above them, at least thirty feet, and Billie wondered why anyone would need such lofty heights.

As they made their way through the home, passing by the opulent living room and the elegant dining area, Billie caught a glimpse of a pickleball court and a full-size swimming pool through the sliding glass doors by the kitchen. She knew that Dennis had acquired the house and all its luxuries in his divorce, which had been particularly bitter. Rumors had circulated that his health had deteriorated from a degenerative spinal disease, and his wife had left him after growing tired of taking care of him. In a cruel twist, she had emptied the house of her belongings and left him a note on the fridge, telling him that she had run off with someone half his age and was leaving the country. The divorce that followed had been messy, with Dennis's affairs and harassment suits made public, and it cost him his position as mayor.

They climbed the staircase, and Billie noticed the photographs lining the walls. They were framed in ornate silver and displayed a happy family of four. Dennis Yang, his wife, and their two children, who were now adults. In each photo, they were smiling and carefree.

As they reached the top of the stairs, Billie took in the master bedroom. It was spacious, with a large king-size bed and a bay window that overlooked the backyard. The room was impeccably decorated with plush furnishings, and a crystal chandelier hung from the ceiling.

Billie walked over to the dresser and saw more family photographs. This time, they were candid shots of the family enjoying vacations, birthdays, and holidays.

"He didn't take down her photos," Billie said, turning to Mazie.

"Of the wife?" she asked.

Billie nodded. "They went through a brutal divorce, but he kept her photos up."

Mazie whistled. "Takes balls. I wouldn't even keep this house. It'd just be a constant reminder."

"Maybe he wants to be reminded? Some people are happy in their misery."

The plush carpet beneath their feet on the second floor felt like walking on a cloud. It was thick and luxurious, and probably cost more than Billie's entire living room. She had grown up with very little, and even as an adult, she had never been one for extravagance. But being in this room made her feel small and insignificant, almost like an intruder in a world she could never truly belong in.

An assistant pathologist with latex gloves crouched near the massive four-poster bed, carefully taking tissue and fluid samples with Q-tips and depositing them into clear vials.

Sprawled out on the bed was the corpse of Dennis Yang, once a prominent defense attorney and mayor of the city. Billie had worked with him several times in the past and had always found him to be shrewd and cunning. She had realized long ago that his political rise had been helped along by less than ethical means.

The sheets on the bed were white but soaked with blood. Under the harsh glare of the track lighting, the bloodstains resembled a Jackson Pollock painting: long and thin streaks accented by spatters. The blood had coagulated and slithered off the bed like thick, dark sludge.

Dennis Yang's eyes had glazed over, giving them an eerie, doll-like appearance. His mouth hung open, twisted into an unnatural expression that made her feel almost nauseated. Two massive gashes along his thighs showed where the blood had poured out of his body. Both his femoral arteries had been sawed through with what looked like a linoleum knife that lay near his body. The cuts were deep, down to the bone, and his robe was open, revealing the grisly wounds. Blood had splattered up onto his genitals, the sight of which made Billie's stomach churn.

"When SIS is done, ask them to make him modest before they take him out. I don't want anybody taking photos of him nude," she said to Mazie.

The assistant pathologist said, "It's a body, Sheriff. I don't think it's going to care."

"This *body* used to be a man I knew. I'm going to have to call his children to tell them their father is dead, so please, show some respect."

The assistant shrugged and mumbled something. Billie folded her arms, and they watched the assistant medical examiner work for a while.

"Well?" she finally said impatiently.

"Liver temp is eighty-three," he said, "so he's probably been dead about five hours."

Billie looked at Mazie. "Who called it in?"

"He did. Before he died. I haven't heard it yet, though."

Mazie had astute attention to detail; it was one of the reasons Billie kept her close, and she picked up on the phrasing and said, "You said *died*, not *killed himself*."

"Yeah, I did."

"You have some thoughts?" Billie asked.

"I mean, nothing really," she said, averting her eyes with a slight blush in her cheeks.

New officers were like new recruits in a gang, mistreated as part of some hazing ritual. The senior officers had a mentality of *we went through it, so you have to*. Part of what that included was creating insecurity in your skills.

"In this job, people around you will make you doubt everything, especially yourself. Don't let them." She inhaled a deep breath and let it out slowly. "Sorry, I'm a little loopy from lack of sleep. I don't mean to be lecturing."

"No, it's cool. I appreciate it. Hey, and I'm sorry. I know this guy was your friend."

"Not friend, really. He was a well-known defense attorney before he retired and went into politics. If I was charged with a crime, he's who I would've hired."

"But you knew him?"

"I knew him. He asked me out once, actually."

"What'd you say?"

"I told him to go home to his wife."

The assistant ME rose with a sigh as his knees cracked from the motion. He turned to the women and said, "That's all I can do until I get back in the lab, but no other injuries I can see. He died of exsanguination, obviously, but the cuts are incredibly deep, and there are no hesitation marks."

"Hesitation marks?" Mazie said.

"People that stab themselves, or a lot of first-time killers that use a blade, hesitate for the first few cuts because they don't know what to expect. You don't know how a human body is going to feel when you plunge a knife into it for the first time. So, hesitation cuts aren't deep and differ from the more penetrating stab wounds. It'd be incredibly painful to saw into your own thighs like he did, so you'd expect to see some hesitation marks, but there's none."

Billie said, "We'll have to wait for the toxicology report. A man on methamphetamine or PCP can do a lot they couldn't normally do."

"That's probably the right play. But they also found an empty bottle of wine. Chateau Margaux. Eight hundred bucks a bottle. Drink of the gods."

"What's your point?"

"Yeah, sorry. That's just good stuff. And I smell alcohol on him. He may have been so drunk *and* high he didn't much feel the cutting." He closed something on the floor that looked like a tackle box and lifted it by the handle. "That's all I got for now, Sheriff. If you two don't mind, I would like to sleep for a couple hours. I have court at eight."

When he was gone, Billie glanced around the room and said, "Odd, isn't it? Dennis had everything people think they want in life, and it brought him nothing but misery."

Mazie watched the body a moment.

"You've seen a corpse before, right?" Billie asked.

"Yeah, I mean, like DUI accidents and stuff. Never seen one like this. I mean . . . it's just . . ."

"It's stunning how much blood the human body contains, isn't it?"

"Yeah, exactly. It doesn't look real."

"You'll get used to it, or you'll quit and find something else to do. That's how it works."

Billie's phone buzzed insistently in her pocket, the sudden sound jolting her nerves like a bolt of electricity. She felt a tingle of icy fear race up her spine as she wondered if it was Dax again, somehow managing to track down her new number despite her best efforts to keep him away. The last thing he had said to her was that he was going to kill her and then himself. That was two weeks ago, and he hadn't contacted her since, but that somehow was even worse. It was like he enjoyed making her suffer in anticipation of what he was going to do.

She had changed her phone number several times, but it seemed like he always found a way to reach her. He had been locked up by a judge three times already for violation of the stalking injunction, but it didn't seem to slow him down. If anything, he enjoyed the time in court, where he got to stare at her in silence.

Maybe he was going through her trash on Mondays when she put out the bins? She made a mental note to start shredding all her documents before throwing them away, just to be safe. She fished out her phone and checked the notification: just a routine calendar reminder.

"Who's lead on this?" Billie said, slipping the phone back into her pocket.

"Detective Parsons."

"Where is he?"

"Downstairs."

Detective Greg Parsons came into the room just then, his eyes scanning the body on the bed with a clinical detachment that Billie had seen in most of her detectives after decades on the job. He leaned against the wall, his clothes rumpled and his skin mottled with burst capillaries, some medical condition he kept private.

"What are you doing here, Billie?"

"I was in the neighborhood."

"Kinda far from your neck of the woods, ain't it?"

Billie looked at the body. "It'll be receiving a lot of attention. I want to stay in the loop on everything."

He shrugged. "If you want. Seems pretty straightforward."

"How many suicides have you seen where they saw into their thighs, Greg?"

"First time for everything."

As Billie left the room, the stench of death seemed to cling to her.

She was exhausted, but she knew she couldn't let her guard down with Greg. He was one of those old-school cops who believed that women had no place in law enforcement, and he wasn't shy about letting everyone know it. She could almost feel his sneer as she walked away.

She left the house, her mind racing with images of blood on white sheets.

4

Billie sat at her desk in the cramped office, surrounded by stacks of papers and manila folders. She furrowed her brow, her face etched with deep lines of frustration. It had been four long days since the gruesome discovery of Dennis Yang's body, and despite her best efforts, they didn't know anything they hadn't known the first night.

She had been poring over the evidence, trying to piece together the puzzle of what had led to the mayor's brutal death. But the more she dug, the less she thought it was suicide.

The fact that Yang had booked a spa day for the near future and paid in advance, not to mention an upcoming vacation to Saint Croix, seemed at odds with a man who was planning to take his own life. And one of the women he was seeing had told Billie that he was struggling to cope with his recent divorce but was working through it with her. The idea of a monthlong therapeutic getaway to a tropical paradise hardly seemed like the actions of a man in the throes of suicidal despair.

The local media had been circling the case like vultures, peddling baseless conspiracy theories about organized crime and heartless mistresses. Billie could only imagine the pain and humiliation that Yang's kids must be feeling as they were subjected to the lurid speculation.

As she read through the latest news report on her computer screen, she grew angry. The district attorney, Roger Lynch, had taken it upon himself to speak to the press and had positioned himself as the go-to on the case. Promising a quick resolution. Of course, if the resolution wasn't quick, she would be the one Roger would point to as spearheading the case, and blame would fall on her. He had done it to her before.

Her frustration was palpable, and her jaw clenched so tightly that the muscles in her face throbbed with pain. She closed the window on the article and turned to the screen behind it, which displayed graphic photos of Yang's mutilated body. The wounds were so savage that Billie couldn't picture someone doing it to themselves. The idea of someone sawing away at their own flesh and bone until they realized they couldn't go any farther was enough to make her stomach churn.

It seemed like everyone was quick to dismiss the suspicious circumstances surrounding Dennis Yang's death, chalking it up to a man unable to handle the upheaval in his life. She had heard that before. The first judge in her stalking case with Dax had said the same thing about him.

The other department heads, including the assistant sheriff, were pushing her to close the case and move on.

Billie stared at the photo of the body. This was the type of case that would draw massive media attention and public scrutiny. The lieutenant governor had already called, adding to the mounting pressure to solve the case.

Taking a deep breath, Billie picked up her phone and called her assistant. "Elle, where's Deputy Heaton?"

After a brief pause, Elle responded, "Desk duty today."

"Get someone to cover for her and tell her to meet me out front in an hour."

Billie gazed out the cruiser's window as Mazie drove them through downtown Tooele, the falling snow blanketing the streets and sidewalks. This winter had been harsh, with fewer days of sunshine than any on record.

As they hit the freeway, the snowfall intensified, creating a serene white landscape. The route led them around the mountains and into a vast expanse of winter desert, with snow-capped hills and endless stretches of snow-covered terrain. Gas stations and fast-food joints were the only signs of civilization.

Mazie broke the silence. "So, what we doin'?"

"We're going to meet someone that I really need to see."

"Who?" she asked.

"He used to be a prosecutor for the county. One of the best they ever had."

"Solomon Shepard?" Mazie guessed.

Billie's eyebrows furrowed in surprise. "How do you know that name?" she asked.

Mazie shrugged. "I heard some stuff about you two or whatever. Just like, watercooler talk," she admitted. "So, does he know we're coming? I heard he's kinda . . ."

"Kinda what, Deputy?" Billie prompted, her tone betraying annoyance.

Mazie hesitated before continuing. "Nothing, ma'am. Just that he's a little isolated. Like a weird hermit or something."

Billie observed Mazie for a moment, appreciating her blunt honesty. Still, she found it exasperating at times. "No, he doesn't know we're coming," she replied.

"Why not?"

Billie kept her eyes fixed on the snowy landscape outside. "Because the last time we talked, he told me that he never wants to see me again."

5

As they took the exit, the familiar sight of a gas station greeted them, with multiple semis parked in a row behind it. Beyond that, the flat-lands stretched for miles, with only a few homes scattered sparsely across the landscape, most of them abandoned.

The cruiser finally came to a halt in front of a large gate, guarded by an intercom. Mazie rolled down the window and called out, "Hello? Tooele County Sheriff's. Anybody there?"

For a few moments, they received no reply. "Maybe he's not home," Mazie suggested.

Billie leaned over toward the driver's side window and spoke softly. "Solomon, it's Billie."

There was a long silence before the gate slowly slid open. The gravel driveway led to a dilapidated home surrounded by a high fence, giving the impression of a fortress. The lawn was overgrown with weeds that burst through the snow like spears, and the windows were so dirty that it was nearly impossible to see through them. Bars had been installed.

"Paranoid much," Mazie muttered under her breath.

Mazie unbuckled her seat belt, but Billie told her to stay. "I haven't seen him in three years. I don't know how he'll react to another person."

"He really went that batty, huh?" Mazie said.

Billie didn't respond as she got out of the car. She took a deep breath, slipping her hands into her pockets to protect them from the cold wind. The idea of seeing Solomon again made her nauseated.

Solomon's past was a grim tapestry of pain. From the raw wounds of a traumatic childhood to the harrowing courtroom attack he'd endured years prior that left him with a leg that barely worked, his history was marred by suffering. The relentless onslaughts from a vengeful defendant he had once prosecuted served only to thicken the layers of distress that had accumulated in his psyche over the years . . . something had to break, and it had.

He thought, at first, that he had locked them away in a safe place, but emotions can't be locked away for long. All the anger and pain he suppressed began tearing him apart from the inside. He saw connections that weren't there, in everything from their relationship to national politics. Theories became outlandish schemes. Logic became leaps that didn't make sense. Billie had talked to him about it once, but he'd brushed it off as nothing.

Slowly, Solomon changed, and not for the better. He began accusing Billie of using him, of coming to his door years ago to put him through even more trauma to find a killer who had called himself the Reaper. She had denied it, but he refused to believe her. It was the first crack in their relationship, a crack that led to a crevasse.

Eventually, as Solomon slipped further into solitude, Billie had shown up to his door one day to check on him. He looked her in the eyes and said he never wanted to see her again. The words stung and cut, and she had to keep her face passive to hide the shock, but she respected his wishes.

As Billie crossed the expansive lawn, she was amazed by the sheer size of the property. The lawn was almost like a park, with no discernible paths or roads leading through it. It was meant to be traversed by foot, not by car.

The home, which lay ahead, looked like part of an abandoned plantation straight out of an old ghost story, with its white facade falling apart and vegetation slowly taking over the building.

Billie climbed the wooden steps to the front porch. She anticipated this likely wouldn't be a pleasant experience, but he was the one person she knew could help her. Not conjecture or lecture or mansplain to her, but actually help her.

Summoning her courage, Billie knocked on the door, and after a few moments, Solomon Shepard answered.

He had grown a beard since the last time she saw him, and Billie thought it looked good on him except for the fact that his skin was unnaturally pale and his eyes were bloodshot, with dark half moons underneath. He looked sickly, as though he had been bedridden for a long time. He leaned on his cane and wore a T-shirt and gray sweatpants, his lips cracked and dry. Seeing him gave her a sensation she wasn't expecting: butterflies in her stomach. But the pleasant feeling was tinged with uncertainty. Something in his eyes looked different, and she could sense the chaos lurking behind them.

"Hi," was all she could manage to say.

"Hi," he replied.

There was a long pause before she spoke again. "Can I come in?"

He looked down at the floor and tapped his cane softly before looking up at the cruiser and seeing Mazie. "You recruiting from the high schools now?" he said.

"She's twenty-one. Same age I was when I put on a badge," Billie said. "She's tougher than I am, though. Maybe a little more naive."

"She'll lose that quick on the streets," Solomon remarked, tapping his cane again.

Billie watched him for a moment. "Solomon, I'd like to come in and speak with you."

He nodded. "Yeah, all right."

Billie stepped inside and glanced back once to Mazie before shutting the door behind them.

The home was a disaster, but somehow not dirty. There wasn't any garbage or dishes with crusted food, but nothing was arranged in a way that was aesthetically pleasing. There was no order, no patterns. When Billie was a child and had once refused to clean her room, her father had told her that if you wanted to know what a person's mind looked like, just take a look at the space they lived in.

Solomon sat down in a recliner. She moved a red quilt aside from the cushions of a couch and sat across from him.

"You look good," he said.

"So do you."

"Bullshit, but thank you."

She glanced to the kitchen. Amber pill bottles were lined up near the sink. A stuffed owl, or at least what she thought was a stuffed owl, with large orange eyes sat on a perch in the living room.

"Interesting decor."

"Most of it came with the house. Actually, I think all of it came with the house." He tapped his cane on the carpet. "I asked you not to come here again, Billie."

"I know."

"But you did anyway."

"It's important."

"It's always important. That's the thing I'm realizing: maybe everything is important, or maybe nothing is, and we'll never know which."

She glanced around the room. "Have you talked to Gesell lately?"

Gesell had been his girlfriend. After he'd pulled her into his life and exposed her to a dangerous ex-con that was after Solomon, Gesell had left him, and he didn't fight for her.

He shook his head. "No. I asked her not to call or come by anymore. She actually listened."

Billie leaned forward and softly said, "Solomon, you can't live like this."

"Like what?"

"Locked away in a fortress."

"Suddenly you're worried about me?"

"I've always been worried about you."

They sat in the silence a while, and she could hear a grandfather clock chime the hour, which she guessed was around ten. The sound was pleasant and reminded her of her grandparents' home and the large clock her grandfather had in his study.

"You need help, Solomon."

"So, you want me to go from being locked away in a fortress to being locked away in a hospital?"

"I just said help. I didn't say anything about being locked away. And getting treatment is not being locked away. It's about being with people that can help people like . . ."

"People like *me*? What is a person like me? Tell me, Sheriff, what penumbra have you classified me as? Psychotic? Delusional? Maybe even psychopathic if—"

"Solomon," she said firmly, "stop."

He ran his tongue along his upper lip and swallowed. He nodded a few times and said, "Sorry. It's, um, funny, there's absolutely nothing constant about a human being. We have dreams that we abandon and get new ones, old friends are lost and we make new ones, families are formed or broken apart, habits dropped and new ones picked up . . . we're just a constant unfinished work, but everyone judges us as if we're the finished product."

"I'm not judging you. I think you needed to do what you did in order to heal. But you tried to heal for too long, and now it's having the opposite effect."

He tapped his cane quietly and didn't respond.

She sighed and noticed the bearskin throw rug over another recliner, and the massive painting of an empty field with golden wheat that hung over the fireplace.

"I like this place."

"Can't beat the price. Do you want some tea?" he said, rising.

"Sure, thank you." She ran her fingers together, feeling the ridges of her fingerprints, as he made his way to the kitchen. "How did you get this house?"

"I rented the mother-in-law in the back, but the elderly gal that owned it before me left it to me in her will."

"You're kidding?"

"No, seriously. I guess she hated her kids and didn't leave them anything. So I got the house and everything in it."

He brought out a cup of tea on a dish and handed it to her. She took it and said, "It's pretty far from everything. You get out much?"

"I take walks occasionally. I have everything else delivered." He sat back down with his own tea. "So, is she the only kindergarten deputy you have?"

"Just her. I recruited her out of POST personally."

"Wow. She must've reminded you of you."

"She does. A little too much perhaps."

Solomon grinned. "She might make a helluva cop, like you, or might be a massive lawsuit waiting to explode."

"Didn't you once say to me that life wouldn't be any fun without risk?"

He sipped his tea. "I've said a lot of things." He set the tea down on the dish on the coffee table in front of him. "What is it you came here for, Billie? Just making sure I haven't killed myself? I'm not there yet. So, you can go back and not worry about it. You're good at doing that."

"That is not fair. I was with you every step of the way when nobody else was. *You* pushed *me* away."

He said nothing, reacted in no way. Sometimes his ability to shut himself down made her uncomfortable.

"What are you here for, Billie?" he said softly.

"Dennis Yang is dead."

Solomon was silent a moment now. "How?"

"Suicide. Allegedly."

"Allegedly?"

"That's what I need your help for," she said, taking out her phone. She pulled up photos of the Yang crime scene and passed her phone to Solomon.

Billie watched as Solomon's pallor went to ashen gray. His hands trembled as he held the phone, and she could see the whites of his knuckles as he gripped it tightly. She felt a pang of regret for showing him the gruesome photos, and wondered if she should have found a way to prepare him for what he was about to see.

The silence lasted so long that she felt the need to talk so it wouldn't be awkward.

"He had gone to work that morning. ME puts the time of death at around eleven p.m. The next morning he had a pickleball lesson scheduled. A few other things that made me think this isn't what it looks like."

Solomon continued staring at the photos.

"Solomon? Are you all right?"

"Yeah," he said, snapping out of wherever he had been. "What does good old Roger think about those cracks in the suicide theory?"

"He says every theory has cracks."

"The cracks are where the good stuff is." He handed the phone back. "Who found him? His wife?"

"His wife left him last year and moved to California. Someone dialed 911 from his home, but there was just silence on the line."

"Why bring this to me?"

"I thought you could help."

"Why would you think I could help?"

"Because you have a talent for this sort of thing."

"I have a talent for the real bad ones, you mean. The ones nobody else wants to touch."

She put her tea on the coffee table with a soft clink, then leaned back on the sofa, crossing her arms loosely over her chest.

"Yes. I believe you have a talent for the bad ones, and that this is going to be a bad one."

"Why do you think that?"

"Aside from scheduling conflicts, there's no evidence of anything other than suicide, but it doesn't feel right to me."

"Few people would cut into their own thighs to kill themselves. Pills and guns are used ninety-nine percent of the time. You're right to suspect something's up." Solomon rose and gripped his cane tightly. "But there's nothing I can do." He made his way to the front door.

She sighed and rose, then crossed the living room and joined him by the front door.

"I'm asking for your help, Solomon."

He looked away from her gaze and to the floor as he softly tapped his cane. "Help you how? Go to court, get warrants, interview witnesses? I couldn't do those things anymore even if I wanted to."

"Then just look at the evidence. That's all I need. If someone really did kill Dennis and made it look like a suicide, I need someone that understands these types of men to look at the evidence and tell me what they see."

"You have plenty of people that can do that."

"Not like you."

He dug his cane into the floor and then tapped it hard. "I can't."

He opened the front door. A surprised Mazie stood with eyes wide.

"Oh, shit," she said, "um, I'm just checking up and seeing if you guys need anything."

"Eavesdropping on the sheriff as a rookie, that is just pure balls." He looked at Billie. "I can see why you like her."

Mazie blushed and said, "Um, I'm gonna head back to the car now."

She hurried back to the cruiser.

Billie noticed a gold plate above the door with writing in a language she didn't recognize. The aesthetics were pleasing, swooping curves of letters that looked maybe Persian or Hindi.

"What is that?"

"It's a prayer," Solomon said.

"Prayer for what?"

He finally looked at her. "For peace."

She nodded. "I'm sorry, Solomon. I'm sorry for all of it."

"I know . . . but I can't help you."

She stepped out, and he'd shut the door by the time she turned around to say goodbye.

6

Solomon came out into the cold winter air. The ground was covered in a blanket of white snow. The air crisp and biting, leaving a tingling sensation on his cheeks and nose. The backyard was barren, with only a few trees scattered around the perimeter. They looked skeletal, with no leaves to protect them from the harsh weather. It was a desolate sight, a stark contrast to the vibrant wilderness that would descend here during the spring.

Solomon used to love the tranquility that came with being surrounded by nature. He remembered the feeling of peace he would get when he was alone in the woods. He used to think that the German word *Waldeinsamkeit* described the beauty of solitude in nature, but now he realized it was more a reminder of how indifferent nature was to humanity. The trees and animals continued to thrive and evolve, regardless of the tragedies of human life.

Solomon made his way to the back of the house, carrying a pistol, crunching through the frosted leaves on the ground. The air was frigid and still.

Behind his home loomed a massive mountain, its jagged peak obscured by a dense fog that clung to the trees and rocks. An old mining route wound up the side of the mountain, and Solomon sometimes took walks up there when the morning fog was thick. Walking through the mist, he felt as though he were climbing up into the sky, leaving the world behind him.

A makeshift shooting range had been built at the base of the mountain, with targets set up fifteen yards out. Solomon made his way to the small table in front of the range and leaned his cane against it. The table was littered with empty shell casings and targets with bullet holes, evidence of many hours spent practicing his aim.

He put on a pair of safety glasses and stuffed wax into his ears, then slipped on a pair of thick shooting earmuffs. He hated the sound of guns firing, but it was necessary.

He loaded the pistol with practiced ease, his movements fluid and efficient. As he turned to face the wooden target, he saw the weathered surface, faded and stained from years of exposure to the elements. It was pockmarked with bullet holes.

Assuming his stance, he felt the familiar weight of the firearm settle into his hand. Drawing a deep breath, he steadied his aim along the sight line, then gradually exhaled as he applied steady pressure to the trigger. The gun jerked back with each discharge, but he maintained his grip, firing in measured succession until the magazine was empty.

He walked back to the small table and carefully reloaded the gun, each movement methodical and precise. As he raised the pistol again, he felt a strange sense of comfort in its weight. He had once been indifferent to guns, but now they were a part of his life. They gave him a sense of security in the isolation of his mountain home, a way to protect himself from the outside world.

After he'd gone through five boxes of ammunition, he walked back into the house, the scent of gunpowder still lingering on his hands and clothes. As he put the weapon away, he felt disappointed. Shooting had been a reliable source of emotional relief for him, but today it did nothing.

He took a deep breath and tried to focus on the present, but his thoughts kept drifting to the past, to someone spread-eagle on a bed with thick gashes in their thighs, blood pouring over the sheets onto the floor.

He walked over to the window and looked out at the mountain behind his house. It was a towering mass of rock and snow, silent and stoic. It was here a billion years ago and would be here a billion years after humanity had gone extinct. A reminder of how brief human life really was. He liked standing at the window and staring at it for long periods of time.

Solomon felt his head pounding with a headache as he walked over to his armchair. He sat down heavily and closed his eyes, trying to shut out the thoughts that threatened to overwhelm him. But they persisted, swirling around in his head like a storm.

He opened his eyes and looked around the room. Everything was exactly as it always was, but it all felt foreign to him now. Like he was living in a stranger's house.

He stood, crossed the room, and glanced at the bookshelf, the titles blurring before him. His mind was too preoccupied with the past, with images of the dead. He closed his eyes and took a deep breath, trying to center himself. But the memories were still there, lurking in the shadows of his mind.

He knew he'd been triggered and dysregulated. He went to the kitchen of the old home, where his medications were, and took lorazepam, double the dosage prescribed. He'd found he'd developed a tolerance to it over the last year and had to keep upping his dosage.

As he sipped water out of a tumbler, he caught a reflection of himself in the window over the sink. The beard showed gray hairs when his head didn't have any, and he remembered when his father's beard went gray before his hair.

The thought of his father made him uncomfortable. He was near the same age his father was when he drank himself to death, and they looked similar. He didn't like seeing his reflection anymore.

He took the tumbler and a bottle of Jack Daniel's out to the porch and sat down in a wooden rocking chair that had come with the home.

Before Solomon owned it, the place belonged to Mrs. George Langley III, an elderly widow who insisted on keeping her formal title. She lived alone in the palatial house—twenty thousand square feet of grandeur and ghostly echoes. She had advertised her casita for rent. Solomon, burdened by draining encounters and an apartment that had grown intolerable, responded promptly. He sought solace in the allure of seclusion, yearning to untangle himself from the suffocating web of human interaction.

The price was a bit steep, but Mrs. Langley offered to cut it in half in exchange for Solomon's help with the property's upkeep.

Solomon tackled the landscaping and garbage disposal and handled the myriad problems that came with owning an isolated mountain property as best as he could. After a while, Mrs. Langley refused to accept rent from him, and the two would occasionally share dinner on the porch and chat.

One night, she asked him why he was hiding from the world.

"Who says I'm hiding?" he'd said.

"No one lives in a place like this that isn't hiding or wandering, and I don't see you doing much wandering, do you? Maybe it's time you did a little."

He'd thought about those words a lot: hiding or wandering. He didn't really know what she'd meant by wandering, but he pictured pure freedom. Something he thought he would never have. Not that there were outside forces keeping him locked away; it was much worse than that. If someone else was doing it, he would have something to fight. But sometimes it felt like his own mind had betrayed him and made him perceive reality in a way that wasn't true. How do you fight your own mind?

Mrs. Langley had died on a cold Tuesday morning. Because they hadn't gotten anything in the will, none of her six children came to her funeral. Solomon was the only one who attended. He laid a flower on her grave and stood there for a long time. She had been the best type of person: the type who was kind when they didn't have to be.

As he settled into the creaky wooden chair, he looked out at the empty landscape beyond his property. The snow had been falling steadily all morning, and the world outside was a unicolor blanket of white. The air was cold and bitter, but he barely felt it through the haze of medication and alcohol.

He took a long swig from the tumbler, the fiery liquid burning its way down his throat. The taste was strong, but it was better than feeling nothing.

He closed his eyes and leaned back, letting the chair rock him gently. The medication began to take effect, numbing his mind and body. He wondered if this was what it felt like to die slowly.

For a while, he just sat there, lost in his own thoughts. The only sounds were the occasional creak of the chair and the wind through barren trees. But then he heard something else: a faint rustling in the bushes by the side of the house.

He tensed, his hand instinctively reaching for the gun he'd left inside. The lorazepam made his movements slow and sluggish. He listened, waiting for the sound to come again. When it did, he used his cane to stand and gripped the Jack Daniel's bottle tightly like a club.

He walked cautiously toward the side of the house, his eyes scanning the white landscape for any sign of movement. His heart was pounding, but he forced himself to stay calm. When he reached the bushes, he saw what had caused the noise: a squirrel, foraging for food in the garbage cans.

He breathed a sigh of relief, the image of the blood and bed coming back into his mind.

The photographs had shocked him. He knew Billie was too astute not to have noticed, and he wondered why she didn't say anything.

The image had seared into Solomon's mind: legs spread apart, two massive gashes in the thighs draining the entire body's blood like a broken dam after a heavy rain. The gruesomeness of the scene wasn't the reason it had shocked him. You could see gruesomeness and still maintain a functioning mind. But this image had crippled his mind because it wasn't Dennis Yang he saw.

It was Solomon's mother.

Solomon remembered vividly how his mother had taken his father's old razors, back when they still had real blades, and swallowed enough pills to knock out a horse before cutting deep into her own legs. Blood had gushed from her wounds, covering her and the sheets in a crimson stream that pulsed in time with her dying heart.

He couldn't forget how white she looked, like a ghost had taken over her body. His father had drunk himself to death a year before, but he didn't look as ashen as his mother did that day. Solomon never understood why until a kid at church claimed it was because her soul had been sent to hell, bleaching her flesh white. Solomon confided in his older brother that he was worried their mother was going to hell, but Ethan just said hell didn't really exist because the world was bad enough.

Billie knew his mother had committed suicide, but she didn't know any of the details. Few people did, as the case files had been sealed because Solomon and his brother were minors when it happened.

Solomon snapped out of his thoughts and left the squirrel to its foraging as he went back to the porch and sat down.

He retrieved the forgotten phone from his pocket, its weight foreign in his hand. It had been left untouched in his closet for what felt like ages, a relic from a time he barely recognized. As he turned it on, the screen flickered to life, illuminating his face.

The device was part of a life he no longer had. He scrolled through the old apps and games that once brought him joy, but now only brought a dull ache to his chest. It was a reminder of how much he had changed in such a short amount of time, and how much he had lost.

After the attack by Alonso Hafeez, a former defendant who blamed Solomon for his incarceration, his life had become a hazy blur. The pressure in his chest had grown until it consumed his entire being, leaving him struggling to find a way forward. Pressure was a force of nature, sometimes making people stronger, sometimes breaking them entirely. He had hoped to heal and become more resilient, but the worst of his compulsions had taken hold, leading him down a self-destructive path.

He thought about his options: let it go or call her.

He unlocked the phone and dialed, and a *number does not exist* message played. Billie didn't have the same number anymore. He set the phone down and went to the bathroom. Then he looked at himself in the mirror again and took out some razors.

7

As she waited for Roger Lynch, Billie gazed out the floor-to-ceiling windows of his office, overlooking the breathtaking view of the valley below. The sun peeked above the mountains, casting an ethereal glow over the landscape. The beauty of the moment brought back memories of her childhood, when she would go on drives with her father to admire the fall foliage and they would end up talking about police work the entire time. Zachary Gray was a man who wore his heart on his sleeve and would discuss his work, including cases that were troubling him, with anyone who would listen. Even his ten-year-old daughter.

While she reflected on her father's openness, Billie contrasted it with the closed-off nature of Roger Lynch. He was power hungry, and she wondered if that was the only way he knew how to live.

Tooele was nestled in a snow-covered valley, the cold air from the six months of snowfall they received crisp and sharp. Mountains loomed in every direction, their snowy peaks guarding the quiet streets below. People here were tough and liked to keep to themselves: Billie could even see it in the way they walked with purpose, their breaths visible, faces pink. Cafés and shops offered warmth and light against the cold.

Despite the harsh winter, the city felt alive and strong.

Roger hung up and said, "You'll have to excuse me. Duty calls."

"I imagine preparing to run for governor must take a lot of time."

"Not governor, not yet anyway." He leaned back in his seat and put one foot up against his desk. "I assume sheriff isn't the last stop for you. What's your ambition?"

"I don't have one."

"Everybody has one."

"Not me."

"You have to want something."

"I just want a peaceful life."

"That's it? Peace? That's easy."

"No, it's not." She glanced back to the horizon as the sun completed its rise over the mountains. "What did you want, Roger?"

"I wanted to get an update on the Yang thing."

She sat down across from him. "You could've texted."

"I prefer face to face. It's a dying art. So, you're about to close it as a suicide is what I hear, correct?"

Usually, she was good at telling where she stood with people, but not with Roger. His personality shifted with whoever was around, and she could never tell who he was at any particular time. Solomon was the opposite: what you saw was what you got. She understood why the two detested each other.

"Why do you care, Roger?"

"Lots of people are interested. Dennis was a prominent member of the bar and our former mayor who—"

"You couldn't care less about Dennis Yang. Now tell me why you really asked me to come, or I'm leaving."

He was a man who seemed used to subterfuge and roundabout speech, and being asked something directly made him uncomfortable. It brought her a small pleasure when he shifted in his chair.

"I want what everybody wants: to see the case closed so people can heal."

"And?"

"And because we have other cases to work and this is getting all the media attention. It's hurting morale."

"What?" she said with a mirthless chuckle.

"I don't like when one case gets so much attention. It's too much scrutiny."

"What is it you don't want people to scrutinize? Did you and Dennis have a history?"

He leaned forward and sighed like he was having to deliver a lecture he'd already delivered fifty times. "You said yourself once, I'm not your boss, and you're not mine. I don't have to tell you anything. But I will say this, when our interests align, we work well. When they don't align, everything falls apart. Take your little stalking problem. Our interests align, and look how many resources you have at your disposal to prevent this bastard from hurting you. It benefits both of us when our interests align, is what I'm saying."

Billie knew exactly what he was saying: *Yes, you have a hunch it might be more than a suicide, but I want you to declare it a suicide and get it out of the press.* But she wasn't going to make this easy for him. She wanted to look at his face while he said the words.

"I don't understand what you're asking, Roger. Use plain English."

He sighed again, and she had to suppress a smile.

"I'm asking you to expedite the case of Mr. Yang. It's a suicide, all the evidence points to suicide, we—"

"Not all the evidence. And it's curious that a sitting district attorney would ask the sheriff to declare a death a suicide when there were indications of murder. Almost like you're involved somehow."

He chuckled. "Yeah, that's it. I'm involved in killing a man that donated to my campaign with a blank check. Look, just clear it as fast as you can."

She rose and said, "We'll see," before she left.

Lost in thought as she rode the elevators down and went outside, she mulled over her meeting with the district attorney. Roger Lynch's refusal to say what they both knew he wanted had been smooth, almost as if he suspected he was being recorded. Billie wondered if he was simply being cautious, or if he knew something was looming on the horizon and was taking steps to protect himself. It reminded her of the higher echelons of organized crime, who even in their private lives with their spouses avoided saying anything that could incriminate them.

As she climbed into her truck, she couldn't shake the feeling that something big was coming.

He had placed her in a difficult situation, one where any action she took would result in trouble. If she pursued the investigation into the suicide, it would provoke Roger, and he would retaliate in some way. He had a habit of making life miserable for her detectives by manipulating court dates or refusing to prosecute important cases. But Billie knew that the balance of power was not entirely in his favor. As a sheriff, she held a great deal of public trust and influence. If Roger lost her confidence, it could damage his reputation with the county's residents irreparably. They were both dependent on each other, and both had something to gain or lose.

When she glanced up, she was startled that a man was standing near her truck. She thought to herself that he was handsome and had a warm smile before she recognized Solomon.

She rolled down her window. "I like you without the beard."

"I clean up nice sometimes. How'd your meeting with Roger go?"

"How'd you know I had a meeting with Roger?" she said with a tinge of fear. She'd had enough men surprising her with their knowledge of her routines to last the rest of her life.

"Anyone else in that building would come see you. Roger's the only one that would demand you come see him." He tapped his cane against the pavement of the parking lot. It had a layer of ice covered in fresh salt that sank a little when Solomon pressed down on it. "He still a jackass?"

"Truer words," she said, relaxing into her seat. "What are you doing here, Solomon? You made it pretty clear you wanted nothing to do with me."

He continued tapping on the ice. "I think I need to help with this. But there's some things you should know first."

"Like what?"

8

They sat at a diner while Solomon explained his mother's suicide to her in as much detail as he could remember. Billie knew some of his background, but not all. Not that he was the one who found his mother like that, and not that—only ten at the time—Solomon attempted to give her CPR because he had seen people come back to life in movies when they were given CPR. When the paramedics finally arrived, Solomon was covered in blood and sitting next to his mother's body weeping.

As they talked, she watched his eyes. They hadn't dulled at all in the past few years, and the only thing that had given away that time had passed was the gray in his beard, which was gone now. But he had a sadness there she wasn't used to seeing. Something that she thought he didn't want her to see.

When he finished telling her about his mother, she took a moment to sip coffee out of a white mug. A server asked if they needed anything, and she said they were fine.

"I don't even know what to say. It's just so . . . tragic."

"Yeah, well, all we can do is play the hand we're dealt, right?"

She set her mug down. "So, what do you think it means that they're so similar?" Billie said.

"Not just similar, almost identical. I think there's two possibilities: either this is just a total fluke that Dennis Yang happened to kill himself in the exact same manner as Janet Shepard, or someone that knows about her death—or found out about it—killed Dennis."

"And which way are you leaning?"

He waved his hand. "I'm here, aren't I? I haven't sat down in a restaurant in three years. That's progress, Sheriff."

She grinned. It was good to see him joking again.

"What happened, Solomon? Why three years?"

He took a drink out of a soda cup and then set it down. "Conversation for another time. Right now, you have to get me, just a plain old American citizen with no special security clearance, access to privileged files. You sure you wanna risk an ethical censure and maybe a lawsuit over this?"

She shrugged. "I'm the sheriff. I can do what I want."

"Spoken like a true dictator." He finished his soda and got his cane. "We gotta make a stop really quick."

The Marigold community was an idyllic enclave perched high on the mountain, offering a stunning panoramic view of the valley below. It was the most exclusive and upscale area in the entire county, populated by wealthy residents who wanted to escape from the mundane realities of life.

The winding road leading up to the community was treacherous, slick with ice.

Solomon gazed out at the rugged terrain, the hills rolling white with fresh snow, dotted with grazing cattle that seemed unfazed by the passing traffic. The occasional breach in the fence allowed for a curious calf or cow to wander onto the road, slowing down the traffic to a crawl. Billie honked her horn impatiently, but the animals were unconcerned. Suddenly, a cow let out a loud moo and proceeded to defecate on her bumper. Billie cringed, while Solomon chuckled.

"Is this the glamorous career you imagined yourself having when you were a kid?" he said.

"There're worse jobs to have than sheriff, even with cows relieving themselves on my truck. No police officer in the county would dare arrest me, for example."

"So, you're basically above the law, is what you're saying? Not very PC, Sheriff."

"I'm kidding. But I do get both the mayor and the district attorney trying to always manipulate me into doing what they want, so that's one perk of the job."

"What's Roger want now?"

"He wants me to clear this case."

"Why?"

"He thinks it's getting too much press. But of course Roger can't utter a sentence without at least one lie sneaking in there, so who knows."

"It could be true. If there's not an arrest, both of you look bad."

"I don't care about looking bad."

"You might not, but he does. Don't underestimate the lengths he would go to if he thought it would harm his career."

She stopped at the gate. There was a security shack, but no one was in there. A keypad and intercom were on the driver's side. "So, what are we doing here, Solomon?"

"Gotta see someone really quick. Hit F3, would ya?"

She did, and a gruff male voice said, "Yeah?"

"It's Solomon Shepard. I need to see you."

A silence before the buzz and then the gate opened. Billie glanced at him and then pulled in.

Solomon waited for her, and then they walked through the complex together. The condos were upscale and the cars in the driveways shiny and new.

"Who are we seeing here?" she asked.

"Just a friend. He's helped me with some things before," Solomon replied, his face stoic.

"Your friend seems well off to live here."

"He is. He coulda retired a long time ago, but he's one of those people that has to constantly be doing something. I think he gets in trouble when he doesn't have enough to do."

The double doors they stopped in front of were an imposing sight, with white paint gleaming in the sunlight.

Solomon knocked, the sound echoing through the silent complex. Billie stood next to him, her hands buried deep in the pockets of her coat, watching as Solomon checked the time on his phone and knocked again, his breath visible in the chilly air.

The door creaked as the lock disengaged, revealing a man with long hair tied in a bun and dressed in a flashy shirt and torn jeans that looked very purposely ripped. He had a tattoo on his neck, the cursive letters spelling out a name that Solomon couldn't quite make out.

"Sol," he said with a grin. "Thought you was dead."

"Not yet. Can we come in?"

The man looked at Billie and then back at Solomon. "Tell me you didn't bring the damn sheriff to my door."

"She's cool."

"Even so, I'm retired now, Sol. Guess you didn't hear since you been away. I got the club and the bar, brother, and that's it. I'm streamlining."

"You owe me one, Swiggy. I'm collecting."

"What do I owe you?"

"You know what I'm talking about. You really want me repeating it in front of the sheriff?"

A long pause.

Swiggy folded his arms and leaned against the door. "I'd hoped you'd forget about that."

"I never forget who owes me favors."

Swiggy exhaled. "Come inside."

As they went in, the interior of the condo revealed itself to be a haven of plushness and comfort. The furniture was high quality, and each piece looked meticulously chosen for its placement in the room. The floors gleamed, and the surfaces shone under the soft glow of the overhead lights. It was a sharp contrast to the gritty, rough-looking man that stood waiting for Solomon to speak.

"So? What'd ya need?"

"The former mayor died, you heard that, right?"

"Yeah," Swiggy said with a nod.

"I need to know who he was involved with. Stuff the cops can't find. I need names."

"Why's that? I heard he offed himself."

"Just making sure that's what it was."

"Mm-hmm," he said, eyeing Billie.

He strode across the room, his bare feet silent on the marble floors, and plucked a package of cigarettes from the coffee table. He returned to the foyer and ignited a lighter with a sharp flick of his thumb. A small flame blossomed, and then he took a drag from the cigarette. The smoke swirled and billowed from his lips, appearing thicker and darker than Solomon's breath had outside. "If I do this, we're square. You and me are done. You sure this is important enough to use that up?"

Solomon tapped his cane on the floor and said, "Yeah . . . I think it is."

9

The door to Roger Lynch's office swung open, revealing his secretary standing in the doorway. "I'm leaving, Mr. Lynch. Do you need anything before I go?"

Roger tore his gaze away from the article on his desktop, which detailed his past as a lobbyist before becoming district attorney. "Yeah, can you grab me a Coke from the machine?"

"That's all the way downstairs," his secretary protested.

Roger shrugged nonchalantly.

She sighed. "I'll be right back."

As soon as she left the room, Roger couldn't help the smirk that spread across his face. People always talked about money, but to Roger, it was all about power. He didn't respect those who fought only for financial gain; their vision was too narrow.

He had already planned to leave for the night, but he waited until his secretary returned with the Coke. It brought him a small sense of joy to make her do something she didn't want to do.

"Thanks," he said, taking a few sips before setting it down.

He grabbed his suit coat and left his office.

The District Attorney's Office occupied the most prominent space in the Public Safety Complex, a complex and building that Roger had fought tirelessly to see constructed. It was more centrally located than the Sheriff's Office and larger than the courtrooms, emergency services, and fire administration, which took up only the first few floors of the main building. From his vantage point, he felt like a medieval lord, looking down on all those below him.

As he walked through the quiet floor, with only a few staff and attorneys still working at their desks or in small offices, he felt proud. He had turned this place into an efficient machine, more than tripling the allowable budget from the county council while gaining a reputation as one of Utah's toughest district attorneys. It was his greatest accomplishment . . . so far.

He nodded to someone on his way out and then went to the men's room.

This floor and the one below it were being renovated, and there was visible pink fiberglass where the walls should have been. The crew's paints and tools were stacked on the sides of the hallway in messy piles, the area closed off to everyone except workers for weeks.

When he reached for the door to the bathroom, his cell phone slipped out of his hand and hit the floor. As he bent down to retrieve it, he heard a loud clank from farther down the hallway.

Roger froze, staring in the direction of the sound. It was too dark to see anything, but he couldn't shake the feeling that someone was there, watching him. He quickly picked up his phone and stepped into the bathroom, trying to dismiss the eerie feeling.

The walls were paneled with brick and the brand-new sinks were made of stainless steel. The old buildings had barely held together and were eventually deemed unsafe for the police, courts, emergency services, fire, and paramedics they housed. When Roger saw the opportunity, he quickly spearheaded the campaign for new buildings and had a major hand in selecting the designers. In many ways, he felt like this building was his own.

After he finished his business in the bathroom and made his way to the elevators, he pulled out his phone to text his wife. Before he could tap out the first word, a loud noise startled him, and he spun around.

The sound reverberated through the hallway. It was a sharp, sudden crack that echoed off the walls and made his heart skip a beat. He couldn't quite place what it was, but it sounded heavy, like a stack of boxes tumbling to the floor. Or maybe it was something more significant, like a light fixture coming loose from the ceiling. For a moment, he couldn't move, couldn't think. As the echo faded, he shook his head, chiding himself for thinking like a child.

The sudden sound of a loud bang against an office door made him jump.

"Hello?" he said.

The elevator dinged and opened. He hesitated a moment, glancing toward the office where the sounds had come from, then ignored it and got onto the elevator.

As the elevator doors slid open on the first floor, Roger's eyes immediately darted toward the front desk. It was always manned by a police officer, but now the desk was empty.

"You need something, Mr. Lynch?" someone said near him.

Roger startled again and felt his heart in his throat as he caught sight of the officer assigned to the desk coming out of the bathroom.

"Didn't mean to scare ya," he said.

"You didn't. But I heard some noise up on our floor."

"Like what?"

"Like somebody was there in the sections being renovated. It's taped off and locked. No one should be there."

"Huh. All right, I can check it out when I do my rounds."

"Well, if you find anybody in there, tell them to be in my office at nine sharp on Monday. I made it very clear no one was allowed in the portions under construction. The last thing the county council wants right now is a lawsuit by an employee."

"All righty, I'll let ya know."

Roger nodded but didn't respond as he texted his wife, and then left the building and was hit with a blast of frigid air. The large lots on either side of the building were now empty and silent, except for the occasional gust of wind that caused the trees to sway and moan. The parking garage loomed next to the building like a dark abyss. Roger hurried through it, his footsteps echoing off the concrete walls. As he approached his parking spot on the second floor, he noticed a black Mustang and a Corvette parked next to his silver Mercedes.

He walked toward his car, and the feeling of being watched washed over him like a cold wave. His anger dissolved into fear as he turned around, scanning the dark corners of the garage, but he saw no one. He hurried to his car, fumbling with his keys, and as he finally got the car door open, a sudden noise made him jump. His heart pounded in his chest.

He glanced up and nearly screamed, but instead instinct took over, and he froze.

The BMW zipped past him, missing him by inches.

"What the hell are you doing!" Roger shouted at the top of his lungs.

The car accelerated away, its taillights disappearing around the curve to the parking level below and then the exit. Roger's eyes flicked to the cameras above, knowing they would capture the vehicle's license plate. But right now, he had bigger problems.

His wife had responded to his text, saying she didn't want to go to dinner tomorrow. He swore under his breath.

His pulse throbbed in his temples, an icy dread trickling down his spine. He'd meticulously planned tomorrow evening's dinner for two months. He needed the comptroller on his side if he was going to run for attorney general next year, and his wife knew it. The little power she had in their relationship she wielded like a fencer wields a foil, and tonight, she'd struck a crippling blow.

What can I do to get you to come? he texted, meaning, *What do you want me to buy for you to get you to do this?*

He unlocked his car and reached down to the handle when he felt pressure against his throat. It was soft at first, almost unnoticeable. Then he couldn't breathe, and then the pain hit. A thin pain just below his jaw that ran the length of his neck. It was then he realized someone had opened the door to the Mustang parked next to his car and wrapped something around his throat.

As panic set in, Roger's eyes darted around, trying to catch a glimpse of his attacker. But it was too dark to see anyone, and he could only feel the pressure against his throat growing tighter. He thrashed, trying to fight off the assailant, but it was like trying to break free from a python's grip. He kicked his legs and flailed his arms, hoping to connect with something or someone, but the wire around his throat only cut deeper, and the pain grew sharper. Finally, his hands found the wire, and he clawed desperately at it, but it was like trying to cut steel with his fingernails.

Desperately, Roger fought for his life.

He threw his weight around, bucking and jerking with everything he had. The attacker's grip tightened, and Roger felt his vision dim. The world around him started to spin, and he realized he was losing consciousness. But with a surge of adrenaline, he kicked up both feet and pushed off his car with all his strength, sending the attacker stumbling back.

Roger's heart thundered in his chest, each beat a desperate plea for oxygen as he gulped frantically at the air. His hands clawed at the wire around his neck, trying to loosen its deadly grip. Suddenly, the attacker's hand slipped slightly to the right, and Roger saw his chance. With a wild burst of energy, he sank his teeth into the attacker's fingers, biting down hard and drawing blood through the gloves. The wire loosened just enough for Roger to rip it away from his neck, and he tried to run, gasping for air.

Roger stumbled toward the other side of the parking garage, the sound of his own pounding footsteps echoing in his ears. He could hear the heavy footfalls of the attacker behind him, getting closer with each second. His heart was racing, and he knew he had to find a way to escape.

As he neared the edge of the garage, he saw a railing in front of him and didn't even hesitate before leaping over it. He landed on a thin tree that shook under his weight, grabbing onto branches to steady himself as he fell to the grass below.

The impact was jarring, and he winced as he felt the cuts from sharp bits of wood that had sliced his flesh, but he didn't stop moving. He scrambled to his feet and ran toward a car that was leaving the parking lot.

With a burst of desperation, he waved his hands and shouted for the driver to stop. The car screeched to a halt, and Roger recognized the employee behind the wheel.

Before he could even catch his breath, he looked up to the railing and saw that his attacker had vanished. With a groan of pain, he fell back onto the grass, the metallic taste of blood in his mouth.

10

Billie's eyes widened as she read the text message on her phone. She threw off her covers and sprang out of bed, her mind already racing with thoughts of what happened to Roger Lynch. Hurriedly, she made her way to the bathroom and turned on the shower, the noise of the water masking the sound of her racing thoughts.

As she stepped out of the shower, she wrapped a towel around herself and reached for her phone, checking the time. It was early. She pulled out a black suit from the closet and dressed herself, her movements efficient and practiced. She reached for her gun and checked to make sure it was loaded and secure.

As she made her way out the door, her eyes were drawn to a package on her doorstep. She froze, her heart in her throat. She hesitated for a moment, then cautiously made her way around it. She knew better than to take any chances, and on her phone, she quickly pulled up the footage from her doorbell camera.

A masked figure had left the package and fled.

"Damn it," she muttered under her breath.

Contrary to the glossy portrayals on television, crime scenes were ephemeral creatures. Time, the elements, the unsuspecting passersby, and even the tendrils of air pollution eroded fragile evidence. With each moment that passed, whoever tried to kill Roger slipped farther away.

With some hesitation, she texted one of her detectives to get the bomb squad to her house.

As the bomb squad meticulously inspected the package, unease settled deep in Billie's gut. She watched the robotic arm carefully lift the lid, revealing a pristine white cake with bold red icing. The captain's voice broke the silence, but Billie barely registered his words.

"It's a cake," he said.

At first Billie didn't understand, but then it dawned on her why a cake: it was the anniversary of her first date with Dax.

She told the captain to call in the Special Investigations Section and keep the package under tight surveillance until they arrived. As she retreated to her truck, she couldn't shake the feeling that she was being watched. Her eyes scanned the area around her, but she couldn't see anything out of the ordinary. It was an unsettling feeling. She knew that she couldn't let her guard down. Not when Dax was involved.

As Billie drove, her mind raced with all the possible scenarios of what Dax could have planned. The cake was a reminder that Dax was always there, always thinking about her, and probably always watching her.

How odd that at one time she had loved him. Or . . . was it love? She didn't know. She thought she had been in love before, and looking back now, she wasn't sure that either of them were real. Solomon had told her once that everyone gets three loves in their life, and she had already had two.

She took a deep breath and looked outside the windows. The mountains towered above her, their snow-capped peaks glistening in the morning sunlight. The fields of wild grass, which normally waved gently in the wind, were now shimmering snow.

Her phone buzzed, interrupting her thoughts. It was Mazie, letting her know that they had Dax in custody after waking him up in his apartment.

Billie felt a wave of relief wash over her. At least she knew where he was now.

Just then, a text from Solomon came through. Swiggy, who appeared to be some sort of investigator, had some information that could be valuable. Now she had three places to be at once. Sometimes she wondered how her father had done this job for forty years. The stress tolerance and energy required seemed to drain her to the point that she thought about quitting daily.

She took a deep breath and texted Solomon back that she would be there in a minute.

She adjusted her course and got onto the freeway, heading to Solomon's home. The drive was long, but the beautiful scenery around her provided some solace from the fact that Roger's attacker could be halfway across the state by now.

Solomon waited patiently on the inside of the fenced area, his hands clasped together over his cane. As soon as he saw Billie approaching in her truck, he opened the gate, inputting a code on the keypad before the gate closed shut behind him. When he reached the truck, she couldn't help but notice the state of his clothes. His slacks and sweater were worn out, with frayed edges and visible signs of wear and tear.

"You don't approve of the clothes?" Solomon remarked, with a hint of amusement in his voice. His ability to read Billie's thoughts and emotions from her body language and facial expressions was both impressive and unnerving.

"Don't worry," he added, "I'm not offended. I haven't bought any new clothes in . . . I don't even remember how long. Nothing lasts forever, right? Even the pyramids of Giza are falling apart."

She grinned and said, "We need to make a stop first."

She parked the truck in front of the sprawling Public Safety Complex, the imposing structures looming over them. The concrete facade seemed to stretch on forever, and the sheer space the campus took up was enough to make anyone feel small.

As they made their way through the busy lobby, Solomon kept glancing around nervously, his eyes darting from person to person. He avoided eye contact and didn't even acknowledge the greetings from officers or staff who recognized him. Billie could feel his unease, and she wondered how long he had been away from people. She couldn't imagine living in that massive house all alone. The way Solomon acted now, as though he was ready to sneak out a back door, made her realize that isolation wasn't a gift.

They pushed onto a packed elevator. Whispers and murmurs floated around them like a thick fog. It was clear that the news of the attack on the DA had spread quickly, and people were on edge.

The elevator doors opened, and they stepped out onto the floor. It was like a scene from a movie: people talking in hushed tones, looking up at the two of them as they walked past.

As they approached Roger's office, she could hear him shouting through the door. She glanced over at Solomon, who was tapping his cane nervously on the carpet.

"Are you okay?" she asked softly.

"Just dandy," he replied, his voice shaking. He looked like he was about to have a panic attack.

"You don't have to come in. I'll be out in a minute."

"Um, yeah, I guess I can just have a seat."

The waiting area was dimly lit and smelled faintly of coffee. A young woman sat behind a large desk covered in paperwork. She wore a crisp white blouse and had her hair pulled back into a tight bun. Solomon hesitated for a moment before taking a seat in one of the chairs next to the desk.

Billie walked into Roger's office, his shouting becoming louder as she approached. She could see the assistant district attorney, Mike, a well-groomed man with perfectly styled hair, sitting across from Roger.

He wore an expensive suit, and his shoes looked like they had never touched a single pebble. Despite the tense situation, the man's face remained perfectly calm and collected as he flipped through his phone.

Billie wondered how someone could be so composed in the presence of Roger's explosive anger. She guessed he must spend a lot of time with him to have developed such a thick skin.

Roger slammed the phone down and shouted, "Where were you?"

"Got held up. You doing okay?"

"Do I look like I'm doing okay, Sheriff? Someone tried to kill me in my own parking lot."

She opened her note-taking app on her phone. "I'll need all the details and the video footage from the lot."

"Fine. Mike, get her what she needs."

The assistant DA nodded but didn't take his eyes off his phone.

Roger said, "When I need you in an emergency, you drop everything and get down here."

Solomon opened the door and leaned against the doorframe. Roger looked like a ghost had just come in and said hello. His mouth was partially open, and his eyes were wide.

"Do you just assume everybody has to do what you say, Roger?" Solomon said.

The speed at which Roger regained his composure was impressive. His mouth shut, his eyes returned to normal, and he leaned back in his seat in a comfortable pose as though chatting with a friend he hadn't seen in a while.

"Nice clothes, Solomon. Are you homeless now? I've always thought that's how you would end up."

"Is this your subtle way of asking for fashion advice, Roger?"

Mike snorted as he tried to suppress a laugh. He cleared his throat as Roger's eyes fixed on him with the laser focus that unnerved most people. "Got something in my throat," he said matter-of-factly.

Roger looked to the sheriff. "You brought him in to help you with this? I'm flattered."

"Sure, Roger, it's all about you."

"I'm dealing with enough right now. I don't need your attitude on top of it."

She sighed. "I'll find who did this. But you need to not make my job harder by constantly being on TV talking about this."

"We'll see. Public loves a survivor."

"You won't be much of a survivor if we don't figure out why you were targeted, because it's probably going to happen again."

"Well, then you better hurry and find him, Sheriff," Roger said, his voice stern and severe, "because the clock is ticking."

11

Billie asked Mazie to drive them, and she sat in the passenger seat as Solomon climbed into the back of the cruiser. There was a thick, transparent plastic shield separating the patrol deputies up front from the arrestees in back.

"So, Sol," Mazie said, "Billie said you were a social worker at the prison before becoming a prosecutor."

"Sure was."

"I bet you have some crazy stories."

"Not really. People are pretty much the same everywhere. Those of us outside the mental institutions and prisons aren't much saner than anybody in there."

"Jeez, you're a ray of sunshine."

"You're not the first person to tell me that," he said, glancing at Billie.

As they merged onto the freeway, the rush of cars was more intense than Solomon remembered. The once-open road was now packed with vehicles, their headlights and taillights blurring together in a sea of motion. The sound of engines and honking horns filled the air, a chaotic symphony of urban life. Solomon wondered how fast the population had grown in recent years, or if the crowded conditions were simply a product of his own perception.

"This isn't the way to Swiggy's," Solomon said.

"We're making one more stop," Billie said.

"Where?"

Amara Men's Clothing was a fashionable mom-and-pop setup at the local mall that Solomon had always liked to shop at. The owner, Ralph, was an older man who had lost his wife about ten years prior. He built up the business to three locations and was going to go for a fourth when his wife passed, and he just didn't have the passion for it anymore. He once told Solomon that success was only fun if you had someone to share it with.

"Seriously?" Solomon said as they parked out front of the shopping mall, the last one left in the county. "You don't think we have more important stuff to be doing right now? Like meeting with my investigator who's waiting for us?"

"It'll only take a minute," Billie said.

Mazie added, "Yeah, seriously, Sol, you need some new threads. You can't look like you stepped out of Lawrence Welk or whatever."

"How do you know about Lawrence Welk?"

"I have a grandma. Come on, I'm excited. Let's get you decked out."

The mall was practically empty except for a few people in Gap and a few more in Bath & Body Works. Solomon used to hang out at this mall in his youth. They had both a bookstore and an arcade, so he would save up as much as he could during the week, usually selling candy to other classmates for ridiculously marked-up prices, and then would go on Saturday when the mall opened and leave when it closed. Sometimes his brother, Ethan, would come with him, but Solomon preferred solitude, though at times he was anxious that it was actually isolation he was after.

On the rare occasions Solomon thought about his older brother, it made him melancholy. He'd once, out of curiosity, tracked him down and found that he had joined the military at eighteen and been transferred overseas. Solomon had never reached out to talk to him. He was starting to forget what he looked like.

But he would never forget the arcade: the scent of warm machines, overpowering cologne from the teenage boys who were eager to impress the girls, and occasionally the wafting of marijuana smoke from the employees toking up in the back office. It was the most intoxicating mixture of smells Solomon remembered from youth.

The arcade was gone, replaced by a med spa and a drug-and-alcohol-testing center.

Amara smelled the same: dust and leather. The jackets were near the door with the jeans and shirts in the back. Ralph Amara was behind the register ringing someone up. He had aged over the years. He was hunched over now, and his skin looked sallow. Less hair and dimmer eyes. Solomon smiled at him, and the man smiled back.

"Where you been?" Ralph said in a voice that seemed lower, perhaps weaker, than Solomon remembered.

"Just hiding out. You staying out of trouble?"

"Never." He straightened up. "I read about what happened with that big fella a few years ago in the paper. I was sorry as hell about all that. I sent a gift basket. Did you get it?"

"I did. Thank you. Some seriously delicious stuff."

"Mary used to get it for anyone in the neighborhood that had to go to the hospital." He waved his hand like he was wiping away a thought. "You're not here to listen to an old man ramble. What can I do for you?"

Mazie said, "Just look at him. Isn't it obvious?"

A look of concern came over Ralph's face as he noticed Solomon's clothing for the first time. "All right, I know just what to do."

Solomon was forced into buying three pairs of jeans, several shirts, and a sports jacket with slacks and nice shoes. He drew the line at ties.

He came out of the shop in jeans and a white button-up shirt with a black jacket and a leather bracelet Mazie insisted he get because it looked cool. They chatted a few more minutes with Ralph and then left.

Mazie admired the clothing and said, "You actually look hot."

"Coming from practically a child, that's just sad."

"Whatever. I know hot. Don't you agree, Sheriff?"

"Certainly," Billie said, sensing his embarrassment. "Not being handsome enough has never been Solomon's problem."

Solomon blushed as they got outside to the parking lot and headed to the cruiser. "Wanna grab a shawarma?" he said to change the subject.

Billie got into the passenger seat and said, "I believe you were just berating me for making your investigator wait."

"Yeah, but I'll always stop what I'm doing for shawarma."

Mazie was the last one to get in and turned the car on. She checked her face in the mirror and ran a finger underneath her eye to remove a bit of makeup. She then pulled out, and a song came on her playlist that she turned up. It was Taylor Swift.

"You like Taylor Swift?" she asked Solomon.

"I love all types of music. Not normally what I listen to, though."

"What do you listen to?"

Billie said, "You don't want to know."

Mazie looked in the rearview. "I'm curious now."

Solomon said, "Gimme your phone."

He took the phone and searched for a song. For a moment, there was silence, and then a sudden explosion of sound burst from the speakers. Thunderous drums pounded out a primal beat, followed by screeching guitar riffs and a driving bass line. And then, the front man's voice tore through the air like a growl, raw and intense. It wasn't singing so much as it was a guttural expression of pure emotion.

Mazie shouted over the music, "Black death metal, huh? Who's this band?"

"Stabbed by Satan."

Billie shouted, "Charming, but can we listen to something that doesn't make me think my head's in a blender?"

Solomon turned it off. "That's a very descriptive way to describe this music, Sheriff."

Mazie said, "What'd ya like so much about it? I couldn't understand a word he was saying."

He handed the phone back as they got on the freeway. "It's pure barbarism. We all have some barbarian in us, right?"

The club was a sprawling space situated in the heart of an industrial section of the county. Solomon scanned the exterior of the building, taking in the details of what appeared to be a converted diner. The old orange awnings that once shaded the windows were now faded and tattered, and the outline of the name of an Italian restaurant that had long since closed was barely visible on the front facade. The entire area was devoid of any other signage or distinguishing features, lending an air of secrecy and exclusivity to the club.

Mazie parked in front.

"I don't think I've ever been here," Billie said.

"Swiggy owns it."

"What is it?"

"A sex club."

Solomon got out of the car as Mazie said, "Wait, what?"

Solomon opened the door for Billie and told Mazie, "Sorry, short stuff. Adults only."

"I'm not a kid. I can handle seeing a sex club."

"Fair enough. But if we had two cops in there, especially one in a uniform, it'll make him really nervous, and I need him comfortable."

"Oh, come on. I've never seen the inside of a sex club."

"Google it."

She rolled her eyes and sighed. "Fine. I'll be in the car like always, I guess."

The entrance to the club loomed before them, the imposing double doors painted a deep, inky black. As they drew closer, Solomon could see that the doors were padded, as if they were designed to keep sound from escaping the building.

As they stepped inside, Solomon felt like he was walking into a void, with no discernible source of light. The darkness was so complete that he could barely make out the shapes of people moving around him. The only sound was the muffled thumping of the bass from the music that was turned low, like a heartbeat reverberating through the walls.

Suddenly, Swiggy's voice cut through the darkness, harsh and grating. "Hey! Turn the lights up, will ya?"

The track lighting came on, casting a dim glow across the room. Shadows flickered and danced on the walls, giving the space a dreamlike quality.

"You hiding a vampire in here, Swiggy?"

Now that they had some lighting, Solomon could see Swiggy sitting with stacks of cash at a table.

"My clientele prefers dim lighting. They come here to indulge in things not meant for the eyes of the public. I assumed you, being a shrink, would understand the need for discretion," he said with a sly grin.

"I wasn't a shrink. And I'm a *live and let live* kinda guy. It's just having sex with multiple strangers at the same time doesn't sound appealing to me. Sounds very . . . germy. Good on you for following your bliss, though, man."

Swiggy chuckled. "Lord help me if this is my bliss."

Solomon settled into a battered leather chair, his cane resting between his legs, his hands clasped on top of the lion-shaped handle. He leaned back slightly, taking in his surroundings, while Billie opted to stand, surveying the club with a keen eye.

"I can't believe you brought the sheriff here," Swiggy said. "Sheriff, please forget you ever saw this place."

"Not a problem," she said with a look of disgust as she saw a painting of something with tentacles attacking scantily clad women.

"See?" Solomon said. "Told you she was cool."

Swiggy finished meticulously counting the bills and stacked them neatly in a pile. With a sense of satisfaction, he leaned back in his chair and picked up a tumbler of amber-colored whiskey. He took a long, deep sip and then lowered the glass. "Gimme your phone," Swiggy said.

Solomon extended his phone toward Swiggy, who took it and swiftly swiped his own phone over it, causing Solomon's phone to emit a distinctive ding.

"You got the file. Some photos in there, too."

"Photos of who?" Solomon said, taking back his phone.

"Our good mayor was a dirty dog. At least twenty women he had affairs with in there. I got as much background on all of them as I could. A few of them were married."

Solomon nodded. "The husband of the married lover as murderer . . . that's too cliché, man."

"Clichés are clichés for a reason. It's almost always the husband or boyfriend."

"The operative word is *almost*, Swiggy. What do you do when it's not the husband or boyfriend and you have no evidence to go on?"

"Pfff. You can keep all that. I'm not trying to understand these people."

Solomon was impressed Swiggy understood enough to not want to get involved in these types of cases. Probably one of the reasons Swiggy quit law enforcement as a detective with the Las Vegas Metro PD.

Solomon opened the files on his phone and looked at the first entry. A woman named Nicole Hearst, a legal secretary at Dennis's old firm.

"What else?" Solomon said.

"That's not enough?"

"Any half-decent investigator could've got me this. That's not your style to just do the minimum."

He smirked before taking another sip of whiskey. "Maybe I've gotten lazy in my retirement."

"You? I think you'll work in your coffin. You need to slow down. It's really important to do nothing sometimes. Just sit around and do nothing. It keeps you balanced."

"When I was a kid, I lived in a motel room with my mom and three brothers, so I'm not sitting around on my ass when there's paying work I could be doing." Swiggy leaned back in his chair, his eyes fixed on Solomon. His facial expression was impassive, betraying nothing of his thoughts, and his body language was relaxed, one hand draped over the arm of the chair. Despite his comfortable demeanor, there was an air of intensity about him, as if he was always on the brink of action.

He finished his whiskey and said, "But you're right, I'm trying to slow down. That's why I quit this investigator shit, Solomon."

"I know, and I'm sorry to drag you back into that world, but I need this."

"Yeah, well, there's a few juicy bits, so maybe it is important."

"Like what?"

"He defended some dangerous people, and not all of them were happy with his representation."

"Like who?"

"Like your old pal Bigfoot Tommy."

"Defending doesn't mean anything. Guy was constantly getting arrested."

He shook his head. "Not like this. Tommy had one of his soldiers smuggling H into prison by having some of his girls come visit him with the stash tucked in places it shouldn't be tucked. The balloons the H was wrapped in burst one time, and the girl died. So they busted Tommy's man for it. Dennis defended him. He was looking at life, but Dennis got him a deal to testify against Tommy, and the guy agreed.

Tommy got locked up while trial was pending, and the dude mysteriously disappeared, so Tommy walked. But I know Tommy, and I don't think he'd let a thing like that go."

Solomon leaned back in his seat, rubbing his lion's head cane lightly with his thumbs. Out of everyone he had met, Bigfoot Tommy was one of the most frightening. A former Green Beret who had clawed his way to becoming a high-ranking member of a violent biker gang, which happened to be the perfect profession for a six-foot-seven sociopath.

"Well, that's a problem. Tommy hates my guts."

"Didn't you try to put him away a buncha times?" Swiggy said.

"Guy shouldn't be out on the streets."

He shrugged. "Sometimes that's the system, right? You can't catch 'em all."

Solomon sighed. "Anything else?"

"Just a question. I know you and the mayor weren't close. Why you care so much about all this?"

"I thought it was no questions asked?"

He laughed. "Shit, all right, be that way." He looked over to the thin man in a black T-shirt behind the bar stocking bottles. "Maynard, two shots of Azul."

Solomon said, "Little early for tequila, Swiggy."

"You working right now?"

"Working?"

"Yeah. You got a job?"

"No."

"My old man said if a man don't work, he better drink, otherwise he'll go crazy."

The tequila came in tall shot glasses. Swiggy held his up, and Solomon did the same.

"How 'bout a toast, Counselor?"

They tapped glasses and Solomon said, "May we be good, and if we can't be good, may we crash and burn quickly."

Swiggy chuckled and then threw the tequila down his throat. Solomon shot it down as well, and Swiggy said, "A man that can drink like that probably drinks too much."

"Or he's numb," Solomon said, rising. "Appreciate it, my friend," he said, giving him a fist bump.

"Stay up, brother," Swiggy said, picking up his cash and heading to a back office.

Solomon went up to Billie, who was leaning against a nearby table with her arms folded.

"You look like a fish out of water, Sheriff."

"Made the mistake of going to the back room and saw what was in there. People are into some . . . interesting things."

"Whatever trauma you've gone through comes out in the bedroom."

"That's true. I guess it's better to take control of it."

"Don't kid yourself. None of us control it." He hesitated a second and tapped his cane against the floor. "I need a favor. I need you to take me to the prison and get me a private meeting with an inmate and not ask why, and not record the interview."

She unfolded her arms with a sigh. "This sounds like the type of favor I'm going to regret."

"Definitely."

12

The sun shone bright and warm on the highway as they drove toward the Utah State Prison in Draper, the wide expanse of desert stretching out around them. A cold wind rushed in through the open window and Mazie sang along to the radio with abandon. Solomon sat in the back seat, watching her with a wistful expression. He envied her carefree attitude, the way she seemed to take pleasure in the little things, like a good song on the radio or the feeling of the wind on her face. For him, life had become so complicated, so uncertain. He longed for the days when things were simpler, when he could move through the world without fear.

Billie was speaking on the phone to the warden of the prison, an old friend she had a good relationship with. It was so easy to be nice and took so much effort to be a jerk that Solomon wondered why someone as clearly brilliant as Roger wouldn't see that.

"So, what was the sex club like?" Mazie asked Billie when she was off the phone.

"Exactly what you'd expect," Billie replied.

"Like, chains and stuff?"

"No, not chains. They're much more creative than that."

When they arrived at the prison and parked, Solomon told Mazie to stay with the car. "Car duty, short stuff," he said.

"Are you freaking kidding me?" she protested.

"Hey, you get to spend all day with your boss kissing her butt. You know how many people would step over their own mothers for that opportunity?"

Mazie shouted some profanity as Solomon closed the door.

"I like her," Solomon said.

The path wound around the towering fence, topped with razor wire, and led to an entrance where several inmates were working on repairs. It was likely that they were paid less than forty cents an hour for their labor. As Billie approached, one of the inmates caught her eye and quickly looked away when he saw the badge clipped to her waistband.

"I hate coming here," Solomon muttered as they walked down the narrow corridor, surrounded on both sides by an electrified fence. "The idea of men locked away like animals never sat well with me."

"Some men need to be locked away."

"Maybe. Or maybe in a civilized society we'd ship them to an island to live freely together and still keep society safe."

She glanced at him.

"What? I'm reading a science fiction book where they're doing that, and it's turning out okay so far," he said.

As they entered the front office, he felt a ball of anxiety in his belly. "It's so claustrophobic in here. You don't even have to be locked up to feel like the walls are closing in."

"It's better than the alternative," Billie replied. "There was a time in this country when mob justice was the only justice anyone got."

The guard's desk was situated in the main lobby, which was a vast space with off-white walls, fluorescent lights, and a concrete floor that echoed with every footstep. The sound of heavy metal doors slamming shut could be heard in the distance.

"What have you found on Roger's secret admirer?" Solomon said as they waited in the check-in line for professional visits.

"Seems so far we have a little bit of everything. A jilted former mistress, two former business partners who feel Roger swindled them, and just about every convict in the county who believes they were treated unjustly. So, take your pick, I guess."

"Forensics come up with anything?"

She shook her head. "We know it was a black Mustang. One of the cameras caught it speeding out, but it didn't have any plates, and the windows were tinted."

"No plates, huh? That's weird that he'd risk getting pulled over. I wonder if he stopped somewhere after and put them on?"

"I thought that, too. I'm having videos pulled from the nearby parking lots of grocery stores and restaurants."

After signing in, they were given plastic guest badges with bold black letters that read "VISITOR." A bald man with a scar on his face was sitting in a corner, next to a vending machine that was stocked with snacks and drinks. His wrinkled uniform was stained with what appeared to be dried blood, and his eyes had a distant, almost feral look to them.

Billie handed Solomon the guest badge. "Room 241. The guard will take you there," she said.

"I didn't tell you who I needed to see," Solomon said.

"I know you well enough. Just be careful, okay?"

The guard with the scar on his face led Solomon through the maze of white brick corridors with thick plastic windows. They passed several doors before reaching the visiting rooms. In one room, several circular tables were set up with vending machines against the wall. A place for families of those locked up to visit with their children.

They walked past that room and entered a small windowless space with a table and a few chairs.

The walls of the room were bare and painted a dull gray. A flickering fluorescent light overhead made the space feel even more sterile. The table was chipped and scuffed, and the chairs were old and uncomfortable. The only sound was that of Solomon's cane tapping against the floor as he made his way to the table.

The guard held the door open and said, "I'll be in the hall if you need me. He'll be shackled at all times. Do not pass him anything, and do not touch him. Do you understand?"

"Yes," Solomon replied.

He sat down facing the door. The guard left, and the door closed with a metallic clang. The room was barely bigger than a cell, and he couldn't imagine spending the rest of his life in such a confined space.

The tightness of the room made his chest feel constricted, making it hard to breathe. He closed his eyes and took deep breaths, following the four-seven-eight pattern. Inhale for four, hold for seven, exhale for eight. The timing was important because this type of breathing helped to reset a person's nervous system. He kept his eyes closed, focusing solely on his breath as he inhaled and exhaled.

When he felt himself calm, he opened his eyes just as the guard led in Bigfoot Tommy.

Solomon's eyes widened slightly as he saw Bigfoot Tommy, his massive frame taking up almost the entire space in the small room. The fluorescent lights overhead seemed to make his bulging muscles stand out even more, casting deep shadows in the crevices of his arms. His skin was the color of milk, with tattoos stretching down his thick neck and over his muscular forearms. The sound of the chair groaning under his weight only added to the oppressive feeling of the room, and Solomon had to suppress the urge to shift uncomfortably in his seat.

"Ten minutes," the guard said, shutting the door.

When they were alone, neither of them said anything for a moment, and then Tommy said, "Usually when people come here asking me for favors, they offer me something."

"What makes you think I need a favor?"

"You here to check up on me then? I didn't know you cared."

"Of course I do. It's not every day you meet a pure sociopath."

"Not a psychopath?"

Solomon shook his head. "You can control it when you want to. A pure psychopath wouldn't be able to. Their disorder is innate, where sociopathy is thought to come more from environmental factors."

He grinned. "Guess getting thrown out of a hotel window by your mom when you're a kid will do that."

Solomon felt a pang of sympathy. He already knew about Tommy's history, and even though he felt the man should never be let out of prison, his personal history was just so . . . sad.

Tommy glanced down to Solomon's cane. "It's not so bad. Made me who I am. Gave me the gift of rage."

"Gift?"

He nodded. "When I let go, I mean really let go and don't give a shit about anything, not getting locked up, not dying, not killing, it's pure freedom."

"It's an illusion, Tommy. Look where you are. That type of thinking doesn't bring freedom. Not in the long run."

"In the long run we're all dead."

A beat of silence between them.

"When you outta here?" Solomon said, tapping his cane against the cement floor.

"Four months."

"I didn't see what you're locked up for."

"Same as always. Some new prospect that barely got his training wheels off gets popped for dope or guns, and decides to cut a deal to testify against me. Happens a lot. This generation just don't have a sense of honor."

"I'm guessing this troublesome prospect isn't going to make it to court?"

Tommy said nothing, leaning back in his chair.

"What do you want?" he said.

"What do you know about Dennis Yang?"

"He was a piece a shit person and a worse mayor. No one's gonna miss him."

"I think his kids would disagree."

Tommy folded his arms. "Why you here?"

"Just wanna make sure it actually is a suicide."

"So you're here 'cause you think I killed that little turd?"

"No, I know you didn't kill him. It's not your style. You'd want to send a message, and making us think it's a suicide doesn't send that message. But you might know something that can help me."

He chuckled. "Even if I did, why the hell would I help you?"

"There's gotta be something you want that I can help get."

Solomon tried to keep his body still and his face blank, but he couldn't help the way his pulse quickened and the hair on the back of his neck stood up with anticipation. He felt a thrill of adrenaline course through him as he realized that Tommy might actually know something about this. It was a feeling akin to the rush he got when he played his favorite game of chess and saw a way to gain an advantage over his opponent, the sense of being in control and about to make an important move.

Tommy leaned forward and put his elbows on the table. "There's something you can do. But you ain't gonna like it."

13

Solomon found Billie standing in the front lobby, surrounded by a group of guards who were trying their best to impress her. Men always seemed to be attracted to her, and Solomon initially thought it was because of her natural charisma and confidence, but as he was around her more over the years, he realized other men weren't seeing it. They saw only the body. It shocked him that there were men who could look at Billie and not see the force of energy that she was.

As he approached, the guards dispersed, giving him a nod of recognition.

He remembered a time when he and Billie had attended a Christmas party together, hosted by Roger for the employees of the DA's and sheriff's offices. Billie had shown up in a festive Mrs. Claus outfit, which had caught the attention of one detective who couldn't keep his eyes off her. After a few too many drinks, he made a crude remark to Solomon about her.

Solomon had quickly shut him down, staring into his eyes with a cold intensity that let the detective know this wasn't a conversation he wanted to finish. The first thought Solomon had was just to hit him, something grossly uncharacteristic of him. It was moments like those that reminded him there were parts of him that scared him.

What the detective had done next surprised Solomon. The man's face had registered a look of confusion as he struggled to understand what he had said that was so offensive. After a few awkward moments of silence, he had shrugged, grabbed his next glass of beer, and wandered off into the crowd.

Billie told the guards to have a good day and joined Solomon to stroll out of the lobby and take the path to the front entrance again. They came outside, and the sun was out, poking through clouds.

"So?" she asked.

"We gotta do him a favor."

Mazie was putting on eyeliner, and the car was filled with the scent of her perfume, a floral and musky aroma that seemed to cling to everything. Her movements were precise and practiced, each stroke of the eyeliner pen adding to the intensity of her gaze. She reminded Solomon of a girl he knew once, a girl who had no one but Solomon to look after her and was killed by the two people who should have been protecting her.

He noticed the way Mazie's thin fingers moved and the small furrow in her brow as she concentrated. "So, where we heading next?" she said.

"You guys are really gonna hate me," Solomon said.

The sun beat down on the snowy landscape, casting long shadows on the worn buildings. The main house was massive, with shuttered windows and chipping paint that made it appear fifty years older than it was. A barn was near it, enormous in its own right, along with several smaller buildings. All dilapidated, all with the windows shuttered. Then barren, lifeless desert for twenty miles in every direction.

The gate was closed and locked, and the cruiser stopped in front of it. Three bikers approached the gate, their leather jackets and boots creaking in the cold. One of them, a burly man with a thick beard and a scar across his cheek, reached out to unlock the gate. They'd seen the cruiser long before it had arrived.

Solomon opened his door and said, "I better talk to them myself."

Billie said, "I'm coming with you."

"No offense, Sheriff, but I don't think they're gonna be happy that I brought the top cop in the county to their door. Trust me on this. I've worked with these guys a lot."

"Will you at least tell me what we're doing here?"

"The less you know, the better."

The man's face was rough and scarred, as if he had lived a lifetime of violence. His eyes were small and dark, darting around, constantly searching for a threat. Solomon could feel the tension in the air as the man approached, his hand resting on the hilt of a large knife on his belt. The gate was old and rusted, with flaking paint and dents, and it groaned as the man pulled it open just enough for him to slip through. The smell of gasoline and oil mixed with the stench of his unwashed body.

"You got balls to roll a cop car up here," the biker said.

"I met with Tommy half an hour ago, and he gave me some instructions to give to Comanche."

The man's gaze lingered on him, his eyes scanning him up and down, trying to determine if he posed any danger. Eventually, he let out a contemptuous grunt and spit on the ground. "Stay close to me."

Solomon followed the man through the gate and into the compound. He could feel the pressure in the air as they walked past the other bikers, who all stared at him with suspicion. Solomon tried to ignore their hostile glances and focus.

The man led him to a large building at the center of the compound, where he knocked on the door. A gruff voice from inside told them to come in, and the man pushed the door open.

Solomon followed the biker into the home, his nostrils immediately assaulted by the pungent, acrid smell of burning meth. The surroundings were claustrophobic, and he felt uneasy as he took in the cluttered and dirty environment.

Victor Methos

Trash was scattered everywhere, creating a makeshift obstacle course for anyone navigating the space. The walls were littered with posters of scantily clad women and biker paraphernalia, and the windows were blacked out. No one seemed to notice the stranger.

They took some stairs leading down to the basement.

A swastika flag was tattered and stained, and a Confederate flag looked like it had been passed down for generations. The space was sparsely lit by a few dim bulbs, casting long shadows on the walls.

The basement was unfinished, with exposed pipes and wires dangling from the ceiling. The air was thick with the smell of cigarette smoke.

As Comanche looked up at them from a wood desk that appeared to be a giant butcher block, the dim light cast a shadow over his face, obscuring his features. Solomon strained his eyes to make out the man's expression. The goatee caught the light, making it shimmer like strands of silver. Comanche's chest heaved as he took a deep breath, the bulldog tattoo flexing on his forearm. The smell of cigarette smoke mixed with the scent of sweat and leather, making the air thick and unpleasant. The swastika flag behind Comanche seemed to pulse with a dark energy, its blackness drawing Solomon's gaze.

Comanche nodded at the biker, who then left the room.

Comanche motioned for Solomon to take a seat, and he did, settling into one of the folding chairs and placing his cane between his legs. He felt a sense of discomfort as he sat across from Comanche, knowing that he was in the presence of someone extremely dangerous, someone who wouldn't hesitate to kill if he thought it was in the best interest of his club.

"You remember me?" Solomon asked Comanche, trying to gauge the man's reaction.

"I do," Comanche replied, his expression impassive.

Solomon knew that the low-level members of any gang or criminal organization were often the easiest to manipulate or turn informant, as they were the least experienced and the most afraid of incarceration. People in Comanche's position were, on the other hand, a different breed of criminal. He was old-school gangster, the type who believed that there was still some honor in being an outlaw.

"You want a drink?" Comanche asked.

"I'm good, thank you," Solomon replied.

"Box said you have a message for me from Tommy."

"I do," Solomon said, leaning back in his chair. "He wants me to—"

But before he could finish, Box came rushing into the room, interrupting them. "He brought the sheriff here," he said breathlessly.

Comanche's eyes narrowed as he lifted the gun that had been hidden underneath the desk and pointed it directly at Solomon.

"Whoa, easy, big guy. I'm just a messenger for your boss," Solomon said quickly, holding up his hands in a placating gesture.

"You brought that bitch here, and you think I'm gonna trust a word that comes outta your mouth?" Comanche growled.

"So, I'm guessing you two are acquainted?" Solomon said.

"What are you really doing here? And if you lie, you're not gonna have a good day," Comanche snarled, keeping the gun trained on Solomon.

"I don't know what's going on between you and the sheriff," Solomon replied truthfully. "I'm just here because Tommy asked me to come. He wanted me to give you this message: he wants you to give me the Cadillac."

"Uh-huh. And I'm just supposed to take your word for it?"

Solomon glanced behind him and saw Box holding a semiautomatic pistol against his leg, ready to intervene if necessary. He knew that he would need to tread carefully.

"Tommy said he was going to call you about me coming by," Solomon said, trying to keep the conversation on track. "And I just realized something: I think he thought it would be funnier if you didn't know anything about it. Now, I like having a gun pointed at my face by itchy sociopaths as much as the next guy, but can I just get the car and get out of here?"

Comanche studied Solomon for a moment, then looked up at Box, who nodded and put his gun away. "He called me, but he told me to not make it fun for you. Car's out back."

"I'll take you," Box said, and Solomon rose from his chair, still feeling Comanche's eyes on him. He couldn't shake the feeling that a bullet could come tearing through his back at any moment, and he felt a wave of relief as they turned a corner and he was back on the stairs leading up.

They emerged outside, and Solomon could see Billie leaning against the car with her arms crossed. Several of the bikers were on the other side of the fence, giving her dirty looks but not saying anything. Box led Solomon to the barn, which was locked up tight. All the openings had been boarded up except for the main door, which was bolted shut with a large metal rod. Box opened the door and went inside, and Solomon followed him.

Inside was a red Cadillac, older but well maintained. A bumper sticker proclaimed the number of kids and grandkids the owner had, with stickers of each child running along the bumper to the end, where a puppy on a leash was held by one of the boys. Box handed Solomon a small slip of paper. "Drop it off there. I'll call and let 'em know you're coming," he said.

Solomon said nothing.

"I'll really call, don't worry," Box said, sensing Solomon's hesitation.

Solomon nodded, accepting the keys to the Cadillac from Box. He took a deep breath, debating whether to follow Tommy's instructions or not. He knew that Tommy couldn't be broken or threatened, and if Tommy had information that Solomon wanted, it would only be given willingly.

Box was about to leave when Solomon spoke up. "Can you let the sheriff in?" he asked.

"Why?" Box asked, turning back to face him.

"Because I can't drive."

Box hesitated for a moment, then nodded. "Fine," he said grudgingly. "I'll let her in. But I ain't responsible if anything happens."

14

Solomon watched from the entrance to the barn as Billie was let into the compound. A beefy biker obstructed her near the gate, but Box motioned him aside with a stern gaze. She walked alongside Box through the compound, past rows of gleaming motorcycles, and they reached the aged barn. She got into the Cadillac without a word, and she and Solomon pulled the car out.

Mazie followed closely behind in the cruiser as Billie drove the Cadillac out of the compound. They could see the bikers watching them from behind the gate as they drove away, but soon they turned a corner and were out of sight.

"Solomon, I trust you, but this is getting sketchy. What are we doing with this car?" Billie asked, glancing over at him.

"Just dropping it off."

"To who?"

"I don't totally know."

They continued driving, eventually making their way to downtown Salt Lake City, where the homeless shelters and liquor stores were situated next to high-end restaurants and hotels. In a section of downtown reserved for businesses that needed cheaper space, they found an apartment complex made up of white buildings with yellow trim around the doors and windows.

Billie pulled the car to a stop in the back of the complex, near the dumpsters, just as Tommy had instructed. "Are you going to tell me what's going on or not?" Billie asked, turning to face Solomon.

"We're just dropping this car off, and some guy's picking it up. That's it. That's all I know," Solomon said, trying to brush off her concerns.

"And what's in this car exactly?" Billie said.

"Didn't ask."

"Drugs?" Billie said incredulously, her voice taking on an angry edge.

"Maybe. Didn't ask," Solomon repeated.

"Solomon, we can't deliver this car without knowing what's in it," Billie said, her frustration growing.

"Maybe nothing's in it. I don't know," Solomon said, his tone defensive.

"You're purposely not finding out because you know if you do, you won't be able to do this."

"We have to do it."

"No, we don't."

"We need the information Tommy has."

"We don't."

"We do," he said, looking at her. "We can't threaten someone like Tommy—all we can do is deal with him. He promised nothing like a dead body is in the car, or pounds of cocaine or something. He said he just needs the car delivered. It'll be fine."

The words sounded empty, but Solomon knew that taking on this risk, or almost any risk, was worth it for the information Tommy had. Because sometimes, he could still feel his mother's sticky blood on his hands.

"Why can't one of his men do it?"

"That was the part he wouldn't explain to me. I assume it'll be terrible for me down the line somehow, whatever it is." He sighed, relenting. "Looking back at it, yeah, it was dumb, but I think he knows something about this. If I didn't need someone to drive, I wouldn't have even brought you here."

"Well, I am here, and I would appreciate being told beforehand what exactly we're doing."

"You're right. I'm sorry." She held his gaze. "No, seriously, I'm sorry."

She relented and leaned back in the seat.

As Solomon looked out the windows of the car, he saw the apartments looming before him like a row of decaying teeth. The building's paint was chipping, and the concrete was stained with years of grime and neglect. He almost shivered at the memories that flooded his mind when he saw the run-down place.

"What are you thinking about right now?" Billie said.

"Why?"

"You look so . . . sad. I'm just curious."

Solomon's throat tightened as he struggled to swallow. He could feel the weight of the sadness pressing down on him, like a heavy, wet blanket that threatened to suffocate him.

"I stayed in a place like this once in foster care. It was an older man who didn't want anything to do with us. He'd lock us in the bedroom at night, and some mornings he would be passed out drunk and wouldn't remember to get us out. I just remember thinking what was the purpose of a life if it was going to be lived like that."

Billie observed him a moment. "I'm so sorry."

A long silence passed between them.

Just as Billie was about to say something else, a man's sudden knock on the window startled them both. Solomon jumped, his heart racing as he saw the unfamiliar face outside. The man was Hispanic, with sunglasses and an open button-up shirt, his khaki pants rumpled and dirty. Billie rolled down her window, and the man leaned in, his eyes darting between Solomon and Billie. "I'm here for the car."

"You got something for me first?" Solomon said.

The man pulled out an envelope with a paper stuffed inside. The envelope was crumpled and dirty, a stain adorning the upper-right corner that looked like coffee. At least he hoped it was coffee.

Solomon opened it.

"Tommy told me to give that to you. Now can you get the hell outta the car?"

Billie and Solomon stood in the complex parking lot and watched the man drive away in the Cadillac.

"I'm going to have to get him pulled over right now and arrest him for whatever's in that car, you know that, right?"

"Whatever you gotta do. I just had to get this."

"What is it?"

Solomon handed her the envelope. She opened it up and took out the single sheet inside. There was a name scribbled in pen.

"I still don't understand how you would agree to do this without knowing why."

He shrugged. "Tommy wouldn't say. I told him I wouldn't do it if he didn't tell me why, but he called my bluff. He's just one of those people that can sense desperation and use it against you."

Mazie pulled the cruiser up and said, "Ready?" through the open driver's side window.

They slid into the car, and a heavy silence filled the space between them. Billie's fingers danced across her phone screen as she dialed the dispatch number and requested for the Cadillac to be pulled over. Then she notified one of her detectives that she wanted everything they had on the name they had just received, Alice Flores.

Mazie said, "So you know this could all be bullshit, right? He could be messing with you and doesn't know anything."

Solomon shrugged. "What else we got?"

She sighed. "Yeah, I guess I see your point. Can we at least eat? It's freaking dinnertime and I haven't even had lunch. And I'm off the clock, by the way," Mazie said as she pulled the cruiser out of the parking lot.

Billie said, "It'll be a minute until they get what I need on Alice anyway."

They drove to a restaurant Mazie had gone to on a date once and loved.

The dingy bar and grill was the type of place that seemed to blend into the shadows of the city. It was tucked away in a narrow alley, hidden from view by a tattered awning that flapped in the wind. The windows were grimy, and the sign above the door flickered.

Inside was dark and musty, with a low ceiling and walls that were stained by years of cigarette smoke. The floor was sticky with spilled beer and other fluids.

The bar was filled with a motley assortment of patrons who seemed to have seen better days. There were grizzled old men hunched over their drinks, young men and women with hardened, melancholy eyes, and some who just looked like they didn't particularly care where they were, and one place was as good as any other.

The bartender was a surly-looking man with a bushy mustache and a grease-stained apron. He moved slowly, as if he had been on his feet for days, and he glared at anyone who dared to make eye contact.

Solomon looked up the menu online since he'd never heard of it. Mostly greasy burgers, fries drizzled in cheese, and spicy wings. Cheap and filling. The type of food he loved.

They sat at a booth with tattered upholstery where a waitress took their drink orders and brought some appetizers.

"So guess who I came here with?" Mazie said. "Mark Fitz."

Billie grinned. "He's cute."

"Really cute. He's a little bitch, though. Oh, sorry. I probably shouldn't talk like that when I'm out in public with the sheriff, huh?"

The waitress arrived with a tray of frothy drinks in tall, chilled glasses. The concoction was a rich, creamy blend of beer, ice cream, and a generous shot of Kahlua, with a sprinkle of cocoa powder on top. Solomon took a sip, savoring the smooth and sweet flavor.

"Doesn't taste as bad as I thought it would."

"It's good shit, right?" Mazie said, immediately forgetting what she'd said about profanity in public.

"It's definitely interesting," he said.

"Hell ya it is." A country song came on, and Mazie said, "If we're drinking, we gotta do it to something that rocks."

She left to the jukebox. Solomon shoved half an onion ring in his mouth and let the grease coat his tongue. "Something interesting happened while I was meeting with Comanche," Solomon said while chewing. "When they found out you were with me, they pulled their guns."

Billie took a drink of her soda, since she didn't drink on duty, before setting it down and meeting Solomon's gaze. "I have a history with them."

"Would've been nice if you mentioned it."

"I didn't think it was relevant."

"It was."

She nodded. "I should have mentioned something."

"What happened?"

"Tommy was a suspect in a brutal case," she explained. "A man he did business with couldn't repay what he owed, so they forced his wife into prostitution until the debt was paid off. The husband came to us, and a week later, he disappeared. I know Tommy's responsible, but there's no evidence. No one would talk, and we didn't even have enough to get a warrant."

"I'm guessing for them to be so pissed, you didn't just let it go."

"The opposite. I really lost it, Solomon. If you had seen what they did to this poor woman . . ."

Solomon was quiet a moment. "So what did you do?"

"I had deputies stationed outside their compound who would pull them over for traffic violations when they drove to or from the compound. At first we got some good arrests for drugs and guns, but they learned quickly and didn't carry anything with them anymore. But we got a big bust one day before they smartened up, twenty bricks of cocaine taped under a truck."

Solomon whistled. "That's some serious cash. It's probably retirement money for someone higher up in the club. I wouldn't count on a Christmas card from them."

Just then, Billie's phone buzzed with a text. She glanced at it and said, "The detective has information on Alice Flores. Let's go."

Solomon eagerly stood up, ready to go. Mazie, who had just chosen a song by Soundgarden on the jukebox, returned to the table to find them getting ready to leave. "Seriously? I'm starving," she complained.

"Get it to go," Billie said, not slowing down as she headed for the door.

15

Alice Flores lived in a trailer park on the edge of the desert.

The park was close to old factories and plants, which were now skeletons. They were dilapidated and broken, with rust and shattered windows. The ground had cracks with weeds growing through them. The air smelled bad because of the decay and pollution. It was an area of the county Billie had come to once and avoided now.

Tooele was home to several trailer parks, a vestige of the town's history as a mining and oil-drilling hub. Back when the industries were thriving, bosses would buy up large plots of land, populate them with cheap trailer homes, and charge their workers rent to live there. In many cases, the bosses would also sell alcohol and drugs, and even manage prostitution and gambling rings, effectively taking back all the wages they paid to their workers. When the corrupt system eventually collapsed, the businesses disappeared, but the trailer parks remained, a reminder of a dark chapter in the town's history.

As they got out of the car, Billie turned to Mazie and said, "We may need you for this." Mazie's eyes lit up with excitement, and she practically jumped out of the car.

"What are we doing?" she asked eagerly.

"Just talking to someone," Solomon said nonchalantly.

"Who?" Mazie asked, looking at the run-down trailer park they had stopped in the middle of.

Billie pulled up the information the detective had sent her on her phone and handed it to Mazie, who said, "Who is she?"

"Someone that may know something," Solomon said.

"Sounds like you're desperate."

"I am."

Solomon surveyed the area, taking in the various trailers that lined the fence surrounding the property. Most of them looked abandoned and in disrepair. One had so much rust it looked like blood had overflowed from its windows and doors, coating the exterior.

"You sure this is the right address?" Solomon asked.

Billie took back her phone and checked the address listed for the woman in NCIC. "This is the right place," she confirmed.

"I don't think anyone lives here," Mazie said.

Solomon carefully looked around the trailer park, evaluating it with a critical eye. The trailers were tightly packed together, with a narrow road running through the middle of the park.

In the center of the park was a small run-down playground, covered in snow. As Solomon took in the scene, his attention was drawn to a set of tire tracks leading around the first trailer. They were straight and narrow, clearly made by a motorcycle.

"We need to get back into the car," he said breathlessly, fear churning his stomach.

The sound of gunfire shattered the silence, and a bullet flew past them, narrowly missing all three of them. It struck the metal exterior of a nearby trailer with a loud spark, then ricocheted off the surface and hit the ground.

Billie reacted quickly, pulling out her sidearm and taking cover behind the car. Mazie followed suit, drawing her own weapon. Solomon hit the ground and managed to roll under the cover of a small trailer.

Billie returned fire, and Mazie took two shots before ducking back behind the car. Solomon tried to locate the source of the shots, but all he could see was empty space.

Then, a shot struck the door of the cruiser, creating a massive hole.

Solomon heard Billie shouting into the phone, calling for backup. Mazie took two more shots, but it was doubtful that she had a clear target either. As the shots continued to ring out, they became more rapid and frenzied. It seemed that the shooter had been spooked, possibly by Billie's call for backup or something else.

The shots stopped, and an eerie silence descended.

"Solomon!" Billie shouted out. "Are you hit?"

"No. Do you see where the shots are coming from?" Solomon called back.

"No," Billie responded.

Mazie added, "I hear running."

The three of them listened intently, hearing the sound of footsteps getting farther away on snow. Billie stood up, weapon at the ready, taking cover behind the car door. Mazie, looking pale and shaken, came around the other side of the car. Time seemed to crawl as they waited in tense silence.

"I think they're gone," Billie said.

Solomon let out a deep breath and collapsed back onto the ground, staring up at the underside of the trailer. "Anybody got a change of underwear?" he joked weakly.

Once the trailer park was secured, the SIS team arrived on the scene, bustling about like busy forensic ants. Solomon watched from his perch on the stoop of a trailer, seated in an old chair. He remembered when he was that enthusiastic and eager, but those feelings had long since faded. Now, he just felt tired.

Mazie walked over and sat in the rocking chair next to Solomon, letting out a groan as she leaned back. "You ever lived in a trailer park?" she asked.

"No. You?" Solomon replied.

"Yeah. That was home until I was eighteen. One of my aunts took pity on me and hired me at a grocery store when I graduated high school. I saved up enough to get my own place. It was a studio apartment with cockroaches the size of my fist, but it was mine," Mazie said.

"That first taste of freedom is always the best," Solomon remarked.

"Totally. That first night sleeping in my own place was the best night of my life. Even with the cockroaches," Mazie said with a sad little grin. "Where'd you grow up?"

"Nowhere in particular. My brother and I bounced around foster homes after my mom died."

"Why didn't you stay in any of them?"

Solomon shrugged. "People barely have energy to take care of their own kids. Taking care of someone else's doesn't exactly become a priority."

Mazie shook her head. "That's messed up."

Solomon tapped his cane, which he held between his legs. "You'd never shot your gun before this, had you?"

"How could you tell?" Mazie asked, surprised.

"The first time someone shoots it, they hope they don't hit anyone. A lot of soldiers coming back from war report closing their eyes when they fire, hoping they don't hit anything. That aversion to killing can go away after a while, but not at first. You shot, but you didn't want to hit anybody."

Mazie swallowed nervously and looked out at the techs working on top of a nearby trailer. One of the detectives was in a black suit with latex gloves, and the sheriff was explaining something to him.

"I'd, um, appreciate if you didn't share that little observation with the sheriff," Mazie said.

"Why? You think she didn't do the same thing the first time?" Solomon asked with a raised eyebrow.

Billie shouted to Solomon, and he rose. Mazie followed him out toward where the sheriff was, and Billie said, "Found his nest."

"Nest?" Mazie said.

Billie said, "Sniper. Right up there. They found some canvas and burlap."

"How much?"

"Just a few bits."

"Probably a ghillie suit to blend in with his surroundings. But you'd have to make something like that to match the trailers."

Billie nodded. "This has been in the works more than today. We didn't surprise anybody—we were set up."

Solomon tapped his cane and glanced up to a black triangle on the trailer. The gunshot residue cone. When someone lay flat on their belly with a rifle and fired, the GSR would leave what looked like a cone or triangle shape in front of the muzzle.

"We weren't set up. I was. Tommy saw this as his chance to take me out."

Billie's jaw muscles flexed, but Solomon was the only one who knew her well enough to know what it meant.

"He'll regret it," she said.

"We both knew that's what it could be. Granted, I didn't think he'd take a shot at the sheriff."

"Meth heads, man," Mazie said. "Just can't trust 'em."

He let out a sigh as he glanced around. "Even in prison, he can get a sniper in a ghillie suit on short notice."

Mazie said, "So I guess Alice is made up then?"

"Looks like it," Solomon said.

A couple of the male techs saw Mazie and gazed at her. She looked away and folded her arms, focusing on the sheriff and Solomon again. "So what now?" she said.

Billie said, "We need to interview the list of women Solomon's investigator gave us."

Solomon said, "Actually, there's something I gotta do alone. I'll catch an Uber and call you after."

"Where you going?" Billie said.

"Better you don't know."

"That's twice you've said that. I don't think that's a phrase I like."

"Get used to it, Sheriff. If anyone is going down in flames for anything we do, it's gonna be me, not you."

16

As Billie and her team worked to uncover what exactly had happened at the trailer park, the next day seemed to drag on endlessly. The park was owned by a man who was ill equipped to deal with the situation at hand. He stuttered and stumbled through his explanations, and Billie could tell he was hiding something. Despite her suspicions, she let him go for the time being.

The park itself was eerily quiet and still, as if it had been abandoned for centuries.

As the deputies searched the trailers, they found evidence of a shutdown mobile methamphetamine operation, and the health department had to be called out. The manufacturing cells consisted of two different trailers and had been carefully set up and equipped, but they had been cleaned out and abandoned long ago. Despite the lack of any current activity, the presence of such a dangerous operation meant this place had to be cordoned off, and Billie couldn't shake the feeling they were still being watched.

As Billie checked her messages, she felt relieved that there were no other calls besides those from Roger.

The mere idea of receiving another call from Dax sent shivers down her spine, leaving her uneasy. His menacing words lingered in her mind, but what really troubled her was the fact that a part of her still had feelings for him.

Once, she had believed herself to be in love with him, or at least as close to love as she was capable of experiencing. But when he presented her with a marriage proposal, her heart inexplicably whispered a resolute no, which ultimately proved to be the correct decision.

As she got into the cruiser with Mazie to leave, Roger called her again. Though one of her least favorite people, she felt a pang of sympathy for him because of his attack and answered the phone.

"Hello, Roger."

"Where the hell are you?" he asked, frustration clear in his voice.

"Little busy right now," Billie replied, trying to keep her own frustration in check.

"Little busy? I was attacked and am probably being stalked, and you're off clothes shopping or whatever you do? I need you here."

Billie took a deep breath and looked at Mazie, who rolled her eyes and shook her head. "Roger, I assigned some of my best deputies to guard you twenty-four hours a day. We don't need more than that."

"I'm the district attorney for this damn county! If I don't feel safe, I can't do my job."

Billie sighed, feeling a migraine beginning to crawl its way into her head. Her hands were still shaky from her getting shot at, but she didn't feel like telling Roger about that right now. "What would make you feel safe, Roger?" she asked with exasperation in her voice.

"What would make me feel safe is if the sheriff, whose job is to protect me, would actually do it," Roger replied.

Billie placed two fingers on her temple and rubbed, trying to alleviate the throbbing in her head. "My job isn't to protect you, but I'll get some more deputies assigned. Anything else?"

"Yes. What are you working on right now?"

"Dennis Yang's suicide," Billie replied.

"You're not trying to find the man that almost killed me?" Roger asked, his voice dripping with disbelief.

"We're doing everything we can, Roger. I have three detectives assigned to your case. They'll find something."

"They better," Roger grumbled before hanging up.

Billie lowered the phone and glanced at Mazie, who had a look on her face like she wanted to tear Roger's throat out. She started the car and pulled away.

"Why does he think he can talk to you like that?" Mazie asked, clearly agitated.

"He talks to his wife like that too," Billie replied with a sigh. "You okay?"

Mazie shrugged. "I don't know. Yeah, I guess. I just . . . I've never had to pull my gun, ya know?"

"What are you feeling right now?" Billie asked.

"Like whether I made the right choice becoming a cop," Mazie replied.

"Why did you become a cop?"

Mazie took a turn and headed to the freeway. "My dad was a cop," she said. "He was a good cop. Good guy. Just wanted to do something that helped people." She looked out the windshield and was silent for a moment. "He was shot on a traffic stop. Just a speeding ticket. Came up to the driver's side and asked for his docs and the guy shot him and took off. Just like that. I was sixteen when he died."

Billie was silent, not knowing what to say.

"Anyway, doesn't matter now, huh?" Mazie said after a moment.

"Everything matters," Billie replied softly.

17

That night, Solomon sat at a small table in the dimly lit coffee shop, lost in the pages of *Crime and Punishment*. The novel, a masterpiece of psychological complexity, tells the story of Rodion Raskolnikov, a struggling young man who commits murder in the belief that he's justified in doing so.

As Solomon read, he felt a sense of familiarity with the themes of the book. The idea of a normal person becoming abnormal through nothing but their own choices resonated with him deeply. He had read the novel a dozen times before, but each time found something new and insightful to ponder. Despite its bleak and gray tone, there was something about *Crime and Punishment* that gave him hope. It seemed to suggest that, even in the darkest of circumstances, people still had the power to choose their own paths.

As night fell outside, Solomon reluctantly closed the book. Some tea had spilled out of his cup because his hands had still been trembling from the shooting. He'd been shot at before, but not like this. Not completely blind to where the shots were even coming from. But he couldn't think about that now; he had to focus.

He stepped out into the frosty evening air and hailed an Uber to take him across town. After the car dropped him off in front of Dennis Yang's house, Solomon stood on the sidewalk and gazed up at the building, his mind swirling with thoughts of *Crime and Punishment*.

Solomon made his way up to the front porch and felt disquiet wash over him. The police tape stretched across the door was a clear indication that something terrible had happened here. He pulled out his keys, attached to a pocketknife, and carefully cut through the tape. Billie had given him the key to the house, as it had been cleared as a crime scene, but the door was unlocked. He cautiously pushed it open, letting his eyes adjust to the darkness inside.

An overpowering smell of cleaning chemicals hit him immediately, and he had to fight the urge to cover his nose and mouth. He reached into his pocket and retrieved some cherry ChapStick, which he rubbed on his finger before running it under his nose in an attempt to mask the overpowering odors.

As he explored the lavish home, Solomon thought it was more of a museum than a lived-in residence. The art on display was impressive, but the house felt impersonal.

He made his way up the circular staircase, peeking into the empty rooms that used to be children's bedrooms. One room contained artifacts picked up during Dennis's travels. A massive golden bull phallus caught Solomon's eye, and he wondered about Dennis's taste in art.

Solomon walked into the master bedroom, where the bed had been removed for forensic examination at the crime lab. The carpets were still stained with blood, despite someone's attempt to wash them.

He pulled out his phone and accessed the police reports on the death of Dennis Yang, which Billie had sent him.

According to the reports, the last person to see Dennis alive was a cashier at a pharmacy, who had helped him when he stopped late at night for some ibuprofen. Solomon could relate. He used to frequent late-night pharmacies in an attempt to stop the migraines that never left. The small connection to Yang felt like a twinge of electricity.

He found the video from the pharmacy's security camera and watched as Dennis joked and laughed with the cashier. Then he watched the footage captured by the medical examiner, which documented the body's condition and served as a record of its state at the time of discovery.

It was always strange to Solomon how differently someone appeared in death, the transition from animate to inanimate. Consciousness to meat.

He couldn't shake the thought that Dennis seemed happy just hours before his death, but he knew that it wasn't uncommon for people who planned to commit suicide to experience a sense of relief before their final act. But why would Dennis pick up ibuprofen if he intended to take his own life only a few hours later? Unless he wanted to dull the pain of sawing into his own legs, but if that was the case, pain pills or marijuana would have done a much better job.

Suddenly, a surge of adrenaline coursed through his veins as an image of his mother, her lifeless eyes staring blankly, forced its way into his mind.

Solomon's heart raced uncontrollably, and beads of cold sweat formed on his brow. He had to physically stop in place, leaning against the wall for support. His breaths came in shallow gasps as the darkness seemed to close in around him, threatening to swallow him.

With trembling hands, Solomon fumbled for the small pill case of lorazepam he kept in his pocket. He hastily swallowed two of the tiny pills, hoping they would bring some semblance of calm. Leaning heavily against the wall, he slid down and closed his eyes, waiting for the medication to work.

Gradually, it took effect, and his frenetic thoughts slowed, allowing his breathing to stabilize. He rose and opened the police reports again as he slowly went down a long hallway.

The reports noted that all the windows in the home were open when police arrived at the scene. Solomon thought it was lazy report writing, since there were so many windows not all of them were likely to have been left open. But he went through the diagrams SIS had drawn of the crime scene and the home and found that the report was correct. All the windows in the home were left open.

If Dennis was killed and then posed to appear like a suicide, the killer was sophisticated. This wasn't a drive-by shooting or a random attack. He planned and waited for the perfect time to strike and then scrubbed as much forensic evidence away as possible. Traces of nail polish remover and rubbing alcohol, both better at destroying evidence than bleach, were found on surfaces in the bedroom and master bathroom.

Someone like that would know to close the windows. The smell from the dead body would notify the neighbors that something was wrong. He could've bought himself a few days or more if he had just closed the windows.

Solomon flipped to the dispatch reports and the logs of the 911 call that got officers to Dennis's home.

The discovery of the body had been a result of a mysterious call made from the home line. The caller had simply hung up, guaranteeing that officers would be dispatched to perform a welfare check. If it wasn't Dennis calling and then changing his mind and hanging up, it was the person who killed him. But why leave the windows open if the police were on their way? . . . it had to be a contingency plan in case the police didn't go inside the house. The unmistakable stench of decay would eventually draw attention.

Why go through the trouble of making it look like suicide if you want us to know you killed him?

Solomon stood in the empty house, surrounded by the remnants of the crime scene. A few slivers of pale moonlight came through the blinds, which hadn't been closed all the way. Solomon closed them and left the house.

He summoned an Uber and waited at the curb, glancing back at the home one more time. Dennis and he had a complicated relationship. The man who had attacked Solomon in court and wounded him, causing permanent nerve damage and partial paralysis of his leg, was represented by Dennis. The trial was a lock, and the defendant was going to go to prison before he attacked Solomon while he was giving closing arguments. The timing was flawless. The defense had gotten to see the prosecution's strategy, and now they got a new trial because a jury couldn't be impartial after seeing that. It was almost as if a lawyer had suggested it to the defendant.

Solomon never had any proof, but he always had his suspicions. Whenever Dennis smiled at him or offered a greeting, Solomon wondered if even seemingly normal, well-adjusted people could smile to your face while they slipped a knife, or had someone else slip a knife, into your back.

He was getting a migraine, and when the Uber rolled to a stop, he told the driver he'd changed his mind and wanted to go somewhere else.

18

Night had fallen as Mazie parked the cruiser in front of the Public Safety Complex. Billie noticed that more cars were here than should have been at this time.

Once inside the building, they were escorted by two police officers to Roger's office, which was heavily guarded by additional police and investigators from agencies other than the sheriff's office. Despite Roger's request, Billie had refused to have a sniper stationed on the rooftop of the adjacent building.

Inside, Roger was angrily criticizing an investigator from the District Attorney's Office for failing to uncover any useful information from the video surveillance footage of the parking lot where Roger had been attacked.

"You know what?" Billie said. "I've changed my mind. I'm starving. Are you hungry?"

"I could eat a rhino's ass." Billie looked at her, and she said, "I mean, yes. I'm hungry."

The restaurant, called Primo Italiano, was a place that Billie recognized from her days as a patrol deputy. The restaurant offered a discount to police officers, likely as a tribute to the owner's grandfather, who had been a police officer in Sicily and died in the line of duty after refusing to comply with a request from a local Mafia boss.

Billie and Mazie took a seat at a table, and Mazie ordered appetizers and two glasses of beer. Billie had texted Solomon earlier and said if he was done, they were grabbing dinner and to join them.

"I shouldn't drink on duty," Billie said.

"You're not on duty. We're both off the clock, and our weapons are secured in our car."

Billie grinned. "You're one of those cops that actually reads the deputy policy manual cover to cover, aren't you?"

"I sure as hell am."

"That had to have been the most boring read of your life."

The beers came, and Mazie took a long drink and had froth on her lip. She licked it off and said, "It wasn't that bad. I've definitely read worse."

"Like what?"

"Before I was a cop, I worked at this tech company that provided support for the social media companies, right. And my job was to see content that people flagged as inappropriate and see if it violated our policies. So I had to read some sick shit. I mean, people are just twisted."

"P. T. Barnum said that nobody ever went broke underestimating the taste of the public."

She chuckled. "You're quoting P. T. Barnum?"

Billie brought the beer up to her lips before saying, "Solomon told me that."

The beer was cold and frothy and tasted good going down.

"Can I ask you something?" Mazie said, her voice low and serious.

She set the glass down. "Go ahead."

"So, that crazy ex that's stalking you, is it legit? Is he trying to kill you?"

Billie took a deep breath and let it out slowly, her eyes fixed on the glass of beer in front of her. "I don't know," she said finally. "I thought

I knew him, but I realize now that I knew nothing about him. When I told him I was getting a stalking injunction, he said he was going to kill me and then himself."

"Shit," Mazie breathed, her eyebrows rising in shock. "That's gotta be scary."

Billie shrugged, a look of resignation on her face. "I expected to be harassed as a female sheriff, but this is something different. Someone I loved once wants to hurt me. I'm not sure anyone can prepare for that. So yes, it is scary."

Mazie leaned forward, her voice soft with concern. "What are you doing about it?"

Billie took a long drink from her beer before answering. "Right now, I'm drinking," she said with a wry smile. "It's not exactly a long-term solution, but it'll work for now."

Solomon made his way around the corner, leaning heavily on his cane as he walked. His face was flushed, and a sloppy grin spread across his face. "Sorry I'm late," he slurred. "Just had to do something."

He collapsed into a chair at the table, and Billie noticed the smell of marijuana on his clothing and the overpowering scent of alcohol on his breath. His eyes were bloodshot, and his movements were slow.

"You gonna finish this beer?" he said to Billie, then reached for her glass and guzzled it down without waiting for a reply.

"Solomon, slow down," Billie said.

"I'm just cutting loose after a hard day on the job. Isn't that what you cops do? Finish a shift and get drunk," Solomon said, his words slurring together. "Where is the server, by the way?" He looked to a young busboy and said, "Excuse me, could you get our server to bring us a fresh round of Guinness beers and tequila shots, please?"

"No, we're fine," Billie said, trying to intervene.

"Hey, what's the deal?" Solomon said, holding out his hands as though shocked at her behavior. "I just wanna have some drinks with my pals."

"Come outside with me, Solomon."

"Why?" Solomon asked, a confused expression on his face.

"Please," Billie said, trying to coax him to follow her.

Solomon struggled to his feet and began making his way outside, leaning on his cane.

Mazie watched them go over the rim of her glass as she took a long drink.

The night air was cold, and the busy street in front of the restaurant was alive with the sound of passing cars. The two stood in front of the restaurant and watched the cars a moment.

Solomon swallowed, his eyes glistening in the streetlights. "I'm sorry," he said, leaning on his cane.

"You don't have to be sorry," Billie said, her voice soft.

Taking a deep breath, Solomon extended his hand, offering the keys to Dennis's home.

Billie took the keys. "What happened?"

He shrugged. "I didn't enjoy it, let's put it that way."

"Did you learn anything?" Billie asked.

Solomon nodded. "The killer's sophisticated enough to know to keep the windows closed, but every single window in the home was open. If Dennis was murdered, the killer wanted the body discovered."

"Why do you think that is?"

He shook his head. "I think . . . I think he wanted me to find it."

Billie hadn't grabbed her jacket. She shivered and hugged herself. She could see her breath swirling in the air like mist with each exhale. Patches of snow were still on the ground, and in the gutters, the ice was blackened by tire tracks and exhaust.

Solomon took off his jacket and put it on her shoulders. It smelled like his cologne and was softly warm.

"Thanks. I'm so sick of this cold," she said. "I wish I could just go somewhere like . . . Aruba."

Solomon was silent a second and then chuckled. "Do you know anything about Aruba?"

"Not really. I've always wanted to hop on a plane and go somewhere I know nothing about. The only thing I know about Aruba is the name." Billie noticed his swaying as he stood watching her and couldn't even guess how much he'd had to drink.

She took his arm. "Come on," she said, "let's get you home."

"He's coming for me," Solomon interjected. "He's coming for me, Billie. That's what this is about. I can feel it."

"Who?"

"It's gotta be Tommy."

"There's no evidence you're connected to this in any way other than a suicide thirty years ago."

He shook his head. "I can feel it . . . he's coming for me. And I don't have a lot of time."

19

Solomon woke up on a couch he didn't recognize, a blanket covering him and his shoes off. He groaned and put his hands over his eyes, trying to block out the streams of sunlight coming through the partially closed blinds. He smelled coffee and heard the sound of dishes being moved around behind him. He turned his head to see Billie, dressed in a black pantsuit with a white blouse and her hair pulled back in an elastic. She saw him and smiled, saying, "Morning."

"Morning," Solomon mumbled, his head pounding. "Guess I didn't make it to my house?"

"It was just easier to come here," Billie said. "I hope the couch wasn't too uncomfortable."

Solomon yawned and stretched his arms over his head before sitting up and looking for his cane. It had fallen to the floor, and he glanced over to make sure Billie wasn't looking before he had to get on his knees to reach it and use it to stand up.

Solomon made his way to the kitchen, where Billie pushed a mug of coffee into his hands. He took a sip and winced at the boiling heat and bitter taste.

"Oh, that's right, you only like tea."

"This is fine. Thanks."

"I'm making eggs," Billie said. "Have a seat."

Solomon sat down at the dining table and looked out the sliding glass doors to the yard. A picnic table was covered with a layer of snow and ice. He wondered if she had ever used the table before.

Billie brought plates of eggs and toast over and sat down across from him. They ate in silence for a moment as Billie returned some texts.

"So this is what it would be like, huh?" Solomon said with a sad little smile.

"What would?" Billie asked.

"Having a normal life."

She took a sip of coffee. "You mean like breakfast with a family and barbecues and opening presents on Christmas?"

"Something like that."

She set the coffee down and picked up her fork again. "One day."

He watched her eat a moment. "One day," Solomon echoed.

Solomon didn't feel like eating, but he moved the eggs around on his plate so he wouldn't offend Billie. After a few minutes, she said, "I have to run to a meeting."

"I'll call an Uber," Solomon said, trying to push himself up from the table.

"Nonsense," Billie said, shaking her head. "You haven't even finished your breakfast." She stood up, straightening her pantsuit. "Take your time. Just text me when you leave, and I'll turn the alarm on."

"Thanks," Solomon said.

He watched her leave, feeling a pang of sadness as the door closed behind her. He was left alone in the quiet house, the sound of his own breathing the only noise he could hear. His own house was bigger, with more things that Mrs. Langley left him, but Billie's house felt like a home. It was a place you'd want to come to for refuge from other people. He wondered what it would be like to have a home like this, a place that felt like a sanctuary rather than a prison.

Solomon washed the dishes off and put them in the dishwasher and then straightened up her kitchen and living room, then decided he might as well vacuum. It didn't appear like the carpet had been vacuumed in a while.

He found a vacuum in the pantry and started with the living room. As he was gliding the vacuum by the windows, gripping his cane with his free hand, he noticed a police cruiser outside. It was parked across the street with two deputies inside. One was asleep and the other was playing on his phone.

After he was done vacuuming, he left the home. He waved to the deputy, who glanced up from his phone long enough to look shocked that someone was leaving the house. Solomon went over to the patrol car. He recognized one of the deputies, Dave Garcia, a younger man that Solomon had worked with for many years when he was a prosecutor.

Dave opened his eyes, and his brow furrowed for a moment before smoothing again.

"Solomon?" he said.

"How are ya, Dave?"

"Hanging in there," he replied, his gaze flicking to a passing car before returning to Solomon. "Where you been? I heard some crazy rumors."

"Yeah, well, they're all true. Especially the ones that aren't," Solomon replied. "What's going on?"

"Sheriff hasn't told you?" Dave asked, surprised. Solomon shook his head. "Her ex has been stalking her and now he's threatening to kill her. We've been assigned to watch her house for the past two weeks."

"Dax?" Solomon asked, recalling the man's quiet, polite demeanor.

"Yeah," Dave replied grimly. "He said he was going to shoot her and then himself. Sounds like a real sick shit."

Solomon couldn't believe that the man he had once thought was too quiet and uninteresting to date Billie could be capable of such threats. It was a reminder that anyone could hide their nature, like a snake coiled beneath the surface.

What really shocked him was that Billie hadn't mentioned it.

"So you and the sheriff . . . you two . . . ," Dave began, then let his words trail off.

"No. I got drunk and passed out on her couch."

"Oh," Dave said, looking disappointed.

"Yeah, exciting life I lead, I know," Solomon said with a shrug, trying to downplay the situation. He tapped the top of the car. "You take care of yourself."

"You too. Come by and say hello sometime."

Solomon started walking and was hit with a calm pleasure. He realized he hadn't gone on a daily walk since Billie had shown up at his door. He already had his jacket and decided to go for a walk now.

He had once read that walking and traveling affected the brain the same way. It was journeying. Human beings evolved as roving tight-knit bands, and our brains haven't changed much since then. A journey helped us to think, to play, to be more aware of our surroundings. To live in the present.

Solomon's daily walks were a source of solace and contemplation for him. He often lost track of time and distance, only realizing he needed to head home when the sun began to set. He was undaunted by the elements, braving cold nights, the snow, and the sweltering summer heat. On one walk, he came across a wolf—or at least, that's what it appeared to be in the moonlit glow. Wolves in Utah had been hunted to extinction, so if it was a wolf, it was the last.

As he walked, he saw litter and cigarette butts line the gutters, and homeless people shivered in corners under snow-covered awnings.

Feeling the need for caffeine, Solomon stopped at a Starbucks and leaned against the redbrick wall. It was then that he noticed a string of missed texts, including one from Billie that made his heart race.

The sniper was in custody.

He summoned an Uber and paced impatiently.

20

Solomon had attended meetings at the District Attorney's Office held in one of the conference rooms, with floor-to-ceiling windows offering a stunning view of the skyline. He remembered being impressed by the state-of-the-art technology and equipment, and the various departments that worked together.

Solomon thanked the Uber driver and got out. Unease gnawed at his belly like rats, and it gave him a sickening taste in his mouth. He checked his pockets for gum and didn't have any. He took a deep breath, tapped his cane, and went inside.

After screening, he had to wait for someone from the DA's office to allow him up. Unfortunately, it was Roger's secretary who got the call. When Roger stepped off the elevators to greet him, he was certain Roger had told his secretary to notify him if Solomon ever showed up again.

"Hello, Counselor," Roger said with a smile. "It is still Counselor, isn't it? You didn't get disbarred or something?"

"Not yet. Roger, I'm in—"

"A hurry? Because we caught your shooter, I'm assuming? Well, you're a little late, Solomon. I struck a deal with him."

Solomon's eyes narrowed a little as he stared at Roger. "What kind of deal?"

"He'll be telling us all about your old friend Bigfoot Tommy's operations and how he hired him to put a bullet in your brain. So you're welcome, Solomon."

Solomon said, "Let me talk to him," and hoped the desperation stayed out of his voice.

Roger chuckled. "You're not one of my prosecutors anymore. You're not going anywhere near him."

Roger turned away, and Solomon grabbed his arm. "Whatever he's telling you is a lie. If he kept his mouth shut and went to prison without saying a word, Tommy would make sure he lived like a king in there. If he snitches, Tommy could reach him anywhere he runs to. There is no way he would make that deal, Roger."

"Even if so, it's not your concern anymore. Go home, Solomon."

"Let me talk to him," Solomon pleaded. "I can get him to tell us what Tommy wants."

Roger's expression was concerned for a moment before it became amused again. "Don't be jealous, Solomon. I've always been the better negotiator between us."

He turned and began walking toward the elevator, but Solomon called out, "This is even stupider than usual, Roger."

Roger stopped and turned back to Solomon. He put his hands in his pockets and approached him, speaking quietly so that only they could hear. "You always looked down on me and thought you were better. But I'm the one who's succeeded, Solomon. I have everything you could have ever wanted, while you're hiding away from the world in some hole." Roger flicked a piece of lint off Solomon's jacket before continuing. "Take care of yourself, Counselor."

He turned away, but then stopped and turned back again. "Oh, I almost forgot. You might want to stay away from the sheriff. She's up for reelection, and you tend to bring bad luck wherever you go." He couldn't help but smile. "I heard your ex-lover moved out of state and left you. I'm guessing she wished she'd never met you. Don't make the sheriff feel the same way. Stay away from her and keep your nose out of this case."

Roger returned to the elevator.

"You kill that guy's goldfish or something?"

Mazie stood next to him, dressed in her uniform. Her hair was pulled back tightly, revealing her makeup-free face. She wore short sleeves, showcasing the tattoos that covered her forearms.

Solomon said, "Were you and Billie separated at birth?"

She chuckled. "I gotta admit, she'd make a pretty cool older sister." She looked toward the elevators. "What was that all about?"

"It was about a very insecure man putting people in danger because he doesn't recognize his insecurity," Solomon replied, exhaling. "Where you headed?"

"I have a meeting with a prosecutor."

Solomon glanced around and put his hand on her arm, leaning heavily on his cane with the other hand, pretending that his injury was worse than it was. "I need you to guide me to the interview rooms at the sheriff's office, milady," he said.

"Interview rooms? Why?" Mazie raised her eyebrows in surprise. "Roger wouldn't let you talk to him, would he?"

"Roger's an idiot. There's no way one of Tommy's men would flip that quickly, especially not on Tommy. If this guy is flipping, it's because Tommy told him to, and I need to know why." Mazie rolled her eyes and let out a groan, and Solomon pressed a little harder. "I just need five minutes, Mazie. If I'm wrong, we've wasted five minutes, but if I'm right and Tommy has something planned, someone's going to get hurt."

She sighed. "I could get in so much trouble for this. You're not even a prosecutor anymore."

"I know, and I hate to ask. But I really need your help."

They looked at each other for a moment, and finally, Mazie said, "Fine. But you owe me for this, and I'm not kidding."

"Whatever your heart desires shall be yours, my queen. But for now," he said, tightening his grip on her arm, "lead the way."

21

After her morning meeting with the city manager, Billie's time was filled with mundane tasks, and she felt frustrated with the never-ending cycle of paperwork that seemed to consume her job as sheriff. Despite her best efforts to stay on top of things, she had fallen behind since the body of the former Honorable Mayor was found.

As she left the Public Safety Complex, a young man in a dirty coat approached her and handed her some papers. "You've been served, ma'am," he said before quickly walking away. The snow had started to fall, and the once-sunny sky was now gray and overcast. She watched the sky a moment before turning to the papers.

Billie assumed the papers were related to a lawsuit filed against the sheriff's office, and she prepared herself for yet another battle to defend her department. But when she looked at the names on the document, she was shocked by what she saw. Her blood went cold as she read:

MOTION FOR TEMPORARY PROTECTIVE ORDER
DAX M. GRANGER
v.
ELIZABETH J. GRAY

Dax had accused Billie of threatening to kill him and asked the courts for protection. As she read through the document, she couldn't believe the lies it contained. Dax claimed that Billie had visited his home two days ago, held a gun to his face, and threatened to shoot him if she saw him again.

She frantically texted Solomon, sending him a picture of the documents and asking if Dax was allowed to do this. When he didn't respond right away, she let out a frustrated breath and stared at the sky, trying to calm herself down. But the anger and emotion inside her were too strong.

She walked to her truck and got in, taking a moment to tap her finger against the steering wheel as she tried to clear her mind. Her emotions were running high, and she remembered her father's advice to do nothing when angry. He had always told her to take a moment to do nothing, to say nothing, and to allow herself time to cool down before making any decisions. She took a deep breath and tried to follow that advice.

Screw that.

As she sped down the freeway, she knew she was going too fast. The ground was slick with ice, and she had to constantly adjust her speed to maintain control. Despite the treacherous conditions, her truck's snow tires kept her stable on the road.

She hadn't heard much about Dax since he was fired from his job for assaulting a coworker, but she knew where he lived now. He had lost his house and was now living in an apartment on the outskirts of the city.

When she finally arrived at the apartment complex, Billie parked the truck and reached for the pistol tucked away in the holster under her coat. She ran her fingertips over the handle.

The apartment complex was a drab brown color, with each building rising three stories. A tall, imposing gray brick wall stood at the edge of the complex, marking the boundary between the apartments and the grocery store next door. The parking lot for the grocery store was on the other side of the wall, a sea of concrete and parked cars.

She approached Dax's second-floor apartment and took the stone steps up to his door. She knocked and could hear footsteps inside. The door swung open, and Dax stood in front of her, shirtless and wearing sweatpants. His skin was pale and flabby, a far cry from the muscular and tanned appearance he had maintained when they were together. Billie had never been particularly concerned with physical attractiveness, but she was struck by how much Dax had changed.

She knew she had to be careful around him, and she braced herself.

"I'm glad you came," Dax said with a smile.

"You didn't leave me much choice. It was either confront you here or in court," Billie replied.

Dax looked her up and down. "You look good," he said.

Billie glanced behind him into the cluttered apartment. It was a mess, with garbage and dirty dishes scattered everywhere. Boxes were stacked up against the walls, overflowing with what appeared to be junk: trinkets, documents, old magazines . . . it was clear that this wasn't the Dax she knew, the one who was fastidious about cleanliness and couldn't stand the thought of germs in the kitchen overnight. Even without looking inside the apartment, she could tell that the Dax she knew was gone, replaced by something far more dangerous.

Dax opened the door and stepped to the side, gesturing for her to come inside. She hesitated for a moment, wondering if it was best to show no fear or exercise caution.

"No, let's go for a walk," Billie said.

The surrounding neighborhood was zoned for mixed use, and the eclectic mix of businesses, storefronts, and residential homes gave the area a disorienting and chaotic feel. It was a part of the city that Billie didn't often visit, as she didn't find it aesthetically pleasing.

Dax led her to the back of the apartment complex, where a chain-link fence separated the residences from the elementary school to the north. There was a hole in the fence where the children had rolled it up to create a shortcut to school rather than going all the way around. Dax held up the section of fence for her to pass through.

"After you," he said with a grin.

"You first. I insist."

He smiled and then went through the opening in the fence.

Billie crossed the school's field, her heart racing as she tried to distance herself from Dax, who walked to the bleachers near a diamond where a group of kids were practicing their hits. Billie sat as far away from Dax as possible, her eyes fixed on the children as they played.

Dax spoke up, his voice laced with nostalgia as he watched the kids. "I come here sometimes to watch them. It calms me down. Reminds me of when I was a kid and had no worries . . ." He trailed off before turning to Billie, his eyes apologetic. "I'm sorry I threatened you. I was drunk and angry."

Billie clenched her fists, struggling to keep her composure. She remained silent, doing her utmost to restrain the overwhelming urge to punch him squarely in the face. Weeks of relentless terror and harassment . . . and all he could muster as an excuse was that he had been drunk.

"What do you expect to gain by filing a protective order against me, Dax?"

He shrugged nonchalantly. "I don't plan to gain anything. This was just the only way I could talk to you."

"You've thrown my life into chaos, and you think all you want is to talk to me?" she snapped.

"That's all I want, I swear. I know what I said, but I'd never hurt you," he insisted, reaching out to touch her.

Billie recoiled, her hand instinctively grasping the concealed weapon under her jacket. "Try to touch me again, and you'll regret it, Dax."

He chuckled, unfazed. "If I wanted to hurt you, I wouldn't have brought you to a field full of kids." He turned back to the children. "I am really sorry how this all happened."

Billie let out a sigh, her voice laced with desperation. "I don't care, Dax. I just want all of this to stop. You said you loved me once, and I truly believe you did. I'm asking you, as someone you loved once, to stop this. Let me live in peace."

Dax seemed lost in his own thoughts, his eyes fixated on the kids as he spoke. "Do you know what I miss most about you? Your smell. I used to stay up sometimes after you had gone to sleep and smell you. It was like flowers after a rain." He leaned in closer to her, as if trying to catch a hint of her scent, causing Billie to recoil again.

Dax slowly pulled away, his voice filled with frustration and sadness. "That's why I can't let this go, because I repulse you. But that won't last. You'll see."

Billie's anger flared as she stood up, her voice spiked with disgust. "The only thing I see is a sick, pathetic man who finds joy in torturing someone who had the audacity to actually care about him."

As she stormed off, Dax called out to her, his words chilling her. "I can wait."

Billie fought back tears as she got into her truck and sped away, her heart heavy with the knowledge that Dax's obsession would not end anytime soon. She pulled over to the side of the road and let out a sob, her head resting against the steering wheel as the tears flowed.

22

The third floor of the sheriff's office contained a series of interview rooms, which were located in a separate area from the main department. These rooms were monitored by CCTV cameras placed at regular intervals along the hallway. There was a total of six interview rooms, with the most comfortable and welcoming room reserved for victims who needed to be interviewed.

To access this room, Mazie and Solomon had to pass through a screening desk, where a girthy deputy was currently seated and speaking on the phone.

Mazie flashed a friendly smile at the deputy as they walked past him, and the deputy responded with a dopey grin, much like a ten-year-old boy might give to his crush. Solomon, on the other hand, kept his eyes fixed on the floor as he walked, exaggerating the limp in his leg and hunching his back slightly. The deputy gave him only a quick glance before returning to his conversation on the phone.

Each of the interview rooms was equipped with a small square window on the door, which was just wide enough for a single person to peer through.

As Mazie and Solomon made their way down the hallway, they passed the first interview room, where one of Billie's detectives was speaking with a man dressed in a blue coat. The man was visibly distressed, and tears were streaming down his face.

The last room on the right was the victim interview room, and Roger had put his prize witness in there. It was a space designed to look as casual and welcoming as possible, with couches, recliners, and a selection of toys and Disney movies on DVD for children. A large, muscular man with a massive potbelly was lying on one of the couches, dressed in jeans and a white tank top. He had several homemade tattoos, including a prominent skull on his neck and a military tattoo on his forearm.

Solomon turned to Mazie and said, "You shouldn't be here when I talk to him. Plausible deniability."

Mazie glanced through the window at the man.

"You want me to leave you alone with *him*?" she asked. "The dude is huge. He looks like a bookshelf."

"The bigger they are and whatever," Solomon replied.

Mazie looked at him skeptically, and Solomon added with a grin, "Don't let the cane fool you. I've got a mean left hook."

Mazie let out a long breath and said, "I'm going to my meeting and will be right back. If you let him kill you, I will be so insanely pissed."

Solomon watched Mazie leave, then turned and entered the victim interview room and closed the door firmly behind him. The room had a distinctive aroma of potpourri, which stood in contrast to the less pleasant smell of body odor.

Solomon made his way over to the love seat using his cane and sat down across from the couch. The man looked at him with a big grin spreading across his lips, seemingly pleased to see Solomon.

He had his head resting on his hands as he watched Solomon. "You remember me?" he said.

"No," Solomon replied.

"Jack Barre. They called me Blackbird. You remember me now?"

Solomon did have a faint memory of Blackbird, recalling an old case where he had prosecuted him for some crime. "Not really, sorry," Solomon said.

"Well, you were pretty cool. Treated me fair considerin' I was guilty as hell."

"Huh. You take a shot at everyone that treats you well?"

Blackbird pushed himself up and leaned against the couch. "If I wanted to tag you, I wouldn't miss. Not from fifteen yards."

Solomon recognized the tattoo on Blackbird's forearm, and he said, "Semper fi."

"Do or die," Blackbird replied.

"Marines are the best snipers in the world. I have no doubt you could've taken me out if you wanted to. Why didn't you?"

Blackbird shrugged and smiled, then put his hands on his prodigious belly in a relaxed gesture. Solomon sensed that Blackbird was trying too hard to appear casual, and that he was actually scared. Something had gone wrong, something he wasn't expecting. "You're really flipping on him, aren't you?" Solomon said.

Blackbird sat up and clasped his hands together. "Your boss talked up witness protection and how Tommy couldn't get anywhere near me. He's so full of shit he's got it coming out of his ears. Tommy can reach me anywhere."

"Then why flip?" Solomon asked.

"It's better than nothin'."

Realization dawned on him. "You were supposed to take me out, but you saw this as your chance to get out of the club. If you actually killed me, they wouldn't have cut a deal with you."

Blackbird spread his arms on the back of the couch and leaned back again, his grin returning as he tilted his head slightly and watched Solomon.

"What happened?" Solomon asked.

"Tommy's on his way out, man. Comanche is taking over the club. And me and him, we got some beef that go way back. It ain't gonna be settled by anything but a bullet, and I ain't trying to end up in no grave at thirty-five," Blackbird said.

"So, what's the plan? Be hidden away somewhere until it's time to testify?"

"New name, new identity, new job. Maybe I'll even pick me up a little housewife and play the good neighbor. Shit, maybe I'll even go to church," Blackbird replied with a shrug.

Solomon shook his head. "You won't live that long."

"We'll see," Blackbird said nonchalantly.

Solomon pushed a toy that was by his feet on the carpet with his cane. "Tommy's hated me for a long time. Why'd he try to take me out now?" he asked.

"Who the hell knows? Maybe he thinks this might be his last chance before they take him out, too."

"What about the suicide? Was that you too?"

"What suicide?" Blackbird replied, his expression genuine.

Just then, the door to the victim interview room opened and the tall, broad-shouldered deputy from down the hallway entered, a look of anger in his eyes. Before he could say anything, Solomon rose and said, "Glad you're here, Deputy. Been waiting for you. He's all yours now. Feel free to call me back in later if you need." He moved past the deputy quickly and looked back into the room at Blackbird, who winked at him before Solomon turned away and headed down the hall.

Solomon sat in a booth at the restaurant, staring out the windows as he waited for Billie to arrive. The restaurant was on a hill near the Public Safety Complex. The sun was setting, casting a warm glow over the city.

When Billie finally joined him, he had already placed their order and didn't notice how late she was.

"So what happened?" she said after sitting down.

Solomon sighed and explained, "Tommy's on his way out of the club. But this sniper doesn't play well with Comanche, who's next in line, so he thinks he has a better chance in witness protection with Roger."

"That seems unwise."

"That's putting it mildly. I know Roger. The best way to afford witness protection for a DA is to bring in a federal agency like the FBI or DEA, but Roger's too arrogant to do that. He'll want all the press for himself and try to arrange witness protection alone."

The waitress brought their food, tacos, and they began to eat.

"So how are you doing?" Solomon asked, changing the subject.

"Considering that I almost got shot this week, I'm holding up pretty well," Billie replied.

Solomon apologized for not responding to her text earlier. Billie brushed it off, saying, "It's okay. I just had a strong reaction. I'm sure the judge will throw this out."

"Not necessarily. There's a gap in the law in Utah. If someone files a protective order or stalking injunction against someone, you can't file the same in return. But the law doesn't include filing one if you have the other type filed against you. You have a stalking injunction against him, so it's not entirely impossible that a court may grant him a protective order. But you're right, they rarely do it because it's against the interests of justice. Still, I think I should handle the hearing for you."

"Are you sure?"

Solomon took a bite of his taco. "If you'd rather have someone else handle it, I understand."

"You're the best lawyer I know. There's nobody else I'd rather have there with me."

Solomon got a slight blush in his cheeks. He took a bite of taco and wiped his lips with a napkin before continuing. "So, what happened with Dax? I couldn't have guessed this is how he would end up in a million years."

She took a small bite of her taco before pushing the plate away and leaning back in her seat. "I'm not entirely sure what happened. I mean, there were little hints along the way, things he would do that made me pause and think. But I never could have imagined this. He told me, calmly and with a straight face, that he was going to put a bullet in my head and then turn the gun on himself so we could be together. He meant it, Solomon. It wasn't just a scare tactic. He really believed it was the only way for us to be together." She sighed. "Did you work with many stalkers when you were a social worker?"

Solomon nodded. "He's what we call a love-scorned stalker," Solomon said, before taking another bite of taco. "There're six types of stalkers, and unfortunately, his type is the most volatile. They can develop something called erotomania, where they believe that the person they're stalking is in love with them. I've had cases where the victim would come home and the stalker would be there, cooking dinner and acting like they're married."

"So he's just psychopathic, then?" she asked.

Solomon shook his head. "Most stalkers aren't psychopaths, but they often have other personality disorders like malignant narcissism or borderline personality. But what's really scary about stalkers is their pathology. They live in a fantasy world where there are no rules. Most women are more afraid of being stalked by a stranger, and that makes sense, but stalkers who are known to the victim are far more dangerous. You're doing the right thing by taking all these precautions."

She hesitated. "I . . . spoke with him."

"Seriously? Why?"

"I thought if I could reason with him . . . but it's not him. He's not the man I knew anymore." She shook her head, looking desperate. "The precautions are just Band-Aids. He's already violated the stalking injunction more times than I can count and is in a revolving door at the jail, but as soon as he's released, it starts all over again. Incarceration doesn't scare him."

"You should come stay with me," Solomon said. "He wouldn't be able to get to you at my house. Your house is too easy for him to break into, even with the deputies outside."

"Are you asking me to move in with you?" she asked with a chuckle.

"I've got ten bedrooms. Might as well start filling them up with beautiful women," Solomon joked. "I'm not kidding about the offer, though. I don't want you to be afraid in your own home."

"I appreciate it, but I won't let him scare me out of my own house."

Solomon wiped his lips with a napkin as he glanced over at a nearby booth where a couple sat quietly eating. "It's an open offer," he said.

"Thanks." She glanced down to the tacos with a look of disgust and pushed them farther away from her. Solomon noticed the puffy, red eyes and knew she'd been crying.

"How are you doing with all this?" she asked.

He let out a long breath. "What if I'm wrong, Billie? What if Dennis's suicide had nothing to do with my mother or Tommy and it's just a coincidence?"

Billie raised an eyebrow. "Do you really believe that?"

Solomon shrugged. "I don't know. Maybe cutting into your thighs is a more common way to commit suicide than we realized?"

Billie shook her head. "I doubt it. All the signs indicate that Dennis wasn't on the verge of suicide."

"Then the only other explanation is that Tommy really did try to take me out, and the suicides are linked somehow. If Blackbird was right and Tommy knows he's on his way out, maybe this is his way of cleaning house. Dennis knew a lot about their operations, and so did Roger."

"You don't have to keep looking into this, you know. You can stop anytime."

Solomon neatly folded his napkin, his fingers nervously twisting its edges. He pondered for a moment before speaking, his voice thoughtful. "Maybe it's better not to know everything about your past."

23

Roger Lynch sat alone in his office, surrounded by the hum of computers and the soft glow of monitors. He thought, with approval, about how the sleek, modern design of the space gave the impression of a high-end tech company rather than a government building. He glanced at the clock on his computer screen and sighed. He had nowhere to go, no one to go home to. His marriage was a sham, built on convenience rather than love. He wondered if his wife felt the same way, if she had married him only to escape her dysfunctional family.

As he exited his office, the jovial chatter of the deputies outside came to a sudden halt. They fell into step behind him as he made his way to the elevators, their silent presence a constant reminder that someone was trying to kill him.

The darkened parking garage loomed ahead, and Roger's heart rate increased as he approached the spot where he had been attacked. He fought to keep his composure in front of his subordinates.

When he had unlocked his car, he thanked the deputies and got in. He pulled away, his eyes always glancing over the dark corners where someone could be hiding. Another defendant his office had prosecuted once attacked him, but he had been caught before he could do any real damage. A copy of *The Catcher in the Rye* had been found in the man's car along with a gun, which he said he was going to use on the district attorney.

Near misses were common, but an actual attack, particularly one where it was clear the attacker was trying to kill him, were rare. Maybe even unheard of in a smaller county tucked away in the mountains of Utah. He had to admit it had rattled him more than he anticipated.

He pulled out of the complex and headed to the freeway entrance. Roger rolled down the window and let the cold night air whip his face. When he was a young man, he had wanted to be a racecar driver. His grandfather on his mother's side had once set the land speed record in the 1960s out on the Salt Flats not far from Tooele.

It was a childish dream, and as his father had told him, a stupid dream, and Roger had promptly given it up. His father was a judge and expected his son to follow in his footsteps. But sitting on a bench casting judgment didn't sound appealing to him. Being in front of a camera, though: there was something about it that sent a shock of electricity through him every time.

Some people would find it pathetic, he knew, but he didn't care. There was no time in his life he felt more alive than when all the attention was focused on him.

As he pulled into his horseshoe driveway, Roger admired his massive home. The striking Spanish red tile roof and the numerous balconies on the second and third floors gave the house an air of opulence, reminiscent of the extravagant mansions that populated the upscale neighborhood of Beverly Hills.

The house was a perfect fit for Roger, who had always dreamed of living in a mansion that would inspire envy in others.

A small twitch of resentment went through him when he remembered the comment Solomon Shepard had made during the office Christmas party. Roger's wife had insisted on hosting the event at their home, and as they looked around, Solomon had quipped that the house looked like something a Colombian drug lord would own. It had slightly bothered him, but the fact that his wife laughed and placed her hand gently on Solomon's shoulder as she did so, giving Roger a quick glance, infuriated him.

Roger sat in his car for a moment, taking a deep breath before stepping out and making his way to the front door. As he entered, he found Mandy reclining on the couch, engrossed in the television. The spacious living room was surrounded by floor-to-ceiling windows, offering a breathtaking view of the lush woods that stretched out behind the house.

Roger's eyes were drawn to the center of the room, where a large bearskin rug lay at Mandy's feet. Her toes, adorned with perfectly painted white nails, curled and uncurled through the soft fur as she sipped from a full glass of wine, wrapped in a silk robe. The room was filled with the sweet aroma of the wine, and Roger could see an already half-empty bottle resting on the sleek marble coffee table in front of her.

"Could you at least not be drunk and in pajamas when I get home," he said as he tossed his keys on the large dining room table past the kitchen.

"Oh sure," she shouted from the front room. "How about I wear a gown and come to the door every night and take your briefcase and get your slippers?"

As Roger entered the living room, he stood for a moment, his hands sliding into the pockets of his expensive suit. Mandy was engrossed in the television, which blared a reality show about wealthy housewives in Miami. The sound of two women shouting at each other over some perceived slight filled the air. "You've been drinking a lot lately."

"Okay, *Dad.*"

Roger felt a twinge of guilt as he watched Mandy take another sip of wine. He knew that she was drinking to numb the pain of their crumbling marriage, but he couldn't deny that he was relieved by how it kept her docile and occupied. The Roman emperors had been wise in providing bread and circuses as distractions for their people, but Roger had found that wine was the best distraction for his wife. He could keep out of her hair, and she could keep out of his. It was a mutually beneficial arrangement, even if it wasn't the ideal situation.

"I don't suppose you made any dinner?" he asked hopefully. "I haven't eaten all day."

"I'm so sorry, my lord. I guess I must've forgot."

"You know, you don't have to be such a bitch all the time."

Mandy let out a laugh, a sound that grated on Roger's nerves. He could tell that she was enjoying the way she had gotten under his skin, reveling in the power she still held over him. He let out a long, exasperated breath as she took another sip of the wine, her cheeks flushed with the alcohol. Despite his contempt for her, he couldn't help but acknowledge the stunning beauty that she possessed.

Her face was playful, a mischievous glint in her eyes that Roger knew all too well. She had always been a master at pushing his buttons, and he had fallen for it time and time again. It was no wonder that men fawned over her. She was a woman who commanded attention, turning heads wherever she went.

But even her beauty couldn't make up for the emptiness that had taken root in their relationship. Roger wondered if there was any way to salvage what was left of their marriage, or if it was too late.

"What's the matter, Roger? Don't you want me?" she asked, teasingly. She loosened her silk robe, revealing her perfectly sculpted breasts and tanned stomach, with each abdominal muscle visible, protruding underneath her flawless skin. Roger couldn't help but compare his own out-of-shape body to her toned physique, and he felt a pang of envy. But he told himself he would be in shape if all he had to do all day was work out and get drunk.

"How about it, Roger?" she said, pulling open her robe a little more. "How about you take me right now? Pull my hair back and kiss me and take me right here on the couch."

The thought of being intimate with Mandy now repulsed him. Though he knew that any man would gladly trade places with him, he felt revulsion toward his wife. Through the years, she had become more and more abhorrent to him, a shadow of the woman he had fallen in love with.

Roger said, "Get some clothes on and I'll order something. Maybe we can at least have a decent dinner together."

After ordering some food, Roger retreated to his lavish bathroom and took a long, hot shower. Once he was finished, he changed into a comfortable Nike sweatsuit, the kind that he used to wear to the gym before his busy work schedule made it impossible to maintain a regular exercise routine.

He turned his attention to the medicine cabinet, where several amber pill bottles were lined up neatly. He opened each one carefully and took the pills, one by one. Most of them were for his abnormally high blood pressure, which had spiked since he stopped taking his antidepressants.

He made his way to the study, where the patio overlooked the sprawling neighborhood. The evening air was cool, and he poured himself a generous amount of whiskey from the well-stocked bar. He sank into the soft chair on the patio and took a long sip, savoring the smoky flavor.

As he drank, he gazed up at the starless sky, the only sound the quiet hum of the city in the distance. He inhaled deeply through his nose, the scent of whiskey mingling with the crisp night air, and exhaled slowly. A single thought kept crossing his mind: *Is this all there is?*

When he got too reflective, he shut down his thinking. There was no point to it.

A sharp snap echoed from the right of the patio, causing Roger to freeze in his seat. He strained his ears, trying to identify the source of the noise. Something heavy seemed to step on the twigs from the giant fir tree that Mandy had insisted on planting next to the house, to keep prying eyes away.

Roger stared intently at the bushes that encircled the house. "Hello?" he called out tentatively.

There was no response, except for the sound of a slight breeze rustling some bushes. Roger turned back to his drink, trying to ignore the unease that was starting to gnaw at his insides. He stared at the sky, lost in thought.

His mind swirled, and his headache pounded harder. At first, he thought it was just the whiskey, too much drink too fast. But the warmth in his belly didn't dissipate, and his body began to feel heavy, as though it were being sucked into quicksand. He noticed the odd sensations in his hands and face, a not entirely unpleasant feeling, and realized that it was something else. Drugs.

Suddenly, the bush nearest the patio split open, and a dark figure burst out and leaped over the railing at Roger.

Roger tried to yell, to get the attention of the deputies he had assigned to monitor his house from across the street, but hardly any sound came out of him. His head was spinning, and he wasn't sure if he was standing up or still lying down. Suddenly, the chair slipped out from under him, and he hit the wooden slats of the patio, feeling the cold wood against his hands. He tried to push himself up but felt something tight around his throat.

A wave of panic coursed through him as he realized what was happening. The familiar feeling that he had nightmares about, a wire wrapped tightly around his throat, sucking away his breath and life. He clawed at the wire, trying to loosen its grip, but it was no use.

As he struggled to scream for help, drool and foamy spittle leaked from his mouth. The world spun around him, and he felt himself losing consciousness. His vision darkened, and the last thing he felt was hands on his body, dragging him away.

24

Billie brought her truck to a stop in front of Solomon's home, and he stared at the imposing structure with a sense of apprehension.

Solomon didn't know much about the property, but he had dug up a few things to quench his curiosity. The home had been lived in by Mrs. Langley's family for over a century, and the stories surrounding their wealth and influence were shrouded in mystery. There were rumors of scandals and even darker things that had happened within those walls.

As he gazed at the house, Solomon couldn't shake the feeling of something watching him, an unseen presence that lurked in the shadows. He took a deep breath, trying to push away the sense of foreboding that settled over him like a heavy cloak.

"You know," Billie said as she turned the truck off, "most people work their entire lives to have a house like this."

Solomon kept his gaze on the home, his eyes drawn to its massive structure. It was a testament to a time long gone, now run down and neglected. Corinthian pillars towered over the porch, their once-white paint now faded and peeling, and a wooden railing ran along the front of the house, its paint chipped and worn.

As Solomon looked closer, he noticed the signs of neglect that marred the mansion's once-grand facade. The windows were dirty and smudged, and the lawn was dead. The roof looked like it had seen better days.

Despite the disrepair, there was still a sense of grandeur about the house. Its history was etched into every inch of the peeling paint. Solomon had felt drawn to this place the moment he had seen it.

"Have you ever heard of hedonic adaptation?" Solomon said.

"Can't say that I have."

"It means that we look for happiness outside of ourselves, and when we get something we want, like a new house or new car, the satisfaction we get fades quickly, and we go right back to where we were, because anything outside of ourselves can't actually give us happiness. But I don't even have that anymore. I think I lost the ability to be satisfied for even short bursts of time."

"Why do you think that is?"

He shook his head, his eyes still glued to his home. "Do you ever feel like this is all meaningless, Billie? That we're a cosmic accident that came in the blink of an eye and will be extinguished in the blink of an eye?"

"I think everybody does at times, and I don't think there's anything wrong with it. It's okay to be sad."

"I'm not talking about sadness. I'm talking about something much deeper. About not having the ability to be happy anymore."

She paused for a moment. "If you can't enjoy a nice cup of coffee on a cold day, you won't enjoy a private jet or a yacht. Just try to enjoy the coffee."

He chuckled. "Let me guess, your dad told you that?"

"He did," she said, her eyes gazing out at something rustling in the bushes nearby. Suddenly, a large rodent scampered away, and she turned back to Solomon. "You know, he would be over the moon to see you."

"No," he replied, glancing at her before opening the truck door. "It's best not to stir up old memories. Sometimes it's better to let sleeping dogs lie."

As he leaned on his cane and stepped out of the truck, Solomon felt a sense of weariness settle over him. "I'll call you if I hear anything else. You sure you don't want to stay here?"

She shook her head. "I'm not changing my entire life because of him."

"Okay, well, call me tomorrow if you hear anything."

"I will."

Solomon watched the taillights of her truck disappear into the distance. He had been slightly misleading with her—the truth was that he didn't go to see Zach not because it would bring up bad memories for Zach, but for Solomon himself.

He and her father had worked together on a lot of cases when Zach was sheriff and Solomon a violent crimes prosecutor. Cases that were filled with blood and misery. The kind of cases that kept you up at night, that left a stain on you that never quite faded away. Solomon had tried to tuck those memories away in the corners of his mind, to push them deep down and forget about them, but he knew that the mind forgets nothing.

He opened his gate with the passcode and then locked it behind him. The home seemed imposing today, unwelcoming. He had wanted to be home all day, but as he stood in front of the house and stared at it, he wanted to be anywhere else. But there was nowhere else to go.

Solomon unlocked the front door and stepped inside his home. The air was cold and still, the silence almost deafening. He had turned off the heat when he left, and now the chill seeped into his bones.

As he made his way over to the thermostat by the front door, he felt uneasy.

After turning on the heat, he walked over to the kitchen to prepare some tea. The kettle began to heat on the stove, and he leaned against the counter, lost in thought.

But then something caught his eye—a slight imperfection in the linoleum floor. He bent down for a closer look, and that's when he saw it: a faint shoe print. It wasn't his, and the realization hit him like a fist.

For a moment, he stood frozen, staring at the shoe print. His mind raced with possibilities. The unease that had been gnawing at him since he arrived home now exploded into full-blown fear.

Slowly, his heartbeat starting to quicken in his ears, Solomon went to the cupboard by the sink. Inside, a handgun sat on the first shelf. A gun was in every room of the house that he frequented, including the bathroom. He checked the chamber and then slipped off his shoes. The linoleum was cold.

Solomon stepped out around the fridge and looked down the hallway. It was a long corridor that led to the dining room, which he never used. The dining room was dark; the blinds Mrs. Langley had hung up blocked what little light there was.

Step by slow step, he made his way down the hall, quietly pushing open doors with his cane. When he got to the dining room, he looked both ways and then turned the corner to his right, near the staircase that led up to the bedrooms on the second floor.

The staircase wasn't far, and he made it there and then stood quietly, listening. The house creaked and crackled as though it were speaking. He took the first step.

The stairs had been replaced and were newer than the house, so they didn't creak much. The part that did was the banister, which hadn't been replaced. Old wood with nicks and scratches as proof that children lived here at one time. Now, he couldn't even imagine the sound of children in a place like this.

At the top of the steps, he paused, leaning on his cane, and listened. A branch from a nearby elm tree tapped the window in the first bedroom, but other than that, it was quiet. The shoe print downstairs wasn't recognizable, and with the exception of Billie, he hadn't had anyone inside the home since a plumber came to fix a broken pipe two years ago. His mind was trying to tell him it was nothing, just his own shoe print. The ball of anxiety in his guts told him something else. That something was wrong.

Solomon's heart raced as he surveyed the upstairs floor, his eyes scanning every inch for any sign of danger. He could notice the slightest details, and something caught his attention.

As he looked down at the carpet, his eyes narrowed. There were depressions in the fibers, small but definitely there. Someone had walked through here recently. He kept his home meticulous, vacuuming every day. Housework had, somehow, become cathartic for him. He hadn't been upstairs since he had vacuumed. The depressions shouldn't have been there.

His mind raced as he followed the depressions with his eyes, tracing their path into an unused bedroom.

Solomon's pulse quickened as he approached the door, his grip tightening on both the gun and cane. The weight of the objects in his hands gave him an inflated sense of confidence, but deep down, he knew he was in danger.

As he glanced in, his eyes scanned the room, searching for any sign of movement, and his heart stopped when he saw the bed. He felt like he had been punched in the chest. The air rushed out of his lungs, and he struggled to catch his breath.

Trembling, he took out his phone and dialed 911, his back pressed against the wall as he slid down to the floor. His hand covered his eyes as he waited for the operator to answer.

"911, what's your emergency?"

25

Solomon and Billie leaned against a police cruiser parked in his front yard, surrounded by a swarm of law enforcement vehicles from the county sheriff's office, state crime lab, and city police department. The air was thick with tension as the officers moved about, scouring the scene for evidence.

Solomon's eyes were fixed on the front door of his home, where the assistant medical examiner, Mathew, emerged. Their eyes met, and Mathew gave a curt nod before heading back to his vehicle. There was no small talk, no friendly banter as there had been in the past. Solomon was a suspect now, and they were on opposite sides of the law.

Solomon's mind was in a frenzy as he recalled the disturbing image that had flashed before him when he had peered into his bedroom. It was an image that was now seared into his mind.

The first thing he had noticed had been the face, twisted in a grotesque expression that sent a shiver down his spine.

Roger's face was whiter than snow, his lips tinged a sickly blue-gray hue. It shocked him. He had never liked Roger and in fact found him despicable, but at that moment he felt a sympathy for him that he never thought he could've been capable of feeling.

The body was completely nude, with giant, gaping gashes in Roger's thighs that revealed clean cuts down to the bone. It was clear that the killer had been skilled, precise, and utterly ruthless.

The killer had not used a sawing motion with a knife. Instead, he had brought an automatic carving knife, slicing through the man's flesh in less than a couple of seconds. It was a cold, calculated act of violence that left Solomon feeling sick to his stomach.

It probably took him too long to saw into Dennis's legs, so he had to come up with a faster way. He's learning.

As he had looked at the lifeless body, Solomon saw the terror and pain. He imagined the blood gushing out of Roger like a river, hot and sticky, as he struggled to cling to life.

"I'm putting you into protective custody," Billie said.

Solomon watched strangers going into and out of his home, and it gave him a sense of dread so acute it dried his mouth. "There's nowhere safer than here."

"Oh, obviously," she said angrily. "You're going into protective custody. No questions asked. And if you refuse, I'm going to have you arrested so you can at least be locked up somewhere this maniac can't get to you."

Solomon couldn't think clearly. His mind raced from thought to thought, and he couldn't hang on to any single one for any length of time. It was only when Billie asked him if he'd heard what she'd said that he realized he hadn't.

"I'm sorry. It's hard to concentrate right now."

Her gaze softened. "I'm putting you into protective custody," she said with the anger in her voice gone now.

"I don't need it."

"Are you kidding me?"

"If he was smart enough to get past my alarms and break into my house, then he's smart enough to know the best way to kill me would be to wait until I fall asleep and put a bullet in my head. He didn't do that. He doesn't want me dead. He wants me to see his work."

"Why?"

"How the hell should I know? I don't know anything about him. Don't expect too much from me, Billie."

"I'm not expecting anything from you. But for whatever reason, this person has selected you as the target." She sighed. "We went through this before, Solomon."

"This is different. Alonso wanted me to suffer before he killed me. This isn't that. He wants me to see what he's doing. I think he wanted me to see it first. Before it was swarmed as a crime scene."

She checked the time on her phone and said, "We're going to go through the list of all the defendants you ever prosecuted so we can—"

"A lot of those are paper files that haven't been uploaded into the database, I'm guessing. It would take way too long to put them in so they become searchable. We don't have time like that. The first one was subtle, and with this he's hitting me over the head with a sledgehammer. The next time is . . ." He trailed off and let out a breath instead. "We need to find him."

Mathew emerged from the sleek black Suburban, the vehicle most used by the Medical Examiner's Office, and made his way over to where Solomon and Billie were standing. His voice was somber as he spoke.

"Can we talk in private for a sec, Sheriff?" he said, gesturing for Billie to follow him.

"Whatever you have to say to me, you can say in front of Solomon."

Mathew's eyes met Solomon's for a moment before he cleared his throat, a gloomy expression on his face. He spoke in a low voice, as if he didn't want to be overheard.

"He definitely bled out here, Sheriff," he said, his voice heavy. "It's impossible to give you an exact time of death, but based on liver temp, I would say that it was very recent. Probably just an hour or two before Solomon says he got home."

"Not *says*," Billie remarked with a hint of anger. "I dropped him off. He got home when he told us he got home."

Mathew shrugged. "Whatever you say. But I'll get you a preliminary report by tomorrow."

As he walked away, Billie said, "Sorry about that."

"You find a dead body in your bed, people are gonna have questions," he said, zoning out and staring at his home.

She inhaled through her nose and let it out softly before pushing off the cruiser and saying, "Let's get going. I want to get you somewhere safe."

"You go. I'm gonna gather some stuff, and I'll take an Uber down."

"Solomon—"

"I'll be fine. I'll meet you at the station. Scout's honor."

Solomon entered his home, the scene of the crime now slowing down as people began to leave with armfuls of evidence they thought might be relevant. A few forensic technicians remained, but they had finished their work and were now chatting casually among themselves, as if they were in a coffee shop rather than at a murder scene. Solomon gave them a single nod in greeting before making his way up to his own bedroom.

As he walked, he glanced into the room where Roger had been found. The sight of the drying blood, which looked like buckets of red-black paint had been spilled over the bed where Mrs. Langley had slept, made his stomach churn. He knew that he would have to call a crime scene cleanup crew to take care of the mess, but he wished he could simply burn the entire room to the ground.

Solomon entered his own bedroom. His eyes scanned his closet, taking in the rows of clothing that had long since gone unused. He pulled out a few pairs of jeans and sweatpants, along with some T-shirts and shorts. As he gathered the clothes, he noticed the thin layer of dust that coated some of the garments. It had been so long since he had worn them that he had forgotten they were even there.

As he turned to leave, his eyes fell on the shotgun and pistol that sat on a shelf in the closet.

Some protection you guys were.

Solomon's heart skipped a beat as he glanced over to his nightstand and saw the drawer partially open. It was only a couple of inches, nothing that anyone else would notice, but he was meticulous about closing cupboards and drawers every evening. The thought of them being open all night filled him with anxiety.

As he walked over to the nightstand, he couldn't shake the feeling that something was wrong, that something had been tampered with.

When he opened the drawer, his heart dropped. He saw a cell phone he'd never seen before. The phone's glossy surface reflected the dim light of the room; it was brand new, but an older Nokia phone. He backed away slowly, his mind racing with possibilities.

Solomon knew that he needed to act quickly, and he went to the bathroom to grab some latex gloves that he occasionally used for cleaning. Upon returning to the drawer, he carefully picked up the phone, his heart pounding.

The phone wasn't on, but he powered it up. There was no passcode.

After he waited for a few tense seconds, the phone dinged with a single text message sent hours ago.

26

Mazie breathed a sigh of relief as her shift came to an end, and she made her way to the women's locker room in the sheriff's office. Rows of blue lockers were adorned with little numbers on metal plates on top. The sight of them reminded her of junior high school.

As she undressed from her uniform, an ugly beige-and-brown combination that did nothing for her complexion, Mazie made a mental note to talk to Billie about changing the color back to navy. She couldn't understand why anyone would choose such an unflattering color for a uniform. Who the hell respected someone in beige?

As Mazie undressed down to her bra and underwear and slipped into a pair of well-worn jeans and a sleeveless Metallica shirt, a young woman named Sherri stepped out of the showers and wrapped a white towel around herself. She made her way over to the lockers behind Mazie and greeted her with a warm smile.

"What's up, cupcake? You hanging in there?" Sherri asked.

"Yeah, I'm hanging in there," Mazie said, offering a small smile.

"You got any plans for the weekend?"

She sighed. "I need to find someone to finish my sleeve and all the tattoo artists here suck. I'm gonna have to go to Vegas just to get anything done."

"So?" Sherri said, taking out a bottle of lotion from her locker. "Let's make it a girls' trip. I know this club down there with the hottest male dancers you'll ever see."

"No, thanks. I don't need greasy strippers rubbing on me. But a girls' trip sounds kick ass."

Mazie took her hairbrush and walked to the sink and mirror. She was lost in thought about the shooting and how odd it was to actually fire her gun, when a soft creaking sound broke through the silence. It was a tiny noise, something like a metal scrape, but it was loud enough to make her pause and take notice.

Slowly, she turned to face the source of the sound. Her eyes scanned the room, looking for any sign of movement or disturbance.

As her gaze fell back on the mirror, she noticed a faint glimmer of movement behind her. There was a vent up above the door, and it seemed to be the source of the sound.

"When was the last time you went to Vegas?" Sherri said as she began to dress.

Mazie approached the vent, her eyes glued to the flicker of light that seemed to be coming from within. It was as though something was moving behind the metal grate, casting shadows that danced in the light.

She grabbed one of the thick plastic garbage bins and dumped out its contents.

"What are you doing?" Sherri said.

Mazie flipped the garbage bin upside down and stood on it. Sherri appeared and grabbed her legs like she was about to tumble over Niagara Falls, and it unbalanced her so that she had to jump off.

"Holy shit, Sherri!"

"I was trying to help you."

"I'm like two feet off the ground. I think I'd live if I fell."

"What are you doing anyway?"

"There's something in the vent."

She climbed back onto the garbage can. The vent had two screws, one on each side. "Hey, Shers, do me a favor and grab my keys, will ya?"

Sherri hurried off and came back with the keys. Mazie opened the pocketknife she had and lifted the flathead screwdriver.

"You have a screwdriver on your keys?"

"No, I have a multitool knife on my keys. The knife has a screwdriver."

She unscrewed the cover and lifted it off the wall.

Mazie's eyes were immediately drawn to the thick black wire that was coiled inside the vent. Then, her gaze landed on something else, something that made her blood run cold. At the end of the wire was a small cylindrical object with a glass sphere at the end. The sphere was reflecting the lights of the locker room in small sparkles of light.

It was a camera, and it was pointed straight at the showers.

With Sheriff Gray out, Mazie had no choice but to notify Assistant Sheriff Dobbs. He was a man of average build and height, with a receding hairline and an unassuming demeanor. He listened carefully as Mazie explained the situation, but his response was characteristically passive. He was a man who didn't want to make any decisions because he would be responsible for the consequences. Mazie was grateful that he at least got the IT department to begin looking into it.

Mazie stood in the locker room a little later, watching a technician from the IT department analyze the camera that had been found in the vent. Meanwhile, another tech was running down where the camera led to, tracing its path back to its source.

Mazie stood with her arms folded. Sherri, who had been standing nearby, was visibly shaken by the discovery. She had almost broken down in tears and had to leave the room to collect herself.

"Well?" Mazie said.

The technician, a skinny guy with an oval head and brown hair, said, "Looks like they ran it from the next room over. What's there?"

"Storage room."

"Well, let's go check it out."

Together, Mazie and the technician made their way to the storage room. As they entered, Mazie scanned the shelves and noticed something. There, behind one of the shelves, she spotted a wire. Someone had gone to great lengths to conceal it, drilling a small hole to thread it through the wall.

Mazie's heart sank as the technician followed the wire to its source. It was connected to a small, inconspicuous device that was likely either recording or transmitting footage of the locker room.

"This is pretty low-tech stuff. The kind you'd buy online for like fifty bucks. Not a sophisticated peeper."

"How long?" Mazie asked.

"How long what?"

"How long has he been recording the women's locker room, dipshit."

"Oh," he said, somewhat flustered at her anger, "um, I don't know. I'll have to get into this and see what's there."

Mazie's frustration boiled over as she left the room, shaking her head in disbelief. As she faced Dobbs in the hall, he looked up at her with his typical air of passive detachment.

Mazie didn't say anything right away, waiting for Dobbs to respond. But he just stood there, staring at her with his blank expression. Finally, she couldn't contain her anger any longer.

"Well?" she demanded. "What are you going to do about it?"

Dobbs seemed taken aback by Mazie's outburst. "We need to look into this further," he said with uncertainty in his voice. "We need to figure out what steps to take next."

"Um, how about we find who did this and arrest them?" she said with heavy sarcasm dripping in her voice. "That sounds like a plan to me."

"Just calm down, we don't have enough information yet to know what we should or shouldn't be doing."

Mazie stepped toward him. "Fix this, Dobbs."

"I'm doing everything I can until the sheriff gets back."

Mazie's attention was momentarily drawn away from Dobbs as she noticed two deputies, Aaron Watkins and Dave Garcia, out of the corner of her eye. They were standing a dozen feet away, huddled together and snickering, trying to stifle their laughter.

Mazie's eyes narrowed as she turned her gaze toward them. Aaron and Dave quickly averted their eyes, trying to act casual. But Mazie saw right through them.

"What's so funny?" she demanded.

Aaron and Dave exchanged a glance before bursting out laughing, unable to hold it in any longer. They turned and walked away, their laughter echoing through the hallway.

Mazie's mind drifted back to her high school days, when a group of boys had taken pictures of her in the locker room. They had done a lot of things to the loner tomboy who had to get free lunch because her parents got divorced and her dad was a cop with two mortgages and alimony. Mazie thought she had grown past all that. It had taken her hitting rock bottom to do it. In an alcoholic haze at just sixteen, she had used a fake ID to get into a bar and hit another woman so hard it fractured her jaw.

The bartender, a friend of hers, shuffled her out the back, but the police were waiting, and she was arrested. Only because her father was a sergeant on the same police force was she not charged with a felony. She got a misdemeanor with an agreement that her case would be sealed when she turned eighteen.

It was then her father sat her down on the steps of their porch and read her a poem. It was written on a laminated index card and was folded and stuffed into his wallet.

Good and evil, they're like two folks dancin'
One's got the light, the other's romancin'
Both of 'em inside us, makin' us choose
For one to win, the other's gotta lose

He had asked her what she thought that meant, and she said she didn't know.

"It means," he said in his deep, calm voice, "that between good and evil, for one of them to win, the other has to lose. Do you understand? It *has* to lose. So, you need to make a choice. Which one are you gonna let win in this world?"

She didn't totally understand why it had impacted her so much, because looking back on it, she was a stupid sixteen-year-old kid who didn't know anything and didn't want to know. But for some reason, her father, the most heroic man she had ever met, had this look in his eyes while he spoke to her that day that she never forgot. He wasn't angry, but ashamed.

She had never seen it before and never saw it again, but her father was her entire world, and it had cut so deep into her that she just wanted to crawl into a bottle and never come out. But she did come out. It took three years of relapses, particularly after her father was shot and killed on duty, but she was eventually able to get sober, and when she turned twenty-one, she applied to be a cop at the same precinct her father had worked at.

Mazie's eyes flicked to a nearby cubicle where she spotted a mug of steaming coffee. Without a second thought, she grabbed the mug and stormed after Aaron and Dave, who were now a few steps ahead of her. She reached them and dumped the scalding liquid on both of them, not caring that some of it splashed back on her own hand. Aaron and Dave yelped in surprise and anger, but Mazie didn't stop to look back at them as she stormed off.

Aaron got the worst of it down his neck and started jumping around like a grasshopper while shouting profanity.

"Deputy Heaton!" Dobbs shouted.

Mazie, her temper cooling as she realized it might not have been the best idea to assault two cops inside a police station, stopped and turned to face Dobbs, her arms folded over her chest.

Sheriff Gray came around the corner just then, her coat speckled with snow.

"What's going on?"

Mazie breathed out and closed her eyes.

Oh shit, she thought.

27

Billie sat at her desk, frustration washing over her. She had important things to do: prepare for Dax's protective order hearing, work Dennis's and Roger's murders, and understand why a lunatic was hunting Solomon. But she was stuck dealing with what some of the deputies were calling "Coffee-gate."

She spent a couple of hours interviewing everyone involved, trying to get to the bottom of who set up the camera in the locker room. Finally, when she had everything she needed from the witnesses, she invited Mazie into her office.

"Shut the door, please," Billie said.

Mazie did.

"Sit down."

Mazie sank into the plush oversize chair in front of Billie's desk, her fingers drumming on the armrests. Her wide, doe-like eyes darted around the room, avoiding direct eye contact with the sheriff as though she were a scolded child. Despite her obvious agitation, she tried to maintain a calm facade, but her tapping fingers betrayed her.

"Deputy Watkins has first-degree burns on the back of his neck. He'll be fine, but there might be a scar. Are you aware that an injury that leaves a scar is enhanced to a class A misdemeanor? The level of misdemeanor that a police officer could be fired for. Or at the least, have an IAD investigation and suspension."

"Yeah," she said softly, glancing to the floor. "I know."

"What would possibly make you think you should dump hot coffee on him?"

"Are you freaking kidding me? They were recording us showering."

"And all you had to do was text me and I would have been right there. I would have had them disciplined, fired, and then arrested for voyeurism. Now he's going to file a lawsuit against the department, and the lawyers will have to negotiate a settlement, and you can bet getting fired isn't going to be part of the settlement. So tell me, Deputy Heaton, what good exactly came from your burst of anger?"

She shook her head and mumbled "Bullshit" under her breath.

"Excuse me?"

Mazie held her gaze but was silent.

"You can speak freely," Billie said.

"I said it's bullshit. Ma'am."

"How so?"

Mazie's voice was filled with frustration and anger as she spoke. "You hired me because I stood up to that scumbag who was groping female cadets for months, but now that I stood up to some pervert recording us in the shower and recording our conversations and thoughts . . . it's like no one cares. And if they actually recorded something and have footage, they could put it online at any time . . . I feel like . . ." She paused, her hands shaking.

Billie sat quietly, taking in Mazie's words, waiting until she was done before speaking.

"Do you think I don't understand, Mazie? Hmm? Guess what, I use those locker rooms, too. If there are videos, I'm on them, too. I feel violated, and ashamed, and so angry I actually put my gun in my drawer rather than having it in my holster while I interview everyone. But guess what? I will stay calm. Because being calm gets things done efficiently. Being angry only makes things worse."

Mazie remained quiet.

"You can't be a good cop if you can't control your temper. You're the face of the law, and it would take only one bad interaction for a civilian to never trust another police officer again. Add up a career's worth of people like that, and one police officer's anger can hurt an entire community."

Mazie swallowed and looked down to the floor. "I . . ." She shook her head. "I know. It was just a reaction. I just felt so . . ."

"I know," Billie said softly. "But I'm going to have to discipline you. Four-week suspension, without pay."

She nodded, running her tongue along her lips. "I understand."

"Good."

Her intercom buzzed and the receptionist said, "Sheriff, Deputy Watkins is done with EMS."

"Send him in, please."

She looked at Mazie, her face steely cold. "You're excused."

The door opened, and Deputy Watkins came in with some gauze on the back of his neck.

Mazie brushed past him, and the two gave each other a frigid stare.

"Shut the door, Deputy," Billie said coolly.

He did, and then ran his fingers over the bandages on his neck as though reminding Billie that he's the real victim here.

"How's your neck?"

"Hurts. I have to go to the hospital after this just to be sure I'm not going to get an infection. She's crazy. I think she should be—"

"Shut up."

Aaron looked shocked. "What?"

Billie leaned forward, holding his gaze while swallowing down her fury. "I said—shut. Up."

She took a deep breath. "Why, Aaron? Well, I know why, but why would you think you could get away with it?"

He shrugged. "It was just a prank. We're always messing with each other. Hatfield the other day put shaving cream in my—"

"Have you ever put a camera in the men's locker rooms?"

He didn't say anything.

"Who else was involved? I assume Dave?"

Watkins folded his arms.

Billie fixed her gaze on him and leaned back in her chair, putting her arms casually on the armrests. It was a subtle gesture, but one that conveyed confidence and fearlessness.

"Where are the recordings?" Billie asked.

"There aren't any. It was cast live."

She sighed. "Aaron, listen to me, I'm going to have you arrested when you walk out of here—"

"What the hell are you talking about? Because of that bitch's—"

"Say one more word and I swear I will mace you in the face."

The blip of rage had slipped out of a facade she usually carefully kept in check. She regretted it instantly, but by the reaction on Watkins's face, he at least understood now that this wasn't a situation he was going to talk his way out of.

"As I was saying, I'm going to have you arrested. The question is, am I going to have you arrested for misdemeanor unlawful surveillance, or am I going to have you arrested for felony voyeurism? Or maybe you intended to upload those videos for some sort of financial gain? Maybe interstate distribution of unlawful pornography would be a fitting charge? Ten years minimum and registration as a sex offender for the rest of your life."

The sheriff sat quietly a moment, seeing what reaction he would have. The best way to hear what someone was really saying wasn't to ask questions, but to sit quietly and force them to talk to break the silence.

"Yeah, I recorded them as a prank. So the hell what? They're grown women. No harm, no foul. But she burned me. She physically attacked me and tried to kill me."

Billie grinned. "You have to know how stupid that sounds."

He inhaled deeply and said sternly, "I'm calling my union rep, and we're gonna file a lawsuit so big—"

"What you're going to do is give me those recordings. Every last copy. Along with every computer, iPad, and phone in your possession. Then you're going to plead no contest to unlawful surveillance as a misdemeanor, with an agreement that you will not serve jail time but you will never wear a badge again."

She leaned forward, locking her eyes with his as he seethed with rage.

Billie's voice was stern as she spoke. "If you don't cooperate, I'll personally arrest you, parade you through this office in handcuffs, and lock you up in the holding cell until your arraignment. And if you're convicted, you won't be sent to jail, you'll be sent to prison with the worst offenders out there, some of which you probably put in there. You better hope the guards don't go on their lunch break at the wrong time, right, Aaron?" She paused for a moment and leaned back in her chair, her arms crossed. "So, what's it going to be? It's up to you."

His eyes narrowed, and she could feel the tension radiating off him. He opened his mouth as if to say something, but then thought better of it and swallowed heavily. She could see the effort it took for him to rein in his anger and respond with a curt nod.

"Smart choice. Turn everything in to Lisa, and tell Deputy Garcia to come in here. I have an offer for him, too."

28

Solomon's heart raced, and his breaths came in short, quick gasps, his body feeling weak and unsteady. With shaking hands, he'd been clutching the phone tightly for what seemed like an eternity, willing himself to steady his breathing. He closed his eyes, trying to focus on the darkness behind his lids and the feeling of the cold wall against his back. Slowly, he drew in a deep breath, held it for a few seconds, and then let it out. He repeated this process, feeling his racing heart begin to calm as he regained control over his breathing.

Finally, he opened his eyes.

Two words had been texted to the phone: Hello, Solomon.

Who are you? Solomon texted.

A couple of minutes later, the response came.

Is that really the question you want to ask? Be honest or I'll know

Solomon hesitated and then texted, How do you know about my mother?

There it is. That's the right question. How about I show you?

Confirmation of his worst fears: this was about him.

Show me how?

Where's the fun in ruining surprises?

Solomon's shock quickly turned to anger as he started typing out a long message, filled with berating words and threats toward whoever was on the other end. But he soon realized that it was pointless and deleted it.

Taking a deep breath to calm himself, he put on his jacket, slipped the phone into his pocket, and summoned an Uber.

Tooele lacked the fast pace of a big city but still had enough trendy shops and businesses to occupy someone wanting to take a stroll down Main Street. Solomon remembered doing just that on his lunch breaks at the DA's office.

He felt the handle of his cane. After he had to use it, he no longer went on those walks.

The Uber dropped him off on a corner where a coffee shop and bookstore stood on one side of the street, and a piano bar, trinket shops, and thrift stores on the other.

As he crossed the intersection, the sky began to darken. On the opposite side of the street, a group of young men walked into the piano bar and gave him a critical look, sizing up his cane and the unevenness of his gait.

Solomon entered the dimly lit bar, the last ray of light from the setting sun vanishing behind him. The place was already starting to fill up with young and vibrant people, their voices and laughter filling the room with a lively energy. He showed his state ID to be scanned since he no longer had a driver's license, and took a seat at the bar, watching the crowd. There was something infectious about youth, the way it saw the world as full of possibilities and not limitations, as something worth celebrating and fighting for. It was a stark contrast to the darkness he felt inside him right now.

"Just a Guinness, please," he said to the bartender.

The beer came in a cold glass and was frothy. He took a long drink and then decided it wasn't what he wanted, so he just turned and watched a group of college-age kids playing a drinking game, though the night was clearly just getting going.

Solomon sat in the warmth of the bar and watched people a long time. Something he could do for hours. Words were empty and too easily manipulated, so to understand people, he liked sitting somewhere and just watching. The way someone glanced away and slipped their hand out of their lover's, or whether they leaned in to kiss someone or pulled away first. Those were the actions that spoke volumes.

When he was a social worker attempting to help the prison population, he would frequently just sit quietly and let the inmates talk. Sometimes he wouldn't say anything for an entire session. He knew they had hit a sensitive spot when fidgeting started. Rubbing the thumb and fingers together or tapping the foot in a frantic motion. It was the nervous system processing whatever it was they were speaking about, and that's when Solomon knew it was a trauma that they hadn't processed yet. But by the time someone had killed another human being and was serving a fifty-year sentence—because of a long criminal history going back to when they were in grammar school—it was impossible to bring all that trauma to the surface in the one hour per week Solomon had gotten with the inmates. It was the reason he left and went to law school. The system was set up to punish, not to heal, and it was too difficult for him to function within it.

Solomon finished his beer and left a good tip for the bartender.

He exited the piano bar into the cold night and strolled leisurely along the frosty sidewalks. A gentle breeze picked up, sending swirls of snowflakes in every direction, some of them landing softly on his face and melting into droplets of icy water.

He was about half a block away when he noticed the car.

It was black with tinted windows and was slowly following behind him.

He started walking faster. The car sped up and pulled alongside him, and he could hear the low hum of the engine. The tinted windows made it impossible to see who was inside, but he could feel their gaze on him.

He quickened his pace, but the car matched his speed.

It sped past him, and he felt relief wash over him.

Then it flipped a U-turn.

Solomon felt his heart pounding as he rushed across the street, glancing nervously over his shoulder at the car with the tinted windows. As he made it to the other side, the light still hadn't changed, and he could feel the car's presence looming closer. Distracted by the menacing vehicle tailing him, Solomon didn't notice the other car that came hurtling toward him from the opposite direction, its tires slipping on the ice and the driver frantically laying on the horn. Solomon narrowly dodged the speeding car, his heart skipping a beat as he stumbled, nearly falling to the ground. Regaining his balance, he hurried inside the safety of the bookstore.

Solomon cautiously moved to the center of the store, his eyes darting around, scanning for a second exit. He felt a chill running down his spine, knowing he was being followed. Tommy had managed to hire a marine sniper on short notice; Solomon had no doubt he could find another one just as quickly. But why toy with him? Why leave him the phone and send him cryptic texts? In the past, the old-school mobsters and bikers who wanted a hit carried out would hire gunmen who simply walked up to the mark on the street—perhaps waiting for a crosswalk light or browsing through shops—slipped a bullet into the back of their head, dropped the gun, and calmly walked away. It was a cold, calculated method that increased the odds of getting away with murder more than anything else. Killing successfully was smooth and efficient; stalking was not. Tommy had something else planned for him.

He saw an employee nearby, busy shelving books, and approached her.

"Excuse me, is there another way out of this store?" he asked, trying to keep his voice calm.

The employee looked at him with surprise. "No, sorry. This is the only public exit. Is everything okay?"

Solomon hesitated for a moment before nodding and quickly left, making his way toward the front of the store. He tried to keep his head down, not wanting to draw any attention to himself. As he reached the entrance, he saw the black car parked outside. Fear crept up his spine, and he knew that he needed to get out of there right now.

Solomon quickly scanned the front windows before making a bee-line toward the back of the bookstore. He passed by the coffee shop and the restrooms, and found the entrance to a dimly lit hallway that was marked with an "Employees Only" sign. Without hesitation, he rushed down the corridor, past several storage rooms and offices.

As he made his way toward the back exit, a woman's voice called out to him from one of the offices. "Can I help you?" she asked, but Solomon didn't stop.

He nudged the groaning door open and stepped into the frosty outside air that bit his skin instantly. The world was draped in darkness, except for a lone light above the door. It cast a ghostly glow, barely disrupting the night's thick shroud.

Taking a moment to catch his breath, he realized that he was in a shared parking lot that was surrounded by a chain-link fence. He spotted an opening on the far side of the lot that led to a residential neighborhood behind the stores.

The snow crunched underneath his feet, and a few times he slipped. The neighborhood hadn't been plowed as well as the streets in front of the businesses, and it was hard to make his way through with his cane.

Solomon hauled himself over a towering mound of snow, finally reaching a relatively snow-free sidewalk. His chest heaved as he gasped for breath, his lungs aching with the effort of each inhale. His legs felt like lead, burning with exertion, and he struggled to keep moving. His cane was useless in the soft snow. Every time he took a step, a sharp pain shot through his lower back, radiating down his legs and up into his hips. It happened whenever he walked too fast.

It felt like a vise grip squeezing the life out of him, suffocating him with each labored breath. The pain was so intense that he thought he might collapse at any moment, but he gritted his teeth and pushed on, determined to put as much distance as possible between himself and that car.

Solomon paused by a gnarled tree, bracing himself against the trunk as the biting wind whipped his face. The cold sensation sent a shiver down his spine and triggered a long-forgotten childhood memory. He'd been walking home from school when a group of bullies cornered him between two houses. There were three of them, and they had tackled him to the ground and shoved snow into his mouth, eyes, and nose until he was coughing and choking.

Solomon remembered crying uncontrollably, but he'd forced himself to stop before he got home. His father had strictly disallowed crying in their household, claiming that it was not manly. If Solomon ever cried, his father, in a drunken rage, would force him to hold up the Bible while he whipped him with a belt, leaving welts on his skin that would take days to heal.

It had taken Solomon a long time to come to terms with the fact that he could feel contradictory emotions at the same time. He loved his father, as a son would, but he also hated him.

What a thin line between the two emotions, Solomon thought.

He pushed himself away from the tree and continued down the quiet neighborhood, taking in the modest homes that lined the street. Most of the houses were no more than a couple of stories and somewhat small, with only a few sporting fences. As he walked, Solomon noticed a distinct lack of toys or basketball hoops in the yards, which made him wonder if there were any children living in the area.

He approached an intersection, and a bright streetlamp overhead illuminated his path. Just as he was about to cross the street, a sudden flash of lights caught his attention. He looked up to see a car parked across the street, facing him. The engine roared to life and jerked forward a foot or two.

Solomon's mouth was dry as he took a few hurried steps back, his mind racing with fear and uncertainty. He considered turning and running back the way he came, but the thought of slogging through the deep snow and ice made him hesitate. He didn't have enough time to call Billie or anyone else. The only option was to run.

He turned and hurried in the opposite direction of the car as fast as he could, his heart a jackhammer in his chest. But as he limped over the icy sidewalk, a sharp, intense burning sensation shot up his leg, jolting his sciatic nerve and threatening to render his leg useless. The pain was so intense that he collapsed into the snow.

The car lurched up onto the curb, its engine roaring as it careened toward Solomon. He barely had time to react before the vehicle slammed on its brakes just feet away from him. Solomon rose and looked at the car, but the lights were bright, and he couldn't see the figure inside.

Solomon bolted.

He used his cane to approximate the closest thing he could do to running and went across the nearest lawn and ran toward the driveway. As he hurried, he could hear the car's tires screeching behind him.

Reaching a tall wooden fence, Solomon frantically searched for a way to escape. He stumbled upon a small gate that was luckily unlocked, and he quickly pushed it open. He staggered into the backyard of a stranger's home, not sure if he was any safer than he was before.

With the car's headlights glaring in his direction, Solomon moved quickly, darting across the backyard and falling several times.

The fence loomed high above him, seeming impossible to climb, but he had no choice. He made a desperate leap toward the top, his fingers barely managing to grasp the wooden planks. He pulled himself up, his heart thumping as he felt the car coming closer and closer behind him.

Motion sensors in the yard tripped, abruptly setting off floodlights. The stark brightness revealed a window on the second floor of the home. Behind the blinds, an elderly figure held a large handgun. Clad in pajamas, the man sternly peered out, his face streaked with lines of concern.

Great, I can either get run over or blown away by Elderly Dirty Harry.

With a sense of relief, Solomon watched as the car's lights turned away from him, and he heard the rumble of the engine fade into the distance. He let go of the fence and slumped against it, gasping for air, feeling like he could pass out right there.

Just as he began to catch his breath, he heard the back door of the nearby house creak open. The old man stepped out, holding the gun in his hand.

29

Billie's phone buzzed with a text from Solomon while she was still at the station, her nerves already frayed from the day's events. The stress had been building up inside her, and she knew she needed to leave the office to find some relief. After her meeting with Dave Garcia had gone about as expected—with him losing his temper and flipping over his chair on the way out—she felt like she needed nothing more than a glass of wine and a hot bath to soothe her frayed nerves.

But as she read Solomon's urgent message, she knew she had to go right now.

As Billie's truck entered the residential neighborhood, her eyes scanned the quiet streets until she saw Solomon sitting on a porch with an old man. They each held mugs that billowed steam into the chilly air. Solomon noticed her arrival and stood up, exchanging a few words with the old man before shaking his hand. Then he moved carefully across the icy sidewalk, a distinct limp in his step, before getting into the passenger side of her truck.

As she drove away, Billie noticed the old man watching them from the porch, his expression unreadable in the dim light.

"New friend?" she said.

"That guy was a fighter pilot in Vietnam. You should've heard his stories, Billie. Actually, after he was done telling me, he said he'd never told anyone those stories and wondered why he had to me."

"What did you say?"

"That it's just my charm." He looked out the window. "Can we stop for a drink?"

"I have beer and wine at my house."

He looked at her. "Are you hitting on me, Billie?"

She grinned. "I'm just not letting you sleep in a house that's already been broken into once." She glanced at him. "You rarely tell me it's an emergency. What's going on?"

Solomon was silent a moment before he said, "Someone tried to run me over. Well, not really. If they had really wanted to, they could've caught up with me."

"Who?"

Solomon shook his head. "I don't know. I couldn't see the driver, but I'm sure it was whoever was in my house."

"When did this happen?"

"About an hour ago. He chased me in his car, but he didn't run me down when he had the chance. I was right. I don't think he wants to kill me. Not yet anyway. Not until I see whatever it is he's trying to show me."

"Are you sure it was the man we're after?"

He nodded. "Unless I was just the victim of a really bad case of mistaken identity, yeah, he was gunning for me."

"I meant it might've been someone Tommy sent."

"Running me down wouldn't be Tommy's style. Not outrageous enough. If he was going to take out the prosecutor that tried to put him away for a decade, he'd want to make a big show of it."

"Like a sniper in a trailer park?"

"Or a bomb in my sneaker or poison in my Mountain Dew. It'd be something I wouldn't see coming."

"That doesn't sound comforting."

Solomon's nerves prickled under his skin, making him fidget and twitch with unease as he thought about the phone and what Billie's reaction would be after she eventually found out that the killer had contacted him.

He'd decided to keep the phone to himself, at least for a while. If he told her, they would submit the phone to the crime lab for analysis, but Solomon knew they wouldn't find anything, and it would blow the only line they had to this man. For now, he couldn't tell anybody.

"I think he's law enforcement," Solomon said.

She stayed silent a moment.

"Why would you think that?"

"The way he processes these scenes isn't amateur hour. He's left us only the evidence he wants us to see. It's someone with experience who's had a long time to think about this. I don't think it's Tommy. Not after tonight." He looked at her with a serious expression. "I think he's a cop, Billie."

She shook her head as she ran her tongue along her cheek, using just one hand to steer as she watched the car in front of her drift and slide to the right before the tires caught traction again. "If that's true, Solomon, if he's law enforcement, this is an absolute disaster. A resignation-level disaster."

"I know," he said softly. "I wish it wasn't, but I can't think of anything else that makes sense."

"This just gets better and better."

He puffed up his cheeks and blew out a long, slow breath. "My mind is mush right now. I can't think. So, it's probably the best time to ask you this." She looked at him. "I want to interview your cops."

She was silent and then laughed. "You have got to be joking."

"It doesn't have to be me, if you don't want me involved, but I'm telling you, Billie, he's one of yours."

"How can you possibly know that?"

What Solomon wanted to say was *Because he left a phone at my house and the only people in there were cops*, but what he said instead was "I can't tell you."

"You can't tell me?"

"No."

"So let me get this right: you want me to accuse my police officers of being murderers, and you can't tell me the reason why?"

"Well, when you say it that way, it just sounds stupid."

"Solomon—"

"Do you trust me?"

"Sol—"

"No, not one of those rhetorical *Do you trust me?* lines you see in the movies. Really, truly, do you trust me?"

She looked into his eyes a second and then turned back to the road. "Yes."

"Then we have to interview everybody in your department that would have an advanced knowledge of forensics. It's one of them."

She shook her head. "What you're asking me would—"

"Make your department lose morale, the officers and staff lose their trust in you, piss off the public, and probably end with you losing your job? I know. That's why you have to know that I wouldn't ask this of you if I didn't believe it a hundred percent: the person or persons we're after are cops."

She remained quiet, lost in thought as she navigated the treacherous, snow-covered road. Solomon didn't say anything, either, just let her digest it. He wasn't entirely sure she would say yes.

"Okay," she finally said, "what do you want to do?"

"Make a list and get it narrowed down to only the personnel that were at my house with Roger and cross it with a list of all the personnel at Dennis Yang's house. This person was definitely at my house, so they were probably at Dennis's house, too. Sometimes these types of killers love mingling with the police and talking about their own cases."

"We have to get IAD involved."

"Having internal affairs interview all your detectives and deputies isn't exactly going to play well at the next Christmas party."

"I can't see a scenario where I come out looking good in this, Solomon. At least with IAD, people might believe they were forcing me to do this."

He shook his head. "He's too smart. He would see that coming."

"What does that mean?"

"It means if he wants me, maybe we should give him what he wants?"

30

Solomon slept on Billie's couch and woke up to the smell of coffee. He rose and went to the bathroom, where he attempted to fix his hair and ran some toothpaste with water over his teeth. When he was done, he went into the kitchen, where Billie was already dressed for the day in a black suit with pumps.

As Billie prepared their breakfast, the smell of bacon and eggs filled the cozy kitchen. "You coming to the press conference?" she asked as she set a plate down in front of Solomon.

"Which one is that again?"

"The one with the interim mayor and county council discussing Roger's death."

"Oh, right. Maybe." Solomon took a bite of his eggs. Billie sat down across from him, sipping her coffee and scrolling through her phone replying to messages.

After a moment of silence, Solomon's expression turned somber. "He was a malicious oaf, but Roger didn't deserve to die like that."

Billie looked up from her phone. She set the device down, giving him her full attention. "I didn't even ask how you're doing with it. You two knew each other a long time."

"Yeah," Solomon agreed, a heavy sigh escaping him. He pushed his eggs around on the plate, lost in thought. "I never liked him, but finding him on that bed . . . it's just so tragic that his life had to end that way. Maybe it was always going to end that way. I don't know."

"What do you mean?" Billie asked, her brow furrowing with curiosity.

"Whatever you put into the world is what it gives back to you," Solomon said, pushing his plate away. He didn't want to eat anymore. "A DA being murdered will upset people. The press conference might make them scared."

"I told them that. But politicians do what they want." Her phone buzzed, but she didn't want to answer it, so she silenced it.

"Um," Solomon said, "I almost forgot. Can you ask Mazie to drive me today? I need to go to some places."

"I don't see why not. She's on administrative leave until IAD gives her the go-ahead to get back to work."

"Wait, what?"

"Oh, that's right, you haven't heard. She poured hot coffee on two deputies who put a camera in the women's locker room."

"Really? On their heads?"

"Yes."

He grinned. "I knew I liked her."

"Solomon, I should have her arrested."

"You need her close, Sheriff. She's tough. Maybe she's not good for detective work, but something like SWAT could be right up her alley."

"Huh. I never thought of that."

"She's got heart. Will they clear her soon?"

"How would I know?"

"Come on, you're the sheriff. You have pull."

She shook her head. "IAD isn't like that anymore. They don't officially work for me, they work for the county. So that the sheriff can't influence them. My word wouldn't mean much to them. But I'm still going to stick up for her."

When breakfast was done, Billie hurried out of the home, leaving Solomon there by himself. He wandered around the house, starting with the living room. Some pictures of Billie's parents were on the side table by the couch, and he glanced at them and saw Zach, her father, with his arm around Billie in every photo.

Moving on to the kitchen, Solomon glanced around, hoping to find something interesting. But aside from a few basic kitchen supplies and utensils, there was nothing out of the ordinary. He opened the refrigerator, hoping to find something that might pique his interest, but all he saw were a few condiments and some breakfast items.

As Solomon stood in the hallway, he paused outside Billie's bedroom and considered whether it would be appropriate to go in without her permission. After a moment of hesitation, he decided that it would be best to respect her privacy and moved on.

As he continued down the hallway, Solomon's thoughts turned to the fascinating nature of other people's homes. He marveled at how every person and family lived in their own unique way, even if they were from identical socioeconomic backgrounds. To him, people's lives were shaped by the traumas they had experienced, and each person's trauma was as unique as a fingerprint.

Solomon had always been intrigued by the way people coped with their trauma and how it manifested in their daily lives. He believed that the way a person decorated their home or arranged their belongings was a reflection of their inner world.

The one dead zone was that he couldn't tell what his external world said about his internal. As astute as he was at reading other people, he felt utterly blind when it came to himself.

Upon entering the storage room at the back of the house, Solomon quickly realized that there was nothing of interest in there. Disappointed, he made his way back to the kitchen, where he rinsed off his plate and left it in the sink. Without any further reason to stay, he made his way to the front door and stepped outside into the cold air.

Despite the chill, the weather had taken a turn for the better, and the snow had stopped falling. The clouds had cleared, leaving a blinding sun in their wake. Solomon squinted in the brightness, wishing he had brought his sunglasses.

A beat-up Honda came around the corner and pulled up in front of Billie's house. Mazie was behind the wheel, her hood up and her sunglasses on. Solomon made his way over to the car, opened the door, and got in.

"You trying to pass for the Unabomber or something?"

"Cold as shit and my heater's busted."

As he settled into the passenger seat, Solomon took in the state of the car. Despite the pleasant smell, it was an absolute mess. Fast-food containers littered the floors, empty cans of energy drinks were stuffed into every available space, and a ripped-open box of tampons sat on the back seat.

"Sorry," Mazie said. "Kind of a disaster."

"Whatever floats your boat. Thanks for doing this, by the way."

"I don't got anything else to do, so at least it gets me out of the house."

"Yeah, I heard you went She-Hulk on some deputies."

"Well, they deserved it. Even if I do get fired." She let out a long breath. "Is it okay if we don't talk about it?"

"Of course."

"Cool. So, where we going?"

"I need to visit someone. Hop on the freeway."

As they merged onto the freeway, Mazie rolled down her window and stuck her hand out, moving it up and down in the wind. It was a carefree, childlike gesture that brought a grin to Solomon's face. He watched as her hand danced in the wind, and thought to himself that he genuinely liked Mazie, and he didn't genuinely like many people.

Mazie glanced over at Solomon, a mischievous glint in her eye. "You know, I heard about you before," she said.

Solomon raised an eyebrow. "Oh? Do tell."

"It's not good."

"I wouldn't think it would be."

Mazie said, "People said you almost died a buncha times and that you snapped and went crazy and live with a bunch of pigeons that you think you can talk to."

Solomon burst out laughing. "I don't even like pigeons. I'm more of a raven man."

She kept her eyes on the road but would glance at him out of the corner of her eye. "So? What really happened?"

"Bad luck happened."

"You believe in luck?"

"I believe in randomness, and when randomness works in your favor, we call it good luck, and when it works against you, we call it bad luck."

"You're into some deep shit, aren't you?"

He turned his gaze toward her. "Now I get to ask you a question."

"Okay, but I'm not that interesting."

"Somehow I doubt that."

She shrugged. "Go ahead."

"Why'd you punch a superior at your graduation?"

"Heard about that, huh?"

"Afraid so."

She let out a long breath. "Guy was such a creeper. He was always coming by the academy and lurking around and trying to get the girls alone, impress them with his badges and buttons 'n' shit. There was a party and one of my friends got drunk, and he tried driving away with her. Like thank Buddha that someone saw it and asked him where he was going, because if no one had seen him, he would've taken off and done whatever."

"Yeah, but why wait until graduation? You could've waited outside his house in the dark and hit him with something and taken off without anybody seeing you. Why do it in front of hundreds of people?"

She hesitated. "Because he slapped my ass, and every female cadet that saw him do it needed to see him get punched."

Solomon nodded. "Respect."

The rest of the ride was spent chatting about his and Billie's relationship and what made him want to be a prosecutor. Mazie told him about what life was like growing up in the barrio of Miami as a poor white kid and how much she missed Cuban food and the homemade rum made with family recipes handed down through generations.

"It's this exit," Solomon said.

The off-ramp snaked down, hugging the edge of the freeway before looping around to the other side. As they descended, the landscape around them changed—the asphalt and concrete giving way to barren, desolate earth, dotted here and there with scraggly bushes and large patches of snow.

A few minutes down the road, they came to a planned suburban community. The homes were tastefully designed, with well-manicured lawns and freshly painted exteriors. But despite their apparent luxury, the area seemed eerily empty, as though the houses were mere facades.

"Right here," he said, directing Mazie to the house.

Mazie drove into a parking spot in front of a grandiose house. Solomon was struck by the unpolished, almost unfinished quality of the yard that surrounded the home. Though it was clear that the yard had been intended to be grand and meticulously manicured, it was instead a patchwork of snow and exposed earth.

The snow had melted in places, leaving behind muddy, hardened dirt that cracked underfoot.

"Lemme guess, wait here?" Mazie said.

He looked at her and said, "No. I prefer to have someone with me with this guy. He's not exactly stable."

"Stable how?"

"You'll see. Just don't touch anything. He's really freaky about his stuff."

Solomon stepped out of the car, his cane tapping against the icy driveway as he carefully made his way to the front door of the home. Mazie followed closely behind, her presence offering some comfort, despite the fact that neither of them was armed.

Solomon pushed a button on an intercom. A voice that always had a hint of panic in it responded with, "I thought you were dead."

"I did too."

"What do you want?"

"You gonna let us in or not? I'm freezing my butt off out here."

A second later, the door creaked open, revealing a thin man with glasses and pasty skin. He peered at Solomon through the lenses, then pushed them up onto his forehead as his eyes flicked over to Mazie. The two of them were around the same age, and Solomon could see the man's initial guardedness soften as he took in Mazie's easy smile and open demeanor.

"Hi," he said to Mazie.

She smiled. "Hi."

There was silence before Solomon said, "Hi, I'm here, too."

He looked at Solomon now, and there wasn't as much agitation in his eyes. "Solomon."

"Einstein."

"What're you doing here?"

"Need your help with something."

"What?"

He glanced at Mazie, who stood with her thumbs in the loops of her jeans. Einstein was staring at her as he spoke.

"Mazie, this is Brian, better known around town as Einstein. He's a genius at electronics."

He smiled awkwardly, as though not used to smiling, and said, "Mazie. I like that name."

"Thanks."

He blushed.

Einstein looked at Solomon and said, "Okay, come in."

Solomon held the door open for Mazie as Einstein disappeared inside the home.

"I guess now I know why I'm not waiting in the car. I'm eye candy."

"You're way too perceptive for how young you are, milady."

As they stepped inside the home, Solomon took in his surroundings. It had been years since he was last there. The space was sparsely furnished, with few decorations or personal touches to make it feel like a lived-in home. It was as though Einstein used the space only for basic shelter and sleeping, with no other purpose in mind.

"Who is this guy?" Mazie whispered as they crossed the living room to a hallway.

"Used to work as a cyberinvestigator for the sheriff's office, but he has severe agoraphobia and stopped leaving his house."

"Huh. So you guys can relate?"

Solomon glanced at her and kept walking, surprised he had never seen anything of himself in Einstein.

Einstein motioned for them to follow him down the stairs, and the musty smell of damp earth and mildew grew stronger as they descended. The weak light from the stairs barely penetrated the darkness, and Solomon had to be careful not to trip or lose his footing. He could hear the sound of dripping water and the low hum of an electrical generator somewhere in the distance. After they reached the bottom of the stairs, Einstein led them into a dimly lit room with concrete walls and cement floors.

"You live in a mansion," Solomon said. "Why do you work in a cave?"

"Keeps me hungry and grounded. You try hacking a Pakistani Intelligence communication sitting on an alligator-leather chair with an expensive oak desk and you'll know what I'm talking about."

The basement was packed with computer equipment, from sleek laptops to towering servers, filling every corner of the room. A maze of cables snaked along the walls and floor, connecting the devices to one another. In the center of the room, multiple monitors displayed lines of code, charts, and diagrams, flashing with information in a hypnotic rhythm. Mazie's eyes widened as she approached a metal shelf loaded with rows of graphics processors, their blinking lights casting a psychedelic glow over her face.

"What is all this stuff?" she asked.

Einstein adjusted his glasses and said, "Those things you're looking at are the most powerful graphics processors in the world. I mine cryptocurrency." He adjusted his glasses again. "I'm rich," he said matter-of-factly.

"No shit?"

"Yeah," he said with an awkward chuckle.

Solomon said, "As cute as this is, I need your help."

He sat down at a computer station and said, "What do you need?"

Solomon looked at Mazie. "I'm afraid this isn't for your ears, milady."

"What?"

"You don't want to hear what I'm about to say. Trust me."

She sighed and said, "Fine. I'll go wander around the mansion."

As she walked away, Einstein said, "Don't go in the locked room on the third floor, please."

"Why? You got dead bodies in there?"

"No," he said with an awkward laugh.

Solomon waited until she was back upstairs before he took out the phone that had been left at his house. "I need to find out everything I can about this."

Einstein took the phone and immediately used a thin tool to remove the cover and look inside. Then he connected a wire to it that went into a terminal and punched a few keys, bringing up reams of data on the screen. Solomon watched the screen as the data loaded, lines of code scrolling across the screen like a waterfall.

"Part of an investigation?" Einstein said.

"Yeah. It was left in my house by whoever we're looking for."

"Hmm."

"What?"

"Well, the phone has pretty sophisticated malware on it. It's conditional, though, and hasn't been triggered yet. I'm guessing if you had a lesser technician looking at this, it would already have triggered and wiped the phone clean."

"In other words?"

"In other words, you did the right thing not turning this in."

"Can you get anything off it?"

He scanned a few pages of code and said, "Not without triggering the malware, but let me think about it for a couple days."

"I'm not sure I have that long. Can you tell me anything else about it?"

"It was purchased at a Big Lots in the county. The serial number is an exclusive made by Nokia and sold exclusively at Big Lots, and looks like it was activated eleven days ago. I don't know, maybe Big Lots has cameras?"

"They do indeed," Solomon said, knocking on the wooden desk with his knuckles. "Einstein, you're seriously the man. Dinner's on me. I'm ordering you a pizza."

Einstein put the phone back together in a second and handed it to Solomon. "I normally charge nine hundred dollars an hour."

"Two pizzas it is."

Solomon knew Einstein didn't like to be touched, so he didn't reach for a handshake. They chatted a few seconds about what he'd been up to, and when Solomon was leaving, he heard Einstein say under his breath, "Finally."

Once they were back in the car, Mazie turned the key and started the engine before saying, "Well, he's interesting."

"No genius has ever existed without a touch of madness."

"Don't nerd out on me, Solomon."

He chuckled. "You wanna be a good cop, right? Well, investigation is all about your network. You're not going to know even a fraction of everything you need to know, so you've got to have people in your network who do."

"Yeah, well, maybe some of us like being the lone she-wolf." She took out some gum and unwrapped it.

There was a pause, and it was clear she was debating something.

Finally, she said, "So you didn't hand in a phone a serial killer left in your house, huh?"

Solomon's eyes went wide, and he opened his mouth to say something, but nothing came out.

"I was coming back down the stairs to ask where the bathroom was when I heard you guys talking. Or I was eavesdropping. We'll never know."

Solomon hesitated and said, "If I had turned it over, the malware on the phone would've been triggered and ruined our best shot at getting him. We'd lose the only link we have."

She nodded. "I get it."

"He's sophisticated. He'll know if someone—"

"Solomon," she said softly, "seriously, I get it." She put the gum in her mouth. "So what'd your pal say?"

"He told me where the phone was bought and the date it was activated. There might be a video."

Solomon's mind raced as he considered the possibility of a video existing, his anxiety morphing into a tight knot of dread in the pit of his stomach. If the person behind this had installed malware on the phone as insurance, they would be too smart to allow themselves to be captured on video. But maybe they hadn't anticipated Solomon enlisting the help of someone like Einstein.

Now in his twenties, Einstein had become a prodigy at fourteen with dual degrees in mathematics and electrical engineering, qualified to work at any major tech company and command a lucrative salary. But instead of going back to the sheriff's office and basking in the accolades of his peers, he had chosen to retreat into an isolated, damp cave and be alone.

Crap, Solomon thought. *We are alike.*

"There's no way he's on video, Sol. Not this guy."

"Who knows? He wants me to know who he is. He might be there on purpose. A little reward for me tracing his phone."

She shook her head, her breath mixing with the cold air as she exhaled a deep sigh. With one hand on the steering wheel, she leaned her arm on the windowsill and stuck her free hand out of the window. "I'm so sick of these crazy bastards."

Solomon looked out the window and didn't say anything.

31

It'd been two days since Solomon had requested the video from the local Big Lots, and he didn't expect it anytime soon. Because of the enormous amount of shoplifting that occurred at big-box retailers, dozens of videos were requested daily, and they were notoriously slow at getting them out.

The phone remained close, always within reach. Despite two text-less days, Solomon hesitated to send a message, paralyzed by indecision over the right move.

Early in the morning, Solomon stood in his backyard, shooting beer cans with a .22 handgun. He liked the clinking sound the cans made when he connected, and after he hit all of them, he slowly limped over and set them up again. If he moved too fast, pain would radiate out of his back and down his leg.

The human body was an elegant machine, and Solomon felt disconnected from that. To him, his body was always something that had to be fought, and it was exhausting.

When he was done shooting, he cleaned his weapon and then showered and dug a suit out of a closet upstairs. It was covered in dust. He slapped off the dust and then put it on. A black suit with a white shirt and blue tie.

Solomon sat on the porch, enjoying the sweet taste of a mango as he cut it with a knife. He left the knife and remaining fruit on the porch and stood as Billie's truck pulled up. As he approached the vehicle, the strong aroma of coffee hit him. The scent was overwhelming, as if an entire pot had spilled out in the truck. Two empty coffees were in the cupholders, with a full one in her hand.

"You planning on not sleeping this year?" he said.

"Long night."

The protective order hearing initial appearance between Dax and Billie was scheduled for an hour from now. Solomon tried to remember if he'd put on deodorant and thought maybe he hadn't, which would be terrible because he hadn't been in court for so long he was certain he would be sweating.

"We have interviews set up all week," Billie said, changing the subject.

"Who'd you include?"

"Everyone."

"Everyone?"

She nodded and sighed. "Everyone. Patrol, Homicide, criminalists . . . even Mathew from the ME's office. If you're wrong, Solomon, I'm out of a job."

"I'm not wrong." Solomon thought a moment. "You mind if I come along to some of the interviews?"

"You know I can't let you anywhere near them, right?"

"I'll just sit behind the window quietly minding my own business."

"If you promise to just observe. I mean it, Solomon. You can't ask anyone anything. You're not a prosecutor anymore."

"I know."

As they approached the courthouse, Solomon noticed the stark contrast of the modern gray stone building to the quaint residential neighborhood. The building had large windows on every floor, giving it an air of transparency that seemed oddly out of place. As they approached the metal detectors, a couple of bailiffs greeted them, chatting with the sheriff, who was technically their boss. Solomon went through the detectors and was then subjected to the wand while Billie watched with a mischievous grin on her face.

"Benefits of being a cop, huh?" Solomon said to the bailiff wanding him.

The bailiff ignored his comment and then let him through.

Solomon caught up to Billie, and they took the elevator to the second floor. The windows overlooked the parking lot on one side and the street on the other. The neighborhood was clean and had a pleasant feel to it.

The courtroom itself was paneled with dark wood but had multiple large windows overlooking the mountains to the west. There were only a few people there, and Solomon went to the docket, a ream of paper with printed court cases on it, at the petitioner's table and found their case as the first one to be called. He sat down at the respondent's table while Billie sat with the observers.

An attorney in a gray suit with a beard the same color came to the petitioner's table to the right of Solomon. He wore large glasses that seemed too big for his face. He set an old-time briefcase on his table and sat down, crossed one leg over the other, and saw Solomon.

"Solomon."

"Chester."

"I saw your name on the docket last night. I had heard you weren't practicing anymore."

"Doesn't everyone come out of retirement at least one time to get their butts kicked?"

Chester didn't grin or smile, and certainly didn't laugh. Solomon remembered him as the type of man that took everything, especially himself, too seriously. People that took themselves too seriously had a tendency to be unpleasant to be around.

Solomon's gaze shifted to the wooden pews behind him, now filling up with people waiting for their hearings. Solomon saw Dax in a corner, staring at him intensely. It was surprising to recognize the pale figure as someone he once knew. The man in the courtroom, with empty eyes, looked like a lifeless copy of the person Solomon knew. With thin cheeks and a grayish face, Dax looked sick.

Billie, however, refused to give him the satisfaction of acknowledging his presence. As Dax's gaze shifted from Solomon to Billie, a smirk crept onto his lips.

"Don't suppose you'd just stipulate to no protective order in place?" Solomon said to Chester.

"We'll pass, thank you."

Chester opened his briefcase and took out a manila folder filled with sheets of paper and a hole punch and stapler. Lawyers have a tendency to only use whatever technology was popular when they first became lawyers.

Most protective order hearings were handled by commissioners, appointed arbiters that were similar to judges but only had narrow functions. A thin woman in a blue skirt and blouse came out and sat at the computer next to the commissioner's. A second later, an old bailiff came out of the commissioner's entrance and said, "All rise. Third District Court is now in session. The Honorable Frank Irving presiding."

Commissioner Irving emerged from a set of double doors, his robe taut against his towering figure. He stood at least six and a half feet tall, with a long, gaunt face and salt-and-pepper hair that hung limply around his shoulders. Solomon knew he also played in a band on the weekends and wouldn't cut his hair for anything.

As he settled into his chair, he beckoned for everyone to sit, his deep voice resonating through the chamber.

He turned to his computer a moment and then said, "First case, please. Counsel will state their appearances."

"Solomon Shepard for Ms. Gray."

"Chester Leonard for the petitioner, Dax Granger."

"All right, would Ms. Gray and Mr. Granger join us at their respective tables, please."

Billie sat next to Solomon and Dax next to his attorney. Billie glanced over at him, and Solomon could see not just disgust and disappointment, but fear. She wasn't one to spook easy. She saw something in Dax that she was genuinely afraid of.

Solomon looked over to the table and was amazed how much Dax had changed. It looked like he'd aged twenty years. His clothes were tattered and his hair unkempt. Scruff was on his cheeks, and his eyes were rimmed red. From a slight sway to his upper body as he tried to sit still, Solomon could tell Dax had been drinking before coming here.

"Mr. Leonard, the floor is yours," the commissioner said.

"We would call Dax Granger to the stand, please."

"Of course. Mr. Granger, please be sworn in by my clerk and seated in the witness chair."

Dax's eyes darted around the room as he settled into the witness chair, his jittery movements suggesting an underlying nervousness. His hands fidgeted with the edge of the witness box, his fingers tapping and tracing over the smooth surface. As he was sworn in, his face twisted into a grimace, as though he resented having to take an oath. The smirk that had been playing on his lips only grew wider as he caught Billie's eye, and he tilted his head slightly in her direction.

"Your Honor," Chester said, "we would ask for stipulation as to time, identity, and location."

"Do you stipulate, Mr. Shepard?"

"Yes, Your Honor."

Chester was standing at the lectern. All the papers he had were spread out on the table, but he wasn't looking at any of them, and Solomon realized they were props. He seemed to be doing it from memory, like all the best trial lawyers.

"Dax," he said as casually as possible, probably attempting to disarm the commissioner and make Dax seem the victim, "you know Ms. Elizabeth Gray here, correct?"

"I do."

Victor Methos

"Tell us about your relationship."

Dax stared at her, and she stared back. For an agonizing few seconds, Dax didn't say anything.

"Dax?" Chester asked.

"Yeah, sorry. It's kinda hard to talk about. Um, I mean, we were in love. I was either at her house every night or she was at mine. It was the perfect relationship. The kinda thing you see in movies."

"It didn't stay that way, though, did it?"

He shook his head. "No. Billie, she likes to be called Billie instead of Elizabeth, started to change."

"Change how?"

"It seemed like the closer we got, the more she pushed me away. And I understood. She's got a lot on her plate being the sheriff, but it started becoming abusive. She would throw plates and threaten me with arrest or that she was going to hurt me. One time she pulled out her mace and sprayed it in my car as I was pulling away. She just was getting more and more bizarre."

"How long did this last?"

"I would say it was probably about three months when this all started happening. I just thought, you know, it was just what it was. We were both coming out of relationships, and I knew it'd take us a long time to adjust. So, I just thought of it as that."

"Did you seek any professional help for Ms. Gray?"

Solomon glanced at Billie, who sat stone faced. Her eyes locked on Dax and her hands firmly pressed together on the table. Solomon could only imagine what thoughts were going through her head.

Solomon leaned over and whispered to her, "I'm guessing none of this is true?"

She shook her head once but didn't say anything.

"We tried counseling, but she was so busy it would never work. I'd just end up being alone there."

188

Solomon rose. "Your Honor, as much as I admire memory lane, could we wander off of it for a second and actually talk about the grounds for this request?"

"I agree. Let's move it along."

"Very well, Your Honor, I was just laying some groundwork. I have here a video that my client gave to me last night that I'd like to introduce to the Court."

Solomon rose. "Objection. The respondent has received no such video and would ask for time to review it."

Unlike trials in a criminal court, the rules of evidence were rarely applied in protective order hearings. Much of the time, they were granted or denied based on whether the commissioner felt the respondent was a real threat or not.

"Mr. Shepard has been out of practice for a number of years, Your Honor, so I would remind him that I have no obligation to turn over evidence prior to a temporary order hearing, and it was designed as such by the legislature in the interests of justice."

"The objection is overruled. Please play the video."

Chester went to the clerk and had a laptop hooked up to the court's system. A screen came down from the wall across from where a jury would sit in the courtroom. Solomon sat down and leaned over to Billie.

"Do you know what this is?" he asked.

She nodded.

The fact that she wouldn't look at him meant Solomon wasn't going to like what he was about to watch.

The video opened in a parking lot. There was no snow and the sky was blue and clear, and Solomon guessed it was sometime in the summer. Billie was coming out of a gym dressed in yoga pants and a tank top, drenched in sweat from a workout and sipping on a water bottle.

The video, which was clearly taken on a phone, was shot from a low angle, probably because Dax was trying to conceal it.

"What are you doing here?" Billie said on the video.

"I just came to talk."

"Leave me alone, Dax."

"How can you expect me to go from wanting to marry you to having you hate me in a month? I can't just turn off my emotions like you."

There was no hesitation in the next motion. Billie moved with a quickness and purpose that left no room for second thoughts. She flung her towel and water bottle into her truck and emerged with her handgun. Dax stumbled backward in alarm as Billie pointed the weapon at his face, her finger poised on the trigger.

Solomon looked at Billie, who stared at Dax on the stand. Dax stared back in turn but had an expression on his face of pure pleasure.

In the video, Dax and Billie argued for a bit, and then the video ended with Billie getting into her truck and driving away.

"What happened there, Dax?" Chester asked from the lectern.

"Just what you saw. I wanted to talk to her, and she pulled her gun on me. If you notice, she clicked off the safety, so it wasn't an idle threat. I think she was going to kill me. That's why I need this protective order."

"But you went to her."

"I did, and it was a mistake. I should've just left her alone, but I loved her." He shook his head as his eyes wet with tears. "I still love her. But I'm scared of her. I'm scared of what she's going to do."

Chester nodded. "Thank you, Dax."

The commissioner said, "Your witness, Mr. Shepard."

Solomon rose and limped to the lectern. His leg caused him pain that radiated out from where the leg connected to the hip. The pain wrapped around his body and made every position uncomfortable.

"You have a stalking injunction taken out against you by Ms. Gray, correct?"

"Yes."

"At the hearing, the Court found a hundred and seventy-two incidents of unwanted contact directed by you to Ms. Gray, is that right?"

"I wouldn't say it that way, but—"

"A simple yes or no will suffice. A hundred and seventy-two incidents, yes?"

"Yes."

"These include phone calls, text messages, messages on social media, and in-person contact, yes?"

"Yes. Like I said, I was—"

"You answered the question, thank you," Solomon interrupted. "Of the in-person contacts, there were four where you showed up at Ms. Gray's office, two where you showed up at her house, and five where you showed up places like the gym, as we saw in the video. Correct?"

"I don't know. I just know I wanted to see her."

"But she didn't want to see you, did she?"

"I don't know what she wanted. She would never talk to me."

"That's right, I'm glad you brought that up, Dax. I'd like to read some of her responses to your text messages." He picked up a stack of documents and read. "You texted that you'd like to speak with her on July eighteenth of this year, and she responded, 'Please stop contacting me. Our relationship is over.' You recall that?"

"I guess."

"Is that a yes or a no?"

Dax glanced to his attorney and said, "Yes."

"You texted her again, two hours later, and said, 'I still want to see you.' She responded, 'No. Don't contact me again.' You remember that?"

"Sure. If you say so."

"Four hours after that, you texted, 'Come to my house so we can talk. I just want to talk.' She responded, 'I don't want to talk. I don't want to see you. I just want to be left alone.' You remember that?"

"Yes."

Solomon went through and read text message after text message of Dax harassing Billie and Billie asking him, eventually pleading with him, to stop. He didn't have to read them all in open court, but he wanted the commissioner to hear them out loud. It sounded far more threatening than just reading them in print.

Chester eventually objected and said that the Court had all the text messages and it was a waste of time to read through them again.

"This incident on the video," Solomon said to Dax when the commissioner asked him to move on, "it took place at the Mountain Fitness on Main Street on August eighth, correct?"

"Yeah."

"At this point, she'd already taken a stalking injunction out against you, correct?"

"No. She'd just filed. It hadn't been granted yet."

"There was a temporary order in place, though, wasn't there?"

"I guess."

"You guess, or yes?"

Dax was silent a moment as he stared at Billie. "Yes."

"How many times before that day would you say she had asked you not to contact her again?"

"I wouldn't know."

"Take a guess. Fifty, a hundred?"

"I don't know," he said with a shake of his head, his voice calming, which to Solomon meant he was trying to keep anger in check. A soft spot had been touched.

"Two hundred? Three hundred? Take a guess, Dax."

"Objection. He's badgering my client."

"I'm simply asking how many times. Even a guess can tell us a lot."

"I'll allow it."

Solomon looked back to Dax. "How many times, Dax?"

He shook his head. "I don't know. Fifty."

"Fifty? So this video was taken in August and you say she had asked you not to contact her fifty times, correct?"

"You said to guess, so I guessed."

"Your Honor, I'd like to introduce the text messages, social media messages, and letters I handed to your clerk earlier."

"So granted."

Solomon limped over to the clerk. His leg was acting up, and pain was starting to spread throughout his hips. When he had the papers, he then stood in front of Dax, as close as possible, with only the banister of the witness box between them.

"What is this?" Solomon said, showing him the first page.

"It's text messages between me and Billie."

"Read the last thing she says to you."

He took a deep breath and said, "I do not want you to contact me in any way, shape, or form. I no longer want you in my life. Please stop contacting me."

"Next text message twenty minutes later. Read the last thing she said to you."

"Dax, stop contacting me."

"Next text message, half an hour after that. Read."

Dax held his gaze and then read. "Stop contacting me immediately or I will take out a stalking injunction against you."

Solomon ran his hand over the edge of the papers, giving them a flipping sound to show how many pages the stack contained. "In fact, from May until August when the incident happened, you had messaged her not fifty times, not a hundred times, but over eight hundred times. The vast majority of those times, when she did actually respond, she responded for you to stop contacting her. Isn't that right?"

Solomon quickly moved on, ignoring the answer Dax was about to give.

"In one day, June fourth, you created a new, fake account and messaged her on Facebook and Instagram a hundred and twelve times before she finally deleted her accounts. A hundred and twelve in one day is about four point six messages per hour. Per hour, Dax."

He shrugged. "I was hurt and upset. All I wanted was to talk to her."

"Maybe you thought that, Dax, but can you understand why someone would be scared of another person messaging them almost five times an hour?"

"Yeah, I understand, but—"

"Thank you. Now when she pulled out her weapon on August eighth, she had changed her phone number three times, canceled all her social media, and had any calls screened coming into her office line. Yet you still showed up as she was coming out of the gym, correct?"

He hesitated. "Yes."

"She wasn't expecting you when she came out of the gym?"

"I guess not."

"She thought you'd moved on because you could no longer message her."

He shrugged. "I guess."

"You guess, or yes?"

He sighed in frustration. "I don't know."

"But you showed up and immediately approached her."

Chester rose and said, "Is there a question in that statement, Your Honor?"

"She cut off all contact with you?" Solomon said before the commissioner could say anything.

"Mr. Shepard," the commissioner said, "please allow me to rule before moving on."

"Of course."

"The objection is overruled. Please go on."

Solomon put both hands on his cane's lion head and stared into Dax's eyes. He'd met him several times, and it was strange how different those eyes looked now. Like there had been a shield over them to prevent anyone from seeing what was behind them. How exhausting,

Solomon thought, to have to put on a mask all day so people don't see who you are.

"She thought you were out of her life."

"I don't know what she thought."

"Really?" he said, picking up the stack of printed-out messages. "Let's see," Solomon said, randomly flipping through the stack, "May twenty-second, 'Dax, I no longer want anything to do with you.' May twenty-seventh, 'You need help, Dax, stop contacting me.' June first, 'I filed a temporary order for a stalking injunction. Stop contacting me . . .' I don't know, Dax, seems she made her intentions pretty clear. You saying you didn't understand what someone telling you hundreds of times to stop contacting them meant?"

Dax opened his mouth to answer, and Solomon said, "After all this, you still decide to show up at the gym and approach her while she isn't paying attention."

"I . . . sure. Whatever."

"Not whatever, Dax. I know you think of this as one sided, but there's another side. Her side. Now think of it objectively: if a woman told you that a man she used to date"—Solomon couldn't help throwing in a jab—"who she had denied twice when he asked her to marry him, if a woman told you this man contacted her against her wishes five times an hour, and then he suddenly showed up someplace she was at, hurrying toward her, that might seriously startle that woman, right?"

"I guess."

"And when people are startled, especially by a man that has shown no regard for their wishes, they may try to defend themselves. Correct?"

"I guess," he said, folding his arms.

Solomon had him now. Dax was trapped in a cadence of answering in the affirmative to every question Solomon posed. "Now let's talk about when you threatened to kill her and then yourself . . ."

Solomon pressed on with his cross-examination, his sharp questions coming one after another with unyielding precision. The clock on the wall seemed to tick by slowly, marking the passing minutes as he grilled the witness relentlessly for over two hours. By the time Solomon finished, Dax was visibly flustered, his face reddened with exertion and his underarms stained with sweat.

Solomon forced himself to sit down, wincing as his knee caught and sent a shooting pain through his leg. He tried to hide his discomfort, but the searing pain made it difficult to focus on anything else.

Chester asked for redirect but was denied. The commissioner stated he had everything he needed.

"I'm going to take this matter under advisement and review the video and the various messages the respondent has provided to this court. Ms. Gray, in the meantime, you are not to have any contact with the petitioner. Mr. Granger, you are not to have any contact with Ms. Gray." The commissioner signed off on something in the file and then moved it to the side. "You'll have my decision soon. Next matter, please."

32

Without work, Mazie struggled to find something to do. She did her yoga and her weight lifting and considered getting lunch with someone but realized her only friends were other cops, and right now on suspension might be a weird time to ask them to lunch. So instead, she busied herself by getting a new book at the bookstore, a romance, and sat in the coffee shop of the bookstore and read.

The draw of the book lasted only a few minutes. She had never liked school and liked reading for leisure even less. Action was what appealed to her. As a teenager, she was always out playing baseball and football with the boys. Her mother had told her she had the devil in her, which was her way of saying she couldn't ever sit still.

Glancing at her phone, she knew Billie was in court. She wanted to support her and be there for her, but respected Billie's desire to keep her life private from colleagues as much as possible. Maybe sometimes the best way to support someone was to just do what the hell they asked.

She let out a sigh and left the coffee shop. It was only noon; she'd done everything she could think of, and it had lasted only a few hours.

She breathed out into the cold air, staring at the gray sky. "This sucks," she mumbled.

"Forget something?"

Behind her, coming out of the bookstore, was a man in jeans and a black shirt, a deep-blue blazer on over it. He had a leather watch and expensive-looking glasses with clear frames. His hair was frizzy, and his cheeks instantly pinched red from the cold. Someone not used to it.

He lifted the book she'd forgotten on the table.

"Oh," she said, "shit. Thanks."

"Looks like quite a read."

"Yeah," she said, certain her own cheeks were turning red, but not from the cold. "I've always had a thing for hot pirates."

"I'm more of a nonfiction reader. Fiction has too much truth in it," he said with a grin.

She grinned, too.

"Joel," he said, holding out his hand.

She placed her hand in his but didn't shake. "Mazie."

"Pearl," he said.

"What?"

"Mazie is short for the Greek word for *pearl*. It's a beautiful name. One you almost never hear."

"Yeah, well, it was my grandmother's."

He let go of her hand. "So I haven't eaten yet today. Feel no obligation to say yes, but I'd love to have lunch with you." He looked down to the book. "Maybe you could tell me what the draw is to pirates."

She glanced away. "I don't know. I got a really busy day planned," she lied.

"Well, look, I'll be over there at Klausie's. If you wanna come by, great. If not, no big deal."

"I'll think about it."

"Better than a no." He began walking away and looked at her one more time as he smiled. "Nice meeting you, Mazie. Hope the book turns out well."

"Thanks."

She turned away from him and started heading back to her car, which was parked on the curb. As she went to the driver's side door, she caught an image of herself in the window. No makeup, her hair a mess, and she didn't remember if she'd brushed her teeth this morning.

Man, that guy deserves a lunch for asking me out like this, she thought.

Klausie's was a German schnitzel joint with a few family members that ran it day to day. Everything made fresh, the hogs even slaughtered one town over. She saw Joel standing in line with his hands in his pockets. His back was wide, like a swimmer's, and he had some muscle on him, but not too much.

"Hi," she said, coming up behind him.

He saw her and smiled. "I'm glad you came."

"Oh, I forgot you were gonna be here. I just felt like some sauerkraut."

"Well, good thing I happened to be here."

"Totally. Weird coincidence."

"Since you're already here, I guess we might as well eat together."

"Might as well."

Stupid, stupid, stupid.

They ordered their food, and Mazie realized too late she had ordered the messiest thing on the menu. Polish sausage slathered with gravy and spicy ketchup. The food was served as they went through the line.

"I got it," Joel said, setting his tray down on the counter and reaching for his wallet.

"Whatever. This isn't 1950." She used her phone and paid with Apple Pay and left a good tip.

They settled into a cozy booth by the windows, which gave them a perfect view of the bustling intersection. Across the street, a bank building towered over the surrounding structures, with the most expensive office space in the entire city. Nestled down the street was the county's only homeless shelter.

"You know that shelter used to be over here," Mazie said.

"The homeless shelter?" Joel said, unfolding a napkin and putting it on his lap.

She nodded. "They kept having to move farther away. It's like people don't want to be reminded that there's suffering in the world, ya know?"

He shrugged. "It's nothing new. It's been that way since the first cities were made."

She watched him cut into his potato and take a bite.

"So can I ask a 1950s date question?" he said. "What do you do?"

She grinned. "I'm a cop."

"Seriously?"

"Serious as shit. My dad was a cop and his dad was a cop. Family genes, I guess. What do you do?"

He chewed a moment, his hazel eyes peering at her in a soft look that made her feel warm. "Isn't it funny that's the question we always ask? What do you do? Where do you live? No one ever asks if we're happy, though. Do they?"

"You asked first."

"Touché. I was just really curious. I'm more curious if you're happy."

She shrugged and took a nibble of some sauerkraut with ham cooked in it. "What does happy even mean, ya know?"

"I think it's like obscenity. We know it when we see it."

She pushed some food around on her plate. "You're good at that."

"What?"

"Dodging questions."

He chuckled. "You are a cop, aren't you? I work in forensics at the crime lab, with computers. None of the cool stuff like blood or trace evidence."

"No shit? That's why you look so familiar. I'm sure we've seen each other before."

"Yeah, probably."

Mazie watched with interest as he bit into the sausage, the juices dripping down onto his napkin and even his pant leg, but he didn't seem to mind and simply dabbed at the stains with another napkin. His lack of pretense put her at ease, and she finally took a large bite of her gravy-soaked sausage. As they talked, the conversation flowed easily and naturally, without any forced small talk or awkward pauses.

After finishing their meal, they ordered some coffee. The sun shone in and warmed their faces as they watched people bustling about on the street. Joel shared with Mazie that he had grown up in the sticky humidity of the South and longed for a change of pace. After his divorce, he decided to uproot his life and moved to Utah, where he secured a job with the crime lab. As they talked, it became clear that they shared a desire for new experiences and were both eager to try new things.

They rose to leave. As Joel hugged her, Mazie took in his scent, a mix of sandalwood and vanilla. It was an understated fragrance, not the overpowering scent that some men tended to wear, and it made her feel a little bit intrigued. She took a deep breath, savoring the aroma, and then pulled away, smiling up at him. Their eyes met, and she saw a spark of interest in his gaze, a hint of something more than just casual friendship. It made her heart race a little faster.

Mazie stared at his butt as he walked away.

Her car wasn't far, but when she got there, she thought it looked odd. It was tilted to the side, and she walked around and saw that the two tires on the driver's side were both flat.

"Shit!"

Her first thought was that she had run over nails or screws, maybe glass if glass could actually pop tires, but when she crouched and examined the tires, she could see the clean slice of a blade entering it near the top. The other tire was the same. Someone had stabbed both her tires . . . and she was pretty damn sure she knew who it was.

She summoned an Uber, rage making her hands shake as she slipped the phone back into her pocket and waited.

33

Solomon took a deep breath as he and Billie entered the small and dimly lit attorney-client room next to the courtroom. The area was sparsely furnished, with a wooden table and a few chairs.

"What the hell was that?" he said when the door was closed. "There's a video of you pulling a gun on him and you decide not to mention it to me before we go into court?"

"I didn't know he was filming that."

"Even if you didn't, you don't think I should've known you threatened to kill him?"

"I threatened to defend myself. And I don't appreciate you raising your voice at me."

Solomon felt his blood boil with anger and frustration, his emotions becoming too much to contain. He gripped his cane tightly and hit it into the wall with a force that left a noticeable dent. He took a deep breath and tried to calm himself down, but the anger still simmered inside him. Without another word, he stormed out of the room.

He limped down the narrow hallway to the elevators and rode one down alone. Once he was outside, he walked to a nearby bus stop and slumped onto the bench. The bench was covered in layers of graffiti; the face of the Realtor who was advertising on it had devil horns and fangs spray-painted on, and the stench of stale urine lingered in the air.

The Nokia phone he'd been carrying with him buzzed. He pulled it out of his pocket and looked at the text message he'd just received.

The text made his heart drop.

What are you so sad for?

Solomon, as casually as possible, took out his sunglasses from his breast pocket and put them on. Then he leaned back on the bench and tried to scan his surroundings without moving his head. He was being watched right now.

Why don't we meet somewhere and talk about it? Solomon texted back.

LOL. If I didn't know you were joking I'd be disappointed you were so obvious. That's the one thing that's the hardest to stand about other people, isn't it? They're so obvious. To everyone but themselves

You don't speak like a batshit crazy sociopath

Neither do you

The response gave Solomon a small shock, and he didn't know why.

So what's on the agenda today? the text came in. Interviews? Or maybe speaking with that annoying assistant medical examiner? My two cents? I wouldn't trust him. Something's wrong with him

I think there's an expression about a kettle and a pot that's appropriate here

LOL. I like you, Solomon. Talk to you soon

Wait . . . what should I call you?

Don't call me anything. I'm a ghost ;)

Solomon sent a few more text messages, but each one was met with silence. He rubbed his temples and considered turning in the phone to get some help. But he knew if he did that, he'd lose his only thread to the killer, and he would disappear . . . like a ghost.

He felt like he was caught in a trap, with no clear way out.

Solomon heard the soft sound of footsteps approaching from behind and saw Billie take a seat on the bench next to him. They sat in silence for a few moments, watching the cars passing on the road in front of them. The morning sunlight cast long shadows, and their breath was visible in the cold air, swirling around them before dissipating into the atmosphere.

"I'm sorry, Billie. You didn't deserve that."

"No, I didn't. But I honestly didn't think of that incident, otherwise I would have told you about it. There were so many like it, I didn't even consider that he could be filming them."

"You were afraid, and I don't think that's an emotion you're used to feeling."

She breathed out deeply and slipped her hands into her pockets. "What do you think the commissioner's going to do?"

"It doesn't matter. It's not about the commissioner or Dax. It's about you and your safety. We'll make sure that you have the protection you need no matter what happens with the petition."

She shook her head. "I hate this."

"I know." He tapped his cane against a small patch of snow near the bench. "Interviews today?"

"Yes."

"Who do you have doing it?"

"A few detectives from IAD are handling it. They don't want me anywhere near it."

"Once IAD gets involved, the first thing any cop would do is ask for their union rep, who'll advise them to keep quiet."

"What do you suggest then?"

"Send IAD the people we can exclude right off the bat. Anyone that's a viable suspect, save for us. I just need a few minutes with this man, Billie. I don't think he wants to hide from me. He wants me to find him. But it has to be me, no one else."

"I've come to think that might be true. But I have to record it."

"No, no equipment. We can't let them think it's an investigation."

A soft, weary sigh escaped her lips, and Solomon's heart sank.

"I know this is a crap position to put you in, and I'm so sorry. But he's going to keep killing, and next it might be . . ."

"Might be you."

Solomon didn't say anything.

Billie took out her phone and began texting her assistant a list of deputies and detectives she wanted to meet with immediately.

34

Mazie had the Uber drop her off at the station because she thought Aaron Watkins might be there. She might've sat in her car a moment to make sure she really wanted to do this, but there was no drivable car, and even thinking about how much it would cost to get two new tires churned her stomach.

As she strode through the metal detectors, they beeped loudly, drawing the attention of a bailiff she knew. She gave him a look that said she was about to bite someone's head off and it might as well be his. The bailiff, sensing her mood, wisely chose to nod in greeting instead of asking her to empty her pockets and go through the metal detectors again.

A restless crowd had gathered in front of the elevator, their murmurs and shuffling creating a low hum that filled the air. With each passing second, the numbers above the elevator ticked agonizingly slowly, causing her impatience and anger to grow.

When the doors finally dinged, she pushed her way to the front to make sure she would get on.

As she leaned against the back of the elevator, her arms tightly folded across her chest, she struggled to keep her hands from shaking with rage.

"Excuse me," a familiar voice said, getting onto the elevator.

Solomon and Sheriff Gray got on. They both saw her, and Solomon said, "Milady. How fares thy day?"

"Where are you going?" Billie asked with a hint of suspicion.

Mazie shook her head. The ferocity of her emotion threatened to burst forth in an explosive tirade, but she held it back, her lips pressed tightly together in a show of stubborn determination. The need to scream and shout until her voice was raw pulsed through her veins, but she knew she had to hold it in.

As the elevator reached the third floor, a flurry of activity erupted, with people surging toward the doors in a chaotic rush to exit. Solomon did, too, but stopped past the elevator doors when he saw Billie wasn't with him.

Billie slipped her arm under Mazie's, preventing her from getting off, and said, "Solomon, I'll catch up with you. Just meet me in my office."

As the elevator doors closed, confining just the two of them in the tight space, Mazie had an urge to climb out the emergency hatch on the top of the elevator and keep climbing until the sheriff couldn't see her anymore.

"I can see the rage just under the surface, Deputy. Whatever you're about to do, don't do it."

"I already have a mom," Mazie said, sensing what was coming.

Billie let go of her arm and fixed her with a penetrating stare. "I'm not your mother, I'm your boss. I think sometimes you forget that."

"Yeah, well, maybe I don't want you to be either?"

"You want to quit?"

She shrugged.

Billie slipped her hands into her pockets in a relaxed gesture and said calmly, "I feel like grabbing a coffee at the cafeteria. Come with me."

As they stepped off the elevator and made their way outside into the frigid air to the cafeteria in the next building over, Mazie trailed behind

Billie, shivering slightly in the cold. She realized she wasn't wearing a jacket, but the biting wind hadn't bothered her until now.

Billie walked with purpose, her strides long and measured. Mazie had always admired her boss's confident gait, a quality that seemed to come naturally to her. It was one of the reasons Mazie had jumped at the opportunity to work with her. She wanted to be like that, to exude the same sense of assuredness that Billie did. That, and no police agency in Florida would hire her since she punched out a captain.

"Where were you going?" Billie asked in a soft voice.

"I don't know."

"Mazie . . ."

"I was going to punch Aaron in the balls, okay?"

A chuckle escaped Billie's lips as she caught a glimpse of Mazie's beet-red face. She shook her head, amused by the younger woman's embarrassment.

"I don't need this shit," Mazie spit, her frustration boiling over as she stopped abruptly in her tracks. She was on the verge of storming off when Billie grasped her elbow, halting her in place.

"I know your rage," Billie said, her voice low and steady. "But you can control it. It doesn't have to control you."

Mazie shook her head, struggling to keep her emotions in check as she felt the telltale prickling of tears behind her eyes. A lump formed in her throat, making it difficult to swallow, and she closed her eyes for a moment, willing herself to regain control. When she spoke again, her voice was calm, though a faint tremor still lingered.

"I, um, I'm just so sick of it, Sheriff."

Billie didn't have to ask what she was sick of. "I know, but the question is what are you going to do about it? Are you going to lash out again, and this time get fired and maybe arrested? Do you think that would teach them some sort of lesson? Or would it confirm every misleading perception they believe?"

Mazie's gaze fell to the cold, hard ground beneath her feet, and she shrugged.

"Do you know what Solomon told me once?" Billie said. "That rage is just your body purging trauma. That it's necessary, but that there's ways to get it out that don't involve destroying your life."

Mazie looked up at her now and hesitantly said, "Like what?"

As they started walking again, Billie led Mazie toward the cafeteria. "It takes a lot of work, but there are things you can do," she said, her voice low and reassuring.

The cafeteria was relatively quiet at this hour, with only a handful of officers, staff, and emergency services personnel scattered among the tables.

Billie led her to the coffeepots, the aroma of freshly brewed coffee filling the air. She poured some into two paper cups, then added sugar and cream to her own. She said, "What did they do?" as she handed a cup to Mazie.

The lump in Mazie's throat had subsided. She took a deep breath, the words spilling out in a rush.

"They slashed my tires," she said, her voice steady despite the anger that simmered just beneath the surface.

"Are you sure it was them?"

"Who else would it be?"

"Maybe someone you arrested who feels wronged?"

Mazie hadn't thought of that, and she was surprised it had slipped past her. "I mean, maybe. But that's a pretty big coincidence that it happens now."

"Aaron and Dave are both under investigation by IAD right now. They know I'm upset and looking for a reason to fire them. Aaron would act stupidly, but Dave is more rational and likes his job and his pension. He would stop Aaron from doing anything stupid, like slashing tires. Maybe before hurting them, you should've made sure they actually committed the crime you're accusing them of?"

Mazie said, "There's no way. It has to be them."

"Maybe. But if you're wrong, it would confirm every single thing they believe about you. An emotional, unreliable little girl who shouldn't be wearing a badge."

She took a sip of the coffee.

"If you really want to beat them, the best way isn't confrontation. It's to work your ass off and become their boss."

Mazie laughed, and the tension and anger left her body.

As they walked out of the cafeteria, a pair of deputies held the doors open for them, and Mazie felt a fleeting sense of gratitude for their small kindness. Billie flashed them a little grin in appreciation, and they stepped out into the frigid air.

"How did you even know I was going to do anything? Do you have like mom-sense or something?"

"You don't need mom-sense to tell when someone is on the verge of losing it."

Mazie was calmer now, and felt a deep sense of shame, but she sure as hell wasn't about to admit that to the sheriff.

"I like standing here," Billie said as they reached the top of the steps leading out to the parking lot. "You can see the mountains behind all the people coming in and out. It's a reminder that the mountain was here millions of years before us and will be here millions of years after. It puts things in perspective."

Mazie looked out over the horizon, her eyes following the jagged outline of the mountains as they stretched toward the sky. She tucked her hand in her pocket and used the other to sip coffee, letting the warmth from the cup heat up her cold fingers.

Billie looked at her and said, "You have the potential to be a great cop. Don't throw it away because revenge briefly feels good."

Mazie felt a slice of humiliation cut through her at Billie's words. As hard as she tried to see it as a superior officer giving her advice, she could only think of the times she had been in trouble with her father when she was a kid.

"Thanks, Sheriff," Mazie said, her voice low and grateful.

Billie grinned at her, a warmth in her eyes that Mazie wasn't used to seeing when people looked at her. It was a look of genuine affection.

"I think you can call me Billie at this point," she said, her voice laced with amusement.

She smiled. "Okay, Billie," she said, enjoying how odd it felt to call the sheriff by her name.

Billie let out a breath into the cold air before taking a sip of coffee and resuming their walk back to the sheriff's office. "What are you doing tonight? We'll be pulling a late night here. I could use your help."

"What about my administrative leave?"

"We can put that on hold for a night."

"Oh. Well, I'll be there then. Actually, I'll come after dinner if that's cool."

"Big plans?"

She grinned. "I got a date at Kaiso."

"Since I've already been called your mother today, I won't ask with whom."

"I didn't mean it. I just said mom-sense 'cause it's weird you totally saw what was about to go down, but Solomon didn't."

"Solomon's anger doesn't come from the same place as ours."

A deputy stopped in front of them, his face red and chapped from the cold. Mazie stared at his bright-red nose, which looked almost comical against the backdrop of his weather-beaten face. He interrupted their conversation to give the sheriff an update on whatever errand she had sent him on.

Mazie looked around while she waited, her eyes scanning the faces of the deputies in the courtyard. She saw a few of them glance at her and then at the sheriff, their expressions unreadable. She had never been one to seek out attention, but there was something compelling about being in the boss's inner circle.

"So?" Billie said when the deputy had finished speaking with her and they headed back to the station. "Who's the date with?"

"His name's Joel. I met him at a coffee shop. He asked me out on a real date. None of this *let's hang out* bullshit. It was awesome."

She grinned at her excitement. "Is he cute?"

"OMG, he's so hot. Like not *romance book cover* hot, but really cute with these dimples that just make your heart melt, ya know?"

"I do."

They stopped in front of the doors, and Mazie said, "I'll come by after I'm done. And, um, thanks. For stopping me from being an idiot . . . again."

"How about the next time you want to hurt someone, you come ask me if it's a good idea first."

"You got it . . . Billie."

Mazie watched as Billie disappeared into the building, her mind a maelstrom of emotions. The conversation had left her feeling both grateful and uneasy. Her anger, overwhelming just moments before, now receded into the background.

As she turned to leave, she felt a sense of calm wash over her, like a gentle breeze blowing in from the mountains. It was a curious feeling, she thought, how quickly her anger could take over, like a flock of birds changing direction midflight. And she knew no matter how quickly the anger faded away, it was always there, lurking in the shadows.

She called a mechanic who she had used before, a brother of one of her fellow officers, and he said he could get some spares on her car right now and got the address to send one of his crew.

Even though it was only midafternoon, and her date wasn't until this evening, she decided to go home and get ready as soon as her car tires were on. She'd been in sweats with no makeup and her hair all over the place when she had hung out with Joel today, so she wanted to knock him off his feet tonight.

She summoned an Uber, completely forgetting the reason she had come here in the first place.

35

Solomon waited in Billie's office, taking a baseball off her desk and tossing it up into the air from her couch and catching it again with one hand. It had been the ball her father kept on his desk, a ball from when Mark McGuire hit a home run right at him and a ten-year-old Elizabeth Gray and Zach managed to get to it before anyone else. It'd never come off the desk since.

Solomon's hand went to his pocket, feeling the buzz of the Nokia phone against his skin. For a moment, he hesitated, his gaze drifting over to the open office door. No one was out in the hall. He retrieved the phone from his pocket and flipped it open, his eyes scanning the message that awaited him.

Miss me? the text had come in.

Depends, Solomon responded. Why don't you tell me who you are and I'll tell you if I miss you?

You crack me up . . . I see you still haven't turned in this phone yet. You must know that I'd stop contacting you instantly, right???

I figured. I'm guessing this is where you can feel smarter than me when I don't stop you in time? Can we just skip that part and have me admit you're smarter and you just turn yourself in?

No response for a long time and then just a smiling emoji.

"I've had my fill of you crazy bastards," he muttered bitterly, his voice laced with resentment and weariness.

What do you want from me?

Billie came in just then, and Solomon slipped the phone back into his pocket. She sighed and sat down at her desk.

"You look tired. You sleeping much?" Solomon said.

"Not really. You?"

He shook his head. "No."

She leaned back in the seat. "IAD will get wind that we're doing our own interviews eventually. We might have only tonight if you want it to just be us."

"Let's hope that's all we need."

They set up in the conference room, deciding it was better not to conduct what were clearly investigative interviews of police officers in the sheriff's office.

Solomon sat at a large gray table next to Billie with chairs across from them. No folders or voice recorders or cameras. With some luck, nobody would think they were possible suspects in the murder of the former mayor and current district attorney.

"Who's up first?"

"Robert Zeeks. He was a deputy at both scenes."

Solomon had seen his name in the reports but said nothing.

Billie's intercom on the conference-room phone buzzed, and her assistant let her know Zeeks was here.

As they sat in silence, the door to the conference room opened, revealing the figure of her assistant, a young woman with a soda in her hand. Behind her came a thin man with a shock of hair on an otherwise bald head, his uniform rumpled after a long night's work.

Solomon watched as the man made his way over, his movements slow and heavy with fatigue. He could see the exhaustion etched into the lines of the man's face, the dark circles under his eyes a testament to the toll his job had taken on him.

"Have a seat, Robert," Billie said. "Have you ever met Solomon?"

"He looks familiar," he said with a glance to Solomon as he sat down.

"He's helping out with all this. We're just interviewing everybody that was at both crime scenes, and your name came up."

He glanced at both of them. "What for?"

"There were some discrepancies we need to see if anyone has any information on."

The man clearly knew this was an investigative interview. Solomon wondered why he thought they could fool a bunch of cops.

"You have any brutality complaints, Robert?" Solomon said.

He turned to him and didn't answer right away.

"No."

"None?"

"None."

"Not a single complaint," Solomon said. "Impressive. How'd you manage that? Even the best cops have a couple."

He shrugged. "I've never had a temper. When other people escalate, I de-escalate."

"My man," he said, holding out his fist for a fist bump. Zeeks ignored him.

Solomon grinned and said, "We've met before. You and I had a case together. Sherrie McDonald. You remember her?"

He shook his head.

"She was a DUI. You pulled her over near the outskirts of Grantsville. She was just over the limit, so not trashed or anything, but

I do remember one thing about the case. She said you made out with her while she was in cuffs in the back seat of the cruiser."

He looked at the sheriff and then back to Solomon. "She was lying."

Solomon glanced at Billie, who had a look that said, *This better be going somewhere.*

"The thing is, when I talked to her, I believed her. I mean, she was a young, beautiful girl. She's cuffed in the back seat and flirting with you to get out of the DUI. I don't think any guy would've been able to resist. I certainly wouldn't have."

Solomon noticed the way his eyes kept darting back to Billie, a flicker of uncertainty and hesitation in his gaze. It was clear that he was holding back, his words carefully chosen to avoid any missteps or mistakes.

"You believe what you want. She's lying."

Solomon wondered if Zeeks would say the same thing if his boss wasn't sitting in front of him.

"Actually, hang tight a second, Rob. Billie, could I talk to you outside really quick?"

They went out into the hallway and shut the door. The conference room wasn't an interview room and didn't have any windows looking in. He wished he could see how Zeeks was behaving right now.

"I don't think it's gonna work with both of us," he said.

"Why not?"

"He looked at you before every answer. Some of these people are going to be intimidated by you. Let me have first crack at them. If I get anything, I'll call you right in."

"Solomon, you're not law enforcement. I can't let you interview a potential suspect to two homicides."

"If it comes back to bite you, I'll say I snuck in when you weren't around."

She folded her arms. "I can't do it."

He leaned on his cane. "You wanna catch this guy or not?"

"Not if it means he's going to walk because I let a civilian interview him. You're not thinking clearly. Let me and my detectives handle this."

"Billie, just—"

"No, you're not interviewing these people by yourself. I'm calling in IAD, and we're doing this by the book."

"Screw the book. This guy we're after, you think he cares about the book? He's going to kill until he dies or we get lucky and catch him. And I can't believe you'd let optics and politics get in the way of that. I didn't think having a political post would change you, but maybe I'm wrong."

She gazed at him quietly a moment before saying, "Out of respect for our friendship, I'm going to forget you said that." She moved toward the door to go back in. "Go home, Solomon."

He tilted his head back, feeling the pull of the muscles in his neck as he gazed up at the ceiling, and blew out a long breath.

Crap.

36

Solomon sat on a bench outside the Public Safety Complex and watched the snow melting on the pavement.

He leaned back, feeling the sun on his face, and breathed in deeply. The scent of melting snow mixed with exhaust fumes and the aroma of coffee from the cafeteria. He wondered if he should go in and get a cup. It would warm him up and give him something to do. But he didn't feel like moving.

Solomon savored the satisfying crunch of the snow under the tip of his cane, the only sound in an otherwise silent afternoon. He fished out the Nokia phone and powered it on, but no new messages greeted him. His thumbs hesitated over the keyboard for a moment; then he typed out a quick text: You there?

No immediate response, but the text did come back eventually: I'm here

Solomon's heart rate spiked as he stared at the screen.

I've had enough. You win. Let's just skip to the end game

All good things to those who wait

There is no way this is a good thing

Opinions vary

Opinions vary. Solomon had used that expression a lot, and his first thought was that this man was listening to him.

I'm too tired for this. At least tell me what to call you, Solomon texted.

He waited for a response for a long time but none came, and he slipped the phone back into his pocket. Pursing his lips, he blew out another breath as he made a decision. He used his cane to stand, then went and leaned against a pillar near the entrance to the building that housed the sheriff's office. Watching the people come in and out.

It was about half an hour later when Rob Zeeks came out of the building and put on some black sunglasses. The sun was bright, and without his own sunglasses Solomon had to squint to see the deputy trudging down the stairs to law enforcement parking around the side of the building.

Solomon stayed a good twenty feet behind him until he rounded the corner and went into the parking garage toward the stairs leading up to the second level. Once in the parking garage, Solomon said, "Deputy," before Zeeks could head up the stairs. Solomon caught up to the man, who had a surprised look and didn't say anything.

"Can I talk to you for a second?"

"The sheriff said you had an emergency."

Solomon leaned against the brick wall and folded his hands over his cane. His leg was causing him pain, but he ignored it as he glanced to a car driving out of the parking garage. "We're all having an emergency. The district attorney was murdered. There's gonna be hell to pay, and guess what, Zeeks: guys like you are standing at the foot of the hill, and the shit's rolling down."

"I didn't do anything."

"Really? Because I remember that interview with the girl you pulled over. She said you did a lot more than make out, didn't she?"

"She was drunk," he said, and followed it up with a flex of his jaw muscles. *Sensitive subject,* Solomon thought. Good.

"She was seventeen. Underage."

"I didn't do anything," he said.

"Sexual touching of a minor who couldn't consent. Kinda hard to erase that, isn't it?"

Zeeks took a step toward him, anger in his eyes as he tried to intimidate him with his superior size.

"You tried to get me fired for it," Zeeks said.

"I knew you remembered me. And actually I wanted you arrested and charged, but my supervisor at the time, the now-deceased district attorney, thought that there wasn't enough evidence. I didn't realize what he was then, but I know now. An aspiring DA has too many cops arrested and suddenly the police union isn't on his side, and it's hard to win an election without their support, isn't it?"

Solomon's hand shot out and grabbed Zeeks's sleeve as he turned away to go up the stairs. Zeeks turned back around, his eyes narrowing in anger.

"I need your help," Solomon said.

Zeeks stood silently.

"I looked at your dispatch logs. You were halfway across the city when Roger was kidnapped. I know you didn't kill him. But I also know you're tight with every cop out there. Just like a unit back in the military, right? Whoever killed Roger is probably working with you. There has to be someone you have doubts about. Someone that maybe acts strangely and gives you pause, but you brush it off because he's so likable."

He stared at Solomon. "I don't know anybody like that."

"Yes, you do. These types of men, they can't hold everything in twenty-four hours a day. They let things slip. An offhanded comment one day, a tasteless joke the next, maybe insisting on talking about the killings at times nobody else wants to talk about them. There's gotta be someone, Zeeks."

Solomon waited until another car drove by and released the man's sleeve.

"Whoever did this is law enforcement. You think your job's hard now, Zeeks, wait until the press finds out a cop killed the DA. What do you think the mayor and the council are going to do? Voters are going to be pissed, and they'll want heads to roll. Maybe it'll come with layoffs and budget cuts, probably a new sheriff chosen by politicians . . . your job is going to get a lot harder. I know you don't want that."

Zeeks thought a moment and then shook his head. "I'm no snitch."

As Zeeks ascended the stairs and vanished around the corner, Solomon remained rooted to the spot, staring after him.

37

Billie didn't finish at the office until nearly ten.

She called the lieutenant over at IAD, a gruff man named Charles, and told him why she thought it could be someone in law enforcement. The lieutenant basically gave her a boilerplate answer, but she knew he couldn't pass up a chance for good press for IAD.

"It'll take some time," he said.

"We don't have much time."

"It'll take as long as it takes," he said before hanging up.

Billie checked her cell phone. She had texted Mazie twice to find out how her date was going and got no reply. A sense of unease settled in her chest. It was unusual, because as far back as she could remember, Mazie had always been fast to reply.

"Sheriff?" a deputy said from the door as Billie was checking her phone.

"Yes?"

"Someone left this outside the front doors."

She looked up and saw him holding what looked like a cellophane-wrapped gift basket. "What is it?"

"I don't know. Looks like candies and stuff. Says it's for you."

A slight thread of fear slithered its way up her spine as she stared at the gift basket. "Put it down very carefully and leave."

The deputy, confused, lowered it to the ground. "Have a good night, Sheriff."

Billie took a folding knife out of a drawer and slowly went over to the basket. It was addressed to her and was sent from a PO box here in town. She bent close and smelled it, then listened to it. She debated what to do. They had an X-ray machine next door at the satellite location for the Utah State Crime Lab, but no one would be there at this hour.

Candies, cheeses, and crackers were meticulously arranged within the basket. Each item was wrapped and visible, with nothing concealed except for a small black box of chocolates. Something told her she knew who this basket was from.

She cut it open and took out the box and opened it.

Inside was a heart.

Having grown up in a rural county where her father owned a small farm he used for livestock and horses, she knew it was a pig heart. It was still bloody and smelled coppery. She lifted the gift basket and took it down with her out of the building.

The drive to Dax's apartment took longer than she thought it would. A crash had occurred on the freeway, and she had to get off and take the paved streets. When she got there, she took the gift basket and went to his door.

Dax had expected her to call the crime lab and analyze the basket. To wait with nervous energy, hoping that he had screwed up and left a fingerprint or DNA somewhere. But she knew it was pointless, not because he didn't leave those things, but because he didn't care. The more times he got locked up, the more interaction she would be forced to have with him through negotiations and court appearances. So, she had decided to do the thing he least expected.

Dax answered the door with a smirk and said, "You know you're not supp—"

She threw the gift basket at him. It hit his face and dropped to the floor, spattering a little blood out when the lid of the chocolate box slid off. Dax touched his lip and pulled away his fingers, staring at the blood. Then he smiled and tasted it.

"I don't need gifts," she said.

She left, ignoring anything he was saying behind her. She got into her truck and only then looked back to the apartment. Dax hadn't moved; he stood at the door shouting at her. When she was storming away, she could've sworn it felt like he was following her.

She pulled out onto the road and noticed her hands shaking. That was terrifying, and yet maybe one of the most exhilarating things she'd ever done. She'd been getting hit for months, and now she got to hit back.

Billie glanced at her phone while she got onto the freeway, hoping the accident hadn't affected the lanes heading back to the city, and saw that Mazie still hadn't returned her text.

Mazie lived in a nice condo community near her gym, because she had said she didn't want any excuses for missing her hour-long intense workouts every morning. The buildings were white and three stories and looked like some nice apartments Billie had lived in during her one year at graduate school.

Memories of that time came flooding back. She had wanted to be a biologist and move to Hawaii to study for her PhD. Her master's degree would've been done in one more year, but she didn't finish. There was something unsatisfying in the work to her, as important as she thought it was.

She went to Mazie's first floor condo and knocked, then rang the doorbell. She did it again a minute later and still got no response. As she was walking away to see if there was a manager or maintenance person that lived on-site that could let her in, she noticed the open window. An open window on a ground floor apartment.

No cop would ever leave their window open on a ground floor apartment, except a rookie.

There was only one other place she could think to check.

As Billie pulled into the strip mall's parking lot, she noticed how the neon signs of the surrounding stores lit up the dark night sky, casting a colorful glow on the concrete pavement. The smell of tobacco from the smoke shop mingled with the scents from nearby restaurants, creating an odd but alluring smell.

Kaiso was a small, unassuming place tucked in between a grocery store and the smoke shop. Its plain exterior was a stark contrast to the lively atmosphere inside. As she slowly circled the lot, Billie scanned the parked cars, searching for Mazie's vehicle.

Billie wondered if maybe she took a taxi or Uber down because she hadn't put spares on her vehicle, but then she spotted the Honda a few spaces down from the restaurant.

Billie pulled her car near Mazie's and got out. As she approached, she noticed that the doors were unlocked. Billie opened the flashlight on her phone and peered into the car. She scanned the interior, looking for any clues or signs of struggle. She examined the seats, the floor, and the dashboard, but found nothing out of the ordinary.

As Billie entered the sushi place, she felt disoriented. The interior looked like a strange amalgamation of an American diner and a traditional sushi restaurant. Kitschy decorations adorned the walls, such as a vintage advertisement announcing "Smoke Lucky Strikes," featuring a dapper cartoon figure in a white T-shirt and slacks about to light up a cigarette. Despite the odd decor, the smell of sushi and soy sauce wafted through the air, making Billie's stomach growl: she couldn't remember when she last ate.

The hostess, a young girl, smiled at her and said, "Just one?"

"Actually, I'm looking for someone." She pulled up a picture of Mazie on her phone.

It was both of them at a bar the night they had gone out with some other people from the department. Mazie was taking a selfie of them and had her mouth open like she was screaming with delight. Billie looked like she always did and was saddened that she couldn't even cut loose for one photograph. She had to always give the appearance of being in control, and now it seemed like she didn't know how to do otherwise.

The girl looked at the picture and said, "Haven't seen her."

"How long have you been here tonight?"

"Since like four."

"You sure you would recognize her? She'd probably be much more dolled up than this."

"I mean, maybe not. I don't know. But I've seated everyone here, and I haven't seen her."

"Would you mind showing the photo around to the other staff and seeing if any of them saw her?"

"Sure."

Billie got her number and texted her the image. The girl said she would be right back and disappeared into the back. When she came out, Billie could see her going to each server and busser and showing them the picture.

"Nobody's seen her," she said when she returned to the front.

Billie thought a moment. "Did you have any single men tonight that were expecting someone that didn't show up?"

She shrugged. "I don't think so, no. I'd probably remember that."

Billie exhaled. "Well, thank you for your help."

"No problem."

Billie went outside and back to Mazie's car. She brought up the flashlight again and went around the car slowly, knowing what she was looking for but hoping she wouldn't find it: blood. But there was nothing.

She called into dispatch and told them to issue a BOLO call for Deputy Mazie Heaton.

38

Solomon stirred from his sleep, and his eyes fluttered open. Disorientation set in as he tried to remember where he was. Slowly, he realized he was on his living room couch, still dressed in the clothes he wore yesterday.

He groaned and rubbed his face, feeling the dull throb of a headache behind his eyes. He'd had a dream that he was standing at his mother's grave. The first time he'd seen her grave, he'd been in foster care already for years. One day, he'd snuck out of school and taken the bus to the cemetery, which was situated in the midst of a quiet residential neighborhood, flanked by a bustling rec center on one side and a vast expanse of well-manicured baseball fields on the other.

Solomon had trudged through the cemetery, feeling the crunch of snow under his feet. The gravestones were all neatly arranged. It was hard to believe that his mother's final resting place was in such a mundane and unremarkable location. But then, he supposed, his mother's life had been anything but remarkable. He couldn't remember much about her except for the bruises and the shouting matches with his father.

The moment he had seen her grave, he knew it was hers. She liked a certain type of flower, marigolds, and there were some marigolds withered and dry near her gravestone. He bent down and touched them, letting his young fingers feel the texture of the dead flowers. When he pulled his hand away, he burst into tears.

He couldn't remember how long he had sat by his mother's grave and cried, but when he was done, he left, and never went back.

Solomon used his cane to stand and stretched his back. His leg was swollen from all the recent use, and he went to the bathroom and got out some ibuprofen, then swallowed it down with water from the faucet. He glanced at his anxiety medication but didn't take any. It slowed his thinking down, and right now, he couldn't afford that.

He turned on the Nokia phone. There were no messages. He had bought a power cord that fit it and plugged it in while he checked his own phone. There was a single message from Billie:

Mazie is missing.

Solomon arrived at Kaiso Sushi around nine in the morning. The sun was just coming up, casting a warm glow on the surrounding buildings and melting the last remnants of frost on the ground. As he stepped out of the Uber, a fierce wind suddenly whipped through the parking lot, picking up bits of snow and stinging his cheeks. Solomon pulled his jacket tighter around him, flipping up the collar for protection against the biting cold. He braced himself and trudged toward the scene.

Forensic techs and a detective were searching Mazie's car while a tow truck waited nearby. Billie was still there, pacing in front of the restaurant with a phone glued to her ear. Solomon approached her and waited.

Solomon looked over to Mazie's car when Billie was off the phone and said, "How long?"

"Best we can tell, she arrived here around seven, got out of her car, and no one saw her again. She didn't make it into the restaurant."

"You've checked all the surrounding businesses for video?"

She nodded. "And my detectives are tracking down anybody that could've seen anything. We'll find her, Solomon," she said, sensing panic.

He wondered what his face must be revealing for her to say that.

The odd thing was he felt nothing. Not panic, not sadness, not anger . . . nothing. Almost like he was drifting above the ground observing what was going on but not really understanding it.

"It's not your fault, Solomon."

Solomon tapped his cane and looked down. "Yes it is."

Billie's phone rang, and she answered.

Solomon went closer to the car and watched two techs going over everything inside with a black light. They wore dark glasses that would help them see any bodily fluids that may have spattered or spilled, even if there had been an attempt to clean it up.

The detective supervising them was Greg Parsons. He wore latex gloves but didn't actually touch the car. He held a flashlight up and ran it along the ground.

"Any cameras?" Solomon said.

Greg glanced up at him, and Solomon expected him to say something like he couldn't discuss an ongoing investigation with a civilian, but instead he said, "No CCTV, no traffic lights. Checked with the businesses that are open and nothing. A few of them are opening soon, though."

Solomon acknowledged Parsons's unspoken message with a subtle nod. Glancing across the street to a row of storefronts, he knew what Parsons meant when he said some of the stores are opening soon. It was his way of giving Solomon a warning to act quickly. Despite the implied threat, Solomon appreciated Parsons's understanding and knew he could count on him to look the other way for a while longer.

Solomon headed across the street toward a row of storefronts, a small barber shop with a faded red-and-white pole twirling outside, a quaint boutique selling luxurious soaps and bath gels with an inviting aroma wafting out onto the street, a busy bagel shop where a line was already forming outside, a bustling deli with fresh sandwich boards on display, and a curious little store called Hometown CBD that was painted in bright greens and yellows, displaying a range of CBD and mild cannabis products, which had recently been legalized in Utah.

Solomon waited on the street corner for the light to turn. Suddenly, he felt a presence behind him and turned to see Billie walking up, her footsteps muffled by the noise of the morning traffic around them.

"Where to?"

He motioned with his head to the other side of the street. "Parsons didn't check all the businesses yet. Some of them were closed when he went to ask about cameras."

"Solomon—"

"If you're about to tell me this isn't my problem or to go home, Billie—"

"I wasn't going to say that. I was going to say just have a police officer with you if you talk to somebody. Please. For me."

"Okay. You're a police officer, so come with me."

The light turned, and they began to cross.

Billie said, "I'm guessing bath gels aren't a hot commodity on a thief's wish list. Which stores were you thinking might have surveillance?"

"The CBD place is the only one that has products expensive enough to justify twenty-four-hour surveillance."

Solomon had an image enter his mind as they got to the other side of the street. Mazie lying on top of bloodstained sheets, her eyes the milky white of the dead.

"Billie," he said with a tremor in his voice, "do you ever feel like everything you touch turns to shit?"

His words hung heavily in the air, the weight of despair and hope-lessness evident in his tone. Billie knew exactly what he meant, the feeling of being trapped in a cycle of failure that seemed impossible to break.

Without hesitation, she stopped and placed a gentle hand on his arm and spoke with conviction. "You are not cursed."

They locked eyes for a moment before Billie pulled away, and they continued crossing the street in silence.

Hometown CBD had two floors and looked like it had once been an army/navy store. Some Halloween decorations were still up, a few lifelike skeletons with spiders crawling on them. The store had just opened, and there were no customers yet, but two employees were busy restocking and tidying up.

Billie asked for the owner, a tall Korean man named Ernie with glasses and wavy black hair. She showed her badge and explained why they were there.

Solomon put both hands on his cane. He watched quietly as Billie said, "Do you have any cameras aimed out toward Kaiso?"

Solomon felt his chest tighten as Ernie glanced at both of them.

"Yeah, we should. We have two interior cameras facing that way."

As he got on the phone with his security company to request the footage, Solomon turned to Billie and said, "Interior cameras facing out are extra. I could marry this guy for not being a cheapskate."

"There might not be anything on it. I would hold off on the wedding plans for a bit."

Within minutes, Ernie had the security footage from all their outward-facing cameras on a link on his phone. Billie had him forward it to the computer analyst at the sheriff's office, and Solomon asked if he could view it.

It was clear footage, nothing grainy, and in high definition. Solomon said, "This is some top-notch gear."

"The extra money's worth a good night's sleep for me. You'd be amazed how many people try to burglarize us. They think that the cops don't take break-ins at cannabis stores as seriously, and they're right. But you people are lucky my father was a police officer and taught me to respect the law, so I'm going to help you."

"We won't say no," Solomon said.

For several minutes, they stayed quiet as Ernie fast-forwarded the video.

"Stop right there," Solomon said. "Back up a little."

The video caught Kaiso from a distance, but it was clear enough to see Mazie's silver Honda pulling into the lot. Ernie magnified the video on his phone, and they could see Mazie in the driver's seat, parked facing the restaurant. She was checking herself in the rearview mirror. Solomon stole a quick glance at Billie, whose face was passive.

Mazie got out of her car and started walking toward the restaurant. Only a few feet away from her car, a figure appeared seemingly out of the dark between two parked cars.

The figure made a sudden move. From his pocket, he retrieved a rag or cloth and swiftly wrapped it around Mazie's mouth. With surprising force, he pulled her into the shadows of the dimly lit parking lot, where the camera's view couldn't reach. Solomon watched in horror as Mazie disappeared, swallowed up by the darkness.

"Play it again," Billie said coolly.

The figure was in a black coat, long sleeves hanging down past the fingers. The hood obscured his face in shadows, leaving only a hint of a jawline and a slight curve of a nose. His movements were quick and precise, like a predator moving in for the kill. Solomon strained to see any other details, but the figure was shrouded in darkness.

The two didn't come back into view.

Solomon swung his cane and bashed it into a display. "Damn it!" he shouted before storming out.

Billie's jaw muscles tightened, and she had to focus on them to get them to relax. "Thank you for your help," she said calmly before walking out and catching up to Solomon, the owner saying something behind her about paying for the display.

The morning sun shone down on Billie and Solomon, casting a pale light on everything around them. Billie noticed the way Solomon's eyes darted back and forth as if he was trying to focus on something but couldn't. She knew that he was struggling with the image of Mazie being taken, and it was affecting him deeply. She decided to give him some space and stood quietly next to him outside at the curb as he watched the traffic for a few minutes.

When they got back to the station, Solomon and Billie headed straight for the computer forensics lab. The small room was crammed with three techs, each hunched over a monitor. Billie approached them and asked them to analyze the video in excruciating detail, to dissect it frame by frame and extract every shred of information they could find. Solomon watched over their shoulders as the techs got to work, his heart racing with anticipation and dread.

On the video, about ten minutes after Mazie arrived, Solomon noticed a man park a GMC truck and get out. He was tall with curly brown hair and stood outside the restaurant. He kept checking his phone, placing a call and several texts. Then he went inside, spent a few minutes in there, and then got into his truck and left.

"How much you wanna bet that's the date," Solomon said.

Billie said to one of the techs, "Can you get the plate?"

He hit a few keys, and the screen widened and focused. Solomon saw the license plate in full, clear view. He looked at Billie and smiled.

39

The owner of the car was Joel Walco, and he lived in a condominium not far from the station. He was thirty-two, college education at the University of Georgia, and something that gave Solomon a little shiver of excitement when he found out: he worked at the Utah State Crime Lab and just happened to have been at Solomon's house when Roger had been found.

Solomon and Billie parked the car in a designated spot and got out. The crunch of snow under their shoes was the only sound in the air.

"This is the kind of place divorced middle-aged men move to when they get busted having an affair," he said.

"That's oddly specific."

"It's just the vibe I'm getting . . . loneliness."

Solomon followed Billie up the stairs, feeling his leg burn with each step. When they reached the second floor, they found the unit they were looking for. Billie knocked, and after a few moments, the door opened to reveal the man they had seen on the video.

He was handsome and had a look of being a mix of Lebanese or Mediterranean. He smiled as he said, "Can I help you?"

"Joel Walco?"

"Yes."

She showed him her badge. "We need to speak with you."

"Oh, wow. Yeah, of course. Come in."

As they stepped into the condo, the small space revealed itself in full. The kitchen was pressed up against one wall, a small dining table and chairs were in the center of the room, and a worn-out couch faced a flat-screen TV on the opposite wall. The entire area had a stale, musky smell to it. A set of sliding glass doors led to a small balcony that overlooked the complex courtyard. A brand-new barbecue sat there, untouched, alongside empty beer bottles that were strewed about. Solomon noticed that the grill itself was completely clean, with no trace of any previous use or char marks.

"You guys want anything to drink? I got orange juice and Coke."

"I'm fine, thank you," Billie said.

"I'll take a Coke."

"Diet or regular?"

"Regular. YOLO."

Joel grinned as he went to the fridge and got the Coke.

He came back and handed Solomon the drink. Billie was staring at a painting the size of a poster. It was a disturbing image of a distorted figure with elongated limbs and a twisted face, a background of dark, swirling colors. Solomon felt uneasy looking at the painting, as if it was somehow alive and watching him.

"So what's this about?" Joel said, sitting on the couch.

"Did you have a date with Mazie Heaton last night?"

"I did, but she didn't show up. Why?"

"We have reason to believe she was kidnapped before her date with you."

He looked shocked. "You're kidding?"

"Afraid not."

"I mean, she's a police officer, right? She mentioned that to me. I didn't hear anything about it on the news," Joel said.

"We're keeping everything close to the chest," Billie replied, turning to face him. She settled into the couch, while Solomon remained standing against the wall. His leg throbbed with a fiery pain that only intensified with each step, and he didn't want to risk aggravating it further by moving.

"So what do you do?" Solomon asked like he didn't know.

"I'm a systems programmer for the crime lab."

"Oh yeah?"

Billie said, "I don't think we've run across each other before."

"No, I've only been with them a few weeks, actually. I transferred down from Boise PD. They had to cut some of the IT department, so all the new guys got the axe. Worked out for the best, though. I mean, besides all this. Do you have any idea who could've taken her?"

Billie said, "We have some idea. But you were the last person to speak with her."

He leaned back now, his eyes going wider. "Oh, okay. I see what this is. Well, look, I went straight to the restaurant from work, and you can check that. I like Mazie. I mean, this is just . . . I've never experienced anything like this."

Billie said, "Why don't you tell us exactly what you remember?"

He shrugged. "We met at a coffee shop and had a date set up for last night at seven at Kaiso, this sushi restaurant. I told her I would meet her in front of the restaurant, but I waited almost half an hour, and she never showed."

"Is there anything you remember that was unusual? Did she mention someone odd, or was there anybody that seemed to be watching you two when you were speaking? Anything at all?"

He thought a moment. "I don't think it's anything."

Solomon said, "How about we judge that."

Joel glanced between them. "There was a guy at the coffee shop where we met. He kept looking at her. I noticed him before I noticed her because it was odd the way he was staring at her."

Solomon felt the first hint of adrenaline. "What did he look like?"

"I don't know, actually. He wore sunglasses and a hat the entire time. White guy, black hair . . . very average. But I don't know. May have just been someone staring at a pretty girl."

Joel brought his hands up to his face and placed both palms over it. He rubbed his face and then blew out a long breath before saying, "I don't know what to do. I mean, can I help in some way?"

Solomon said, "Did anyone else know you two would be at that restaurant?"

"Like who?"

"I don't know. Anyone you told."

He shook his head. "No. Nobody. I mean, a couple guys at the crime lab, but that's it."

Billie said, "We'll need their names."

"Yeah, of course. Anything I can do." He got a melancholic grin and looked out the balcony doors. "I just hope she's okay."

Solomon noticed he put his hands on his lap, palms down on his thighs.

"Could I use your bathroom?"

"Sure. Down the hall to the left."

Solomon went down the narrow hallway. The bedroom was to the right. It was small but clean and had a large bed that took up most of the space. A Grateful Dead emblem on a tie-dye shirt hung on the wall with Jerry Garcia's autograph scribbled in marker near the bottom of the shirt.

He ducked into the bathroom but kept the door open. He took out the Nokia phone and turned it on. No messages. He texted the number and listened to see if a phone dinged anywhere in the condo, but there were no sounds. He shut the door and leaned against the wall, staring at himself in the mirror.

As he looked at himself, he noticed how worn and tired he appeared. His eyes were sunken and his skin was pale, with a few days' worth of stubble on his face. He ran his hand through his hair.

The thought of Mazie's disappearance reminded him of another young woman he had failed to help, Kelly. Her face flashed before him; the memory was still fresh after all these years. Solomon couldn't shake the guilt that lingered inside him, knowing that he could have done more to save her from her stepfather's abuse. The weight of that failure felt heavy on his chest as he stood in the bathroom, staring at his reflection.

He splashed some water on his face and then flushed the toilet and waited a second before going back to the living room. Joel and Billie were speaking about some of the cases he was working on. Something about him seemed too casual with this interview. He was calm and collected. Perhaps it was just his natural personality? Solomon had known enough science nerds that worked at the crime lab to know they weren't exactly the model of chatty or emotional.

They talked for a few more minutes, but it was clear Joel knew nothing about what had happened, or at least didn't give them anything. They thanked him for his time and left. Once in the truck, Solomon said, "He's too calm."

"I know."

"You putting surveillance on him?"

"Sure am," she said, texting someone right then. He was relieved she had gotten the same impression from Joel.

She started the truck and pulled onto the road.

Solomon felt a sudden vibration in his pocket, causing him to remember that he had forgotten to turn off the Nokia. He took it out of his pocket, and the text message that he read caused his heart to plummet and his mouth to go dry. A cold sweat started to form on his forehead as he read the message over and over.

Tell Billie to slow down. She's speeding

Solomon's head whipped around, scanning from corner to corner and from car to car. He was looking for any sign of a person or vehicle that might indicate someone was watching them. Despite his anxiety, he reminded himself that Billie was an exceptional police officer and would likely have detected if someone was tailing her. But he was seeing them somehow . . . Solomon felt vulnerable and on edge.

"What?" Billie said. "You look like you've seen a ghost."

"I think it's seen us actually."

"What does that mean?"

Solomon hesitated, his mind racing as he considered revealing the truth.

"Pull over."

"Why?"

"I'm going to tell you something that's going to make you really angry with me, and I would prefer you not be driving a five-thousand-pound truck when I tell you."

She pulled over. He took a deep breath and shut his eyes a second. Then he retrieved the phone from his pocket and passed it to her, his heart pounding with anxiety.

As she looked at the phone, her eyes widened in horror as she scrolled through the messages. Her mouth hung open in disbelief.

"Tell me this isn't what I think it is," she said, her voice laced with fear and anger.

Solomon's eyes shifted to the street ahead of him, catching sight of a young mother and her daughter crossing the road. The woman held the toddler's hand tightly, guiding her safely across the bustling intersection. As they approached the truck, the little girl's curious gaze locked onto Solomon's, and she smiled.

"He left it at my house."

"And you just decided to tell me now?"

"I didn't have a choice. He said he would cut all communication if I told anyone, and I believed him."

"So? I could've helped you with that. We could have used tracing technology, GPS, who knows what else."

Solomon shook his head. "No, he's too sophisticated for any of that."

He could see her fingers turning white from gripping the phone tightly. "What if we could have prevented this if you had shown me this earlier?"

"It wouldn't have helped. He just would've cut off contact, and that would've been the end of it."

"We won't know that for sure now, will we? Think of chain of custody, Solomon. If we arrest this man, you will have to take the stand and describe what happened with the phone. A good defense attorney could raise reasonable doubt all over the place."

"I wouldn't have normally done this, but this is different. I need to keep this line of communication open with him. And he has Mazie now."

She let out a deep breath. "I suppose I can at least see your reasoning, as misguided as it was." She turned the phone over in her hands. "We need to get this to the crime lab."

"He'll know, and he'll stop using it. We need him talking."

Solomon could feel her anger radiating off her like heat, but he also knew she would eventually understand. She had no choice. Being able to communicate with the man they were after was worth almost any price. Almost.

The two sat in her truck without speaking as she drove. Eventually, she turned on some music. A country station she had been playing earlier. Solomon rolled down his window and let the cold wind hit his face for a while before saying, "So silent treatment, huh?"

"Yes."

"I couldn't tell anybody. You gotta see that."

"I'm not just anybody."

He nodded. "You're not. I should've told you. I'm sorry."

She watched him a second and then turned her attention back to the road.

"How close are you to the sheriff in Boise?" Solomon said.

She shrugged. "Never met him. You think there's dirt on Joel?"

"I don't know. Something's off about him, though. He knows more than he's saying." He paused a moment. "What did you feel when you were looking at that painting on the wall?"

"I don't know. Claustrophobic, I think. Maybe a twinge of anxiety."

"Me too. An odd decoration to have in your house to see every day, don't you think? Unless you relate to the dark, pressing feeling of it. Like if you've got a lot of unacknowledged guilt." He paused and looked out the open window. "Or he could've bought it at Target with his groceries because it's pretty. What the hell do I know?"

"You know something about the man we're after, obviously."

He shook his head, his eyes still out the window. "Not enough."

40

None of the official surveillance officers could follow Joel Walco for the next forty-eight hours, a fact that broke Billie's stone exterior and caused her to speak angrily to the sheriff of the next county over, who'd said he needed the manpower.

Billie had argued with the department heads for official surveillance help, but their hands were tied. Several departments, including the Utah Highway Patrol, the largest law enforcement body in the state, used the same surveillance teams and equipment to save on costs. A pool of cars, surveilling equipment, and sometimes even manpower were shared among the agencies. Something that Billie's father had helped institute. Thirty years ago, such cooperation between agencies would have been impossible. It never ceased to amaze Solomon how territorial human beings really were.

Billie's home had dust on the windowsills that Solomon hadn't seen when he was over before, and he had to fight the urge to get some paper towels and wipe them down.

"Tea?" Billie said.

"Why not? We're gonna be up a while, I'm guessing."

"Why's that?"

"You're not seriously gonna let Joel Sweaty-Hands Walco go unsupervised for two days, are you?"

"I was going to find a couple deputies to sit outside his home."

"I think we should do it."

She filled a teapot with water and put it on the stove. "Are you able to with your leg? It's not easy sitting in a car for hours on end."

"I can do it."

"Don't get offended. I know sitting for longer periods causes you pain."

Solomon breathed out deeply and sat on the couch. "Sorry. Long day."

"Agreed," she said with a sigh.

They sat on the couch and sipped tea. It was a temporary reprieve. Solomon felt the tension in every muscle in his body. Almost like they were cords pulling in opposite directions. He knew Billie felt it, too, because she normally had strict posture, and now she was slouching as she slipped off her shoes and rubbed her feet.

"I miss wearing boots with a uniform sometimes instead of heels," Billie said.

"No way. Beige is not your color." He set the tea down. "Better bring some snacks."

Joel may have already seen Billie's truck, so instead of using that, she got a Tesla from the undercover carpool. Solomon pulled out several CDs he had grabbed from her house and was shocked that there wasn't a CD player.

"Most modern cars don't have one," Billie said.

He shook his head. "March of progress, I guess."

They got to Joel's condo complex, and Billie found a spot near his door to park. It was around a corner, but in view enough that she could see if he left.

"I've never done this," Solomon said, glancing at the condo door.

"Surveillance?"

"Yeah."

"I did this a lot. My father didn't like me out doing anything he considered risky, so sitting somewhere in a car for twelve hours fit the bill. Although I don't know why he let me out on patrol. Seems that's the riskiest of all."

"He knew you had to be thrown into the fire to see if you were really meant for this or not."

"I forget sometimes that you and my father were close."

"One of the best men I've ever known. How's he doing?"

She inhaled deeply. "My mother's gotten worse. We don't know how much longer she has, so my father has been spending every second of his day with her. I keep telling him that he needs to get out of the house and do something, maybe take a community art class or go bowling with friends or something, but he says that as long as she can't go anywhere, he won't either."

"Love makes people do crazy things."

They sat and chatted for a good half an hour before Joel came out of his condo.

Joel had on basketball shorts and a sweatshirt and carried a tennis racket and a white towel. Billie waited until he was pulling out of the complex before she started following him.

"It's been a while since I've tailed anyone."

"Didn't they teach you any tricks at POST?"

"Not much. Tail with three cars and switch up which ones are behind the target is about the only thing I remember. Though I don't think I've ever seen a tail with three teams."

Joel took the surface streets and drove quickly, easily fifteen or twenty miles over the speed limit. He turned down a narrow road up past some snow-capped hills. As Billie trailed behind, her eyes scanned the lavish homes that lined the road, each one flashier than the last.

Solomon and Billie watched as Joel's car turned into the entrance of a nearby country club.

As Joel parked his car and made his way toward a series of tennis courts, Solomon and Billie kept behind him at a safe distance, careful not to draw attention to themselves. The courts were empty of people, but they could see a big white bubble in the distance, likely housing indoor courts.

Joel took a tennis ball from his pocket and bounced it on his racket and headed toward the bubble.

Solomon leaned back in his seat, trying to appear calm even as his mind raced with worry. He knew well that the chances of finding a kidnapping victim decreased by 80 percent if they weren't found within the first forty-eight hours.

"We can't wait," Solomon said.

"That's all this is," Billie said, adjusting the heater. "Waiting and more waiting."

"We don't have the time. Roger and Dennis were killed within twenty-four hours of the last person seeing them alive. If he's sticking to the timeline, we have tonight. Do you really want to spend it sitting outside tennis courts and hoping he goes to where he's holding her?"

"What do you suggest then?"

The cane was between his legs, and he lightly tapped it against the floor of the Tesla.

"This might be one of those instances where the less you know, the better."

"No. Never again. Do you understand me? . . . Solomon, I need you to tell me you understand."

"I understand, but I'm just trying to protect you."

"I don't need protection. I can protect myself. Now what did you have in mind?"

"You're not gonna like it."

"So far, I haven't liked anything about this case. What's one more thing?"

Billie parked the sleek Tesla far from Joel's condo, ensuring that they would remain unnoticed.

As they made their way toward the door of Joel's condo, the tension in the air was intense. They both knew that they were taking a huge risk.

Billie reached into her pocket and pulled out a universal lockpick, her hands moving with the precision of a seasoned professional. She quickly unlocked the cheaper locks on the door, and the sound of them clicking open echoed in the silent hallway.

The two of them stood there for a moment, their hearts pounding.

"You sure about this?" he said. "I could go in alone."

"Let's just get this over with."

Solomon pushed open the door, and they went inside.

41

Solomon walked through the silent condo, taking in his surroundings. The absence of the person who lived there made the place feel different, emptier. Dust swirled in the beams of sunlight that filtered through the partially open windows, the only sign of movement in an otherwise desolate environment.

"Not a good sign," Solomon said. "Guy like this wouldn't leave windows open if he had anything incriminating in here."

Solomon strode over to the laptop on a desk and quickly opened it, but he was immediately met with a password prompt. He considered his options, wondering if he had enough time to take the device to Einstein and have him break into it.

After a moment of contemplation, he decided that it was worth the risk. He quickly closed the laptop and tucked it under his arm, determined to get it to Einstein as soon as possible. He knew that time was running out.

As he turned to face Billie, he saw the disapproving look on her face.

"We've moved up from breaking and entering to burglary."

"I've moved up. You were never here," Solomon said.

Solomon went to the bedroom and opened the closet. It was two sliding brown doors, the type of cheap closets that dorms at colleges would have. Forensic technicians weren't rich, but they weren't starving either. Joel could have likely afforded somewhere nicer—evidenced by the fact that he played tennis at the poshest country club in the city. But Solomon had always believed that people who lived below their means had a type of freedom that most people worked their entire lives for and rarely achieved. He was that way. He wondered if Joel was, too.

Surveying Joel's closet, Solomon found an extravagant array of Armani, Gucci, denim, and more. It contrasted sharply with what appeared to be his frugal lifestyle, resembling a lavish Kardashian wardrobe.

Solomon ran his hand along the shirts and jackets, feeling the soft cloth slide across his fingers, before he looked down to the shoes. At least a dozen pairs, not terribly unusual for professional men his age. Though Solomon preferred one good pair of sneakers and one pair of dress shoes.

The nightstand next to the bed had a drawer with nothing inside but a Bible. Solomon picked it up and flipped through it. A lot of passages were highlighted in yellow marker, and the pages smelled old. The cover was worn out. One of the passages highlighted made him pause and reread it:

They went across the lake to the region of the Gerasenes. When Jesus got out of the boat, a man with an impure spirit came from the tombs to meet him. This man lived in the tombs, and no one could bind him anymore, not even with a chain. For he had often been chained hand and foot, but he tore the chains apart and broke the irons on his feet. No one was strong enough to subdue him. Night and day among the tombs and in the hills he would cry out and cut himself with stones . . .

    Then Jesus asked the unclean spirit, "What is your name?"
    "My name is Legion," he replied, "for we are many."

"Anything interesting?" Billie said.

Solomon was lost in thought when the sound of her voice startled him, causing him to jump slightly. He could feel the heat rising to his cheeks, and he knew she could tell he was embarrassed.

She grinned at his reaction, but then quickly looked away, as if trying to spare him any further embarrassment.

"Yeah, you scared the crap outta me. I'm man enough to admit it."

"Glad to hear it," she said. "What'd you find?"

"Our boy Joel is a religious man," he said, putting the Bible back into the drawer. "But other than that, nothing. You?"

She shook her head. "No."

"Maybe we could get a warrant and come back with—"

"Solomon," she said in a calming voice, "no. This is already too far. We need to leave . . . now."

Solomon looked down to the carpet and tapped his cane. "If she dies . . ."

"I know, but this isn't the way."

Solomon nodded, and they left together. He stopped at the door and glanced back once, and then closed it behind him.

42

Solomon directed Billie to Einstein's house. The home looked pleasant in the afternoon sun, and patches of yellowed grass were visible despite the snow.

"He worked for your dad and now he works for you. Kind of."

"Kind of?"

"Independent consultant. He hates people and prefers not to go out, so hard to maintain a regular nine-to-five that way."

"He sounds lovely."

"You'll like him, promise. There's not many people as interesting as him."

They went up the steps and knocked on the door. Einstein's voice came through a speaker.

"What are you doing here, Solomon?"

"I need another favor."

"Oh no, that's it. That's all I can do. One favor every few years is plenty."

"I need one more and then never again."

"Yeah, right."

"I swear to you, help me this one time and I will never darken your doorstep again. Unless it's to bring you some Twinkies and Mountain Dew Code Red. That's your favorite if I remember, right?"

There was silence and then he said, "How many Twinkies and bottles?"

"A shit ton."

"You and I might have different ideas of what that means."

Solomon scratched his forehead a moment, more to take a pause than because of an itch. Mazie was missing because of him, and he was negotiating over Twinkies.

"Open the door, Brian. I'm not kidding around." He motioned with his head toward Billie. "Maybe you recognize the sheriff?"

"You brought the sheriff to my house? Are you crazy?"

Solomon put his hands on his cane. "Do you know that young woman I came here with?"

"Yeah. She had a thing for me."

"Well, whatever. But she was taken by someone. I need to find her, Brian. Please."

He let out a long breath and said, "All right, come in."

The door unlocked, and Solomon pushed it open, gesturing for Billie to enter ahead of him. She stepped inside, and he shut the door behind them.

They made their way to the basement, the soft sound of their footsteps echoing through the empty space. As they descended the stairs, they could hear the gentle hum of electronics in the distance.

When they finally reached the bottom, they found Einstein sitting at his workstation in front of a wall of monitors, the blue light casting a soft glow over his face. He pushed his glasses up onto his nose and turned to them, a look of intense focus on his face.

"What do you got for me?" he asked with a sigh.

Without a word, Solomon handed Einstein the laptop, the weight of it heavy in his hand. He watched as Einstein quickly got to work, his fingers moving over the keyboard with the precision of a master musician.

"It's password protected," Solomon said.

"That's it?"

"Yeah."

"Gimme something easy, why don't ya," he said with sarcasm dripping in his voice.

Einstein quickly hooked up the computer to a long wire, moving with practiced ease as he worked. He glanced back at Billie, who was lost in admiration of a shelf filled with old toys from the '80s and '90s. The toys looked pristine, as if they had never been touched or played with.

As Billie reached out to touch a Rainbow Brite doll in its box, Einstein spun around, his eyes wide with alarm. "Don't touch that!"

He saw the look on her face and added, "Please and thank you."

Billie looked back to the box. "Quite the collection you have."

"I've been collecting them since I was a kid," he said, turning back to the monitors.

The laptop was unlocked in less than a minute. Einstein motioned with his hand toward it and said, "I'll take my Twinkies now."

"All good things come to something something . . . wait," Solomon said, immediately going onto the laptop and looking through the files.

"What is that?" Einstein said, pushing his glasses up again. "That folder right there."

Solomon clicked on it, and it was secured and wouldn't open without another password. Einstein tried the same one, and it opened.

"Well, that was stupid. People get too lazy with passwords."

"Billie, you better see this."

On the screen was a photograph, black and white but high definition and clear. Billie and Solomon sitting at a café talking. Another photo of Billie leaving her home. Photos of Roger and his wife, of Solomon . . . and of Mazie.

"We had him and we let him go," Solomon said angrily.

Billie was already on the phone to dispatch, but Solomon didn't move.

Einstein said, "What's wrong?"

"We had this guy. We were right there in his condo and could've arrested him."

"So arrest him now."

He shook his head. "If he has half a brain, he's long gone."

Billie hung up the phone and said, "We need to go. Now."

43

Billie drove well over the speed limit, her phone ringing off the hook with calls from dispatch, sergeants, SWAT members, and internal affairs. She tried her best to keep up with the flood of messages, but the constant stream of notifications was overwhelming.

As they raced down the highway, Solomon thought about the implications of Joel Walco's involvement in the case. Though not technically law enforcement, he worked at the Utah State Crime Lab, the primary processing facility for evidence in the state.

The lab handled evidence from every law enforcement agency in Utah, and the thought of how many cases might be affected by Joel's involvement made him feel sick. How many guilty people might walk free? How many innocent people might be wrongly convicted?

The implications were staggering.

Solomon had to hold the grip above the window tightly so he wouldn't slide across the seat when she took a turn so fast her tires were squealing.

"You know there's much more pleasant ways to die than a car crash."

She glanced at him. "Sorry."

He let go of the grip. "We had him, Billie."

"I know."

She got a call just then and listened for a moment before saying, "Are you sure?" After listening to the reply, she said, "Do not engage him. Let me get there first."

She hung up and said, "He's at work. Apparently he went in after tennis."

"Work as in the crime lab?"

"Yes."

Solomon stared straight ahead, tapping his fingers on the grip of his cane.

"I figured you'd be happy at that," Billie said.

He shook his head. "As soon as we left the condo that first time, he should've grabbed a bug-out bag with money and IDs and taken off. That's what I would do."

Billie glanced at him but didn't say anything.

"What?" he said.

"Nothing."

The satellite location of the Utah State Crime Lab in Tooele County was an unremarkable square brick building that looked like it had been built in the '70s. The building was devoid of any character or charm, and its drab exterior seemed to blend in with the bleak, featureless landscape that surrounded it.

Several unmarked cars were already at the crime lab, and the deputies hopped out when Billie did. She hadn't told Solomon to stay in the truck, but the look she gave him said as much. He didn't have a problem with that. He'd seen enough physical altercations to never want to be in one again.

He thought about his home. The comfort of locking himself behind the fences and the motion sensors and alarms, and how much more vulnerable he felt out here. Then he remembered that Joel had already been in his house once, and Solomon still had no idea how he'd done it.

The takedown wasn't much of a takedown. More like a pleasant afternoon walk. Joel came out chatting with the two detectives who held each elbow and was placed in the back of an unmarked SUV. Billie spoke with some of her deputies and then came over to the truck. She had a shocked look on her face, prompting Solomon to ask, "What? What happened?"

"You're not gonna believe this."

Back at the station, Solomon was allowed to watch through the one-way glass as some detectives interviewed Joel.

Solomon gazed into Joel's eyes. Despite the lies people told, the truth always revealed itself through their eyes when they least expected it. It was like a muscle that couldn't be flexed indefinitely.

As Billie approached him, she exhaled heavily before turning to the glass and confirming, "It's true. He's working for the Attorney General's Office."

"You're sure?"

"I spoke with the AG myself. They were conducting an operation investigating corruption in the Tooele County District Attorney's Office. Joel was placed here to gather information about Roger and some higher-ups at the DA's office. And of course me, since Roger and I worked close together occasionally. I'm guessing that's why he was going on a date with Mazie. To get information about me."

Solomon stared at Joel. "I wanna talk to him."

"There's nothing you could do that my detectives can't."

Solomon looked at her. "If this is him, there's no one else that could get him to talk, and you know it."

Billie looked back through the glass at Joel.

"Every victim this guy has taken is dead within twenty-four hours. If Joel's really an undercover investigator from the AG's office, that means we have nothing, and Mazie's twenty-four hours are almost up. We got nothing to lose."

He lightly touched her arm to get her to look at him. "Let me talk to him. Please."

She breathed out through her nose and closed her eyes. "I am so going to regret this."

"Yup, probably. But you're gonna do it anyway because you're awesome like that."

Billie fixed her gaze on him as she approached the door to the interview room. She knocked, then opened it to find her two detectives looking at her with surprise. Parsons spoke up, asking, "What's going on?"

"I need you two to come with me. I want to talk to you about something."

The two detectives exchanged a quick glance; then Parsons shrugged as they both stood up and followed Billie out of the room. As they walked down the hall, Billie discussed a pending case with them, diverting their attention. Once they reached the elevators and the detectives stepped inside, Solomon opened the door and entered the room.

Solomon pulled out the chair and sat down, the scraping sound filling the room with an eerie echo. He used his cane for support and carefully lowered himself onto the seat. Placing the cane between his legs, he rested both hands on the lion's head grip.

"Hi," Solomon said.

Joel let out a sigh and said, "So, what's your role now? The good cop? Did you even speak to the AG?"

Solomon met his gaze, confident in his ability to interrogate suspects. His experience as a social worker in Utah's prison system had given him insight beyond the simplistic use of the Reid technique.

The Reid technique was the prized weapon in a law enforcement interrogator's arsenal, used from Poland to Kenya to Tokyo. It was a calculated and strategic approach that involved building rapport, detecting inconsistencies, and leveraging evidence to extract confessions.

Executing the technique required an air of calmness and a superior ability to solve puzzles and connect dots that others couldn't. However, despite its popularity, the technique was a controversial one that elicited false confessions from innocent individuals.

Solomon was not a fan of the technique and preferred to use other methods. However, he felt compelled to employ it due to the lack of alternative options.

"Don't try to interrogate me," Joel said. "I was a Narcs detective and Vice before that. I don't need your bullshit Reid technique right now."

Solomon didn't say anything.

"That's what you're going to use, right?" Joel said.

"Well . . . not now."

Joel let out a heavy sigh and shook his head before leaning back in the chair, crossing his arms over his chest. "I had nothing to do with Mazie's disappearance," he asserted.

"Really? Because I don't think she would have been at that restaurant if you hadn't been pumping her for information about the sheriff."

"I wasn't—" he said with anger before calming down. "I wasn't pumping her for information."

Solomon tapped his cane against the floor. "She's basically the sheriff's right hand and you wanted dirt on the sheriff. Who better to get it from?"

"Initially I thought that, but I actually liked her."

"So, you weren't going to ask her questions about her work?"

"Not like that."

Solomon held his gaze without saying anything and saw nothing in his eyes but anger and . . . surprise.

"If you had anything to do with this, Joel . . ."

He leaned forward. "I didn't."

Solomon observed him for a moment, feeling a sense of disappointment wash over him as he came to the realization that Joel seemed like he was telling the truth.

"Assume I believe you. Is there anything you can think of that can help me find her?"

Joel hesitated for a moment before finally relenting. He slowly uncrossed his arms and relaxed the tight jaw muscles that had been causing him to clench his teeth. "Were you watching through the glass?"

"I was."

"Then you heard everything I had to say."

"We both know there's always more."

"Not here. Sorry to disappoint, but I don't know anything about her disappearance."

Solomon knew he wasn't going to get anything else, so he rose from his chair and said, "Maybe don't leave town. They'll want to talk to you."

"Who's they?"

"Whoever takes my place."

44

As Solomon exited the interview room, Joel could be heard shouting something about needing to leave. Solomon paid no attention to him and continued down the hallway. Once he was outside, he stood on the steps and took in the view. The sun was starting to set, casting a golden hue on the snow.

He took one last glance at the Public Safety Complex before beginning to walk away. He knew he wouldn't be returning here again.

The frozen sidewalks made a wet crunching sound under his feet, the result of the day's sun melting the ice a little. As he walked, the tip of Solomon's cane became wet, and the small silver cap at the end glinted in the sun. The air was chilly, and he flipped up the collar on his jacket, then tucked his free hand into his pocket.

Mazie's kidnapping and the recent string of murders weighed heavily on him. He couldn't shake the grisly image of Mazie, her body desecrated by the killer's twisted precision, her lifeblood drained away. Her once-vibrant face now pallid, and depending on the time it took to find her, her eyes turning milky white. It was the eyes that haunted him the most, embedding themselves deep into his psyche. His nightmares, growing more frequent as the years wore on, were filled with the unseeing gazes of the dead, their silent accusations echoing in his thoughts.

He had sent a text on the Nokia phone and checked it now for a reply, but there was none.

Solomon had been pondering the identity of the ghost on the other end of that phone nonstop and could come up with nothing.

Why mimic the suicide of his mother? Was it a message, or a taunt aimed at him? He considered the individuals he had encountered throughout his life, searching for connections and patterns that might lead him to something. The people he had helped as a social worker, the ones he had put away as a prosecutor, even those within his personal circle—anyone. But no one fit. The darkness could hide inside anyone.

Strength left him, and he didn't feel he could walk anymore. A metal bench was near him, and he sat down and stared at the ground. A text came through on his phone, Billie asking him where he went. He turned the phone off and took out the Nokia phone. He texted one sentence: Let her live and I'll do whatever you say.

After waiting a long time with no response, Solomon turned off the Nokia and pulled out his own phone to summon an Uber. The cold bit his nose and cheeks and made his fingers feel like icicles around the cane, but he was relieved when a black sedan arrived promptly, and he got into the back seat.

The driver was amiable and tried to initiate a conversation multiple times, but Solomon didn't have the energy to engage and remained silent.

The home was smaller but in a decent neighborhood with snow frosting the roof. Solomon got out of the car and slowly walked the path leading to the front door. There was no porch, and he knocked and waited. A half a minute later, Zachary Gray answered the door.

The old man looked every bit his age. When younger, he was barrel chested, with thick arms from a lifetime of hard labor until he discovered that becoming a police officer was his calling. Now, he was hunched over with a cane. Solomon looked down to Zach's cane and smiled, and the old man smiled back.

"I think mine is bigger than yours," Solomon said.

Zach chuckled. "Come in, smart-ass."

The home had a pleasant fragrance, but the furniture had been covered with transparent plastic sheets. There were no dishes out, no messes. The home was getting ready for its owners' departure.

Zachary Gray had always been a strong and resilient man. For some reason, Solomon had never considered the possibility of the old man's death. But death wasn't necessary to humble someone. Time, the cruelest force in existence, had taken its pound of flesh from Zachary.

Zach motioned with his head toward the couch, and Solomon settled onto the plastic-covered surface, producing a crumpling sound as his weight pressed down. He noticed that the mantel was adorned with nothing but photographs of Billie and her brother from when they were children. On the wall were pictures of them from various stages of their lives.

Solomon's attention was drawn to a photograph of Billie as a toddler, then as a kid, and later as a teenager. In one photo, she had green hair and a giant nose piercing, while in the next, her head was shaved, and she was sporting what was clearly a fake tattoo on her neck.

Zach appeared from the other room carrying a beer and a cup of tea. He placed the tea on the coffee table before settling into the only piece of furniture not covered in plastic, a beat-up recliner. As he sat down, he let out a groan of discomfort. Solomon could see that the old man's ankles were swollen, his skin discolored, and his veins blue and slithery.

Solomon couldn't bring himself to take a sip of tea even to be polite. Instead, he leaned back on the couch and looked up to the photos of Billie.

"I can't imagine her teenage years were easy."

He shook his head as he took a sip of beer. "You wouldn't believe it. Her and her mother. I'd come home from work and find them screaming at each other, and it would end with Billie shouting she hates her and her mother shouting good 'cause I hate you, too."

He grinned. "I can't picture Billie like that. She's so calm and collected."

"It's a wall. She thinks she needs it to be tough, but one day she'll find out being yourself is much less work."

Zach took another sip of beer and then put the bottle down onto the coffee table. Solomon noticed a little splashed up over the lip and onto the table because Zach's hands were trembling. He would get tremors but only when he was at rest, and his movements were slow.

"Parkinson's?" Solomon asked gravely.

Zach stared at him, his eyes narrowing a moment, and Solomon knew it was something he wanted to keep hidden, but it had reached a point that he couldn't.

"Yeah."

Solomon nodded. "Does Billie know?"

"No. And she better not, Sol."

"Of course not. That's between you and her. If you want my two cents—"

"I don't."

Solomon looked away at some other photos. "You were always a cranky bastard when you were sick. I can't tell you how many times I wanted to clock you when you'd come into court while you were sick because you refused to take a day off."

"Man's gotta eat."

"Man's gotta sometimes sit there and do nothing, too. Doing nothing is important if you want to be creative, especially if you're sick."

He smiled and leaned back in his seat with a small groan from whatever pain was in his back. "Was that your philosophy in prosecuting cases?"

"It's my philosophy of life. I'm serious, Zach. You have to sometimes do nothing. That's why everybody's miserable and angry and jumping from compulsion to compulsion. They don't set aside any time to just sit and do nothing."

"My wife doesn't remember who I am, Sol. I bathe her, put her to bed, get her up in the mornings, get her dressed, feed her, give her the million pills she has to take that's shutting her body down, and then I have to start it all over the next morning. Every day of every month of the year . . . some of us don't have the luxury of doing nothing."

"Sorry, I didn't mean it that way."

Solomon tapped his cane a few times.

"Do you remember when I was lying in the hospital after I got stabbed, and they told me that I might never walk again?"

Zach nodded sadly. "I do. You told me that you wanted to kill yourself."

"I meant it."

"I know you did."

Solomon let out a deep breath. "I feel like that now."

"Why?"

"I keep getting people around me hurt." He looked out the windows as the sun had set and twilight began to descend. "My mother once called it the Shepard's Curse."

He finally took a sip of his tea, and it was hot and tasted smooth.

Zach observed Solomon for a brief moment before they were interrupted by the sound of footsteps coming from behind them. Solomon turned around to find Billie's mother emerging from the bedroom, dressed in a nightgown. Her complexion was pale, and even in the fading light, he could see the thin blue veins that started in her neck.

"Don't let them bury me on a Sunday," she said. "They charge too much extra to be buried on a Sunday."

Zach placed his beer down and stood up, approaching his wife with a gentle touch on her arm so as not to startle her. But she barely seemed to notice. Her gaze was fixed forward, possibly lost in a memory from a long time ago.

"Zachary, we have a guest," she suddenly said. "How rude of you not to get him some tea."

"That is rude of me, darling. Let me get you back to your room and I'll get him some."

"And make sure to use the honey from the white honey pot. It's local."

"I will."

As Solomon waited for Zach, he surveyed the living room, taking in his surroundings. His chest felt tight and heavy, and his headache had intensified, and now his neck was hurting, too. It seemed as though his body was gradually shutting down one section at a time, and he wasn't sure if he even cared.

Zach returned and sat down.

"Poor woman forgets everyone, Sol. Don't take it personal."

"Never. Thank her for me for the cookies she would bring me in the hospital. It gave me something to look forward to."

Zach nodded and said, "Remember when you would come over at all hours and we would run through the Reaper case until four or five in the morning and you'd crash for a few hours on that awful couch I had in the basement?"

He smiled. "I can't imagine how much dust I've inhaled from that thing."

"Well, you know what I noticed about all those times? You were stuck. I was like a springboard to you that you needed to bounce ideas off. You would lecture in a way. I found it annoying as horseshit until I figured out that the way you work through a problem is by explaining it to other people. So, am I right?"

Solomon nodded. "How much do you know about all this?"

"A lot. I spoke with Billie last night."

Solomon leaned forward, elbows on knees. "This one took someone, a police officer, in the middle of rush hour traffic in front of a restaurant. He took her because of me. This is my fault, Zach. It's about me."

Zach picked up his beer again and took a sip. "Do you know what your biggest problem is, Sol? You live in your head. It's not your fault, most really smart people do. But the problem is what's in your head isn't what's outside your head."

"Of all my faults you think that's the worst?"

"No, but it does make you blind sometimes. That's why we worked so well together. I don't wanna live anywhere near my head. What I'm saying is you think too damn much, Sol."

He chuckled. "If I had a nickel for every time you said that to me, I'd have like twenty cents, but I still remember it really well."

Zach chuckled. He took a long drink of his beer and then pointed at Solomon and said, "So you've done every fancy trick in the book and you still don't see him. What's left?"

Solomon shrugged. "I don't know. Nothing."

"No, there's something."

"I don't know what else to do, Zach."

He sighed. "You look at dumb shit."

"What?"

"Dumb. Shit."

Solomon at first thought maybe Zach had mixed too much alcohol with medication, but he remembered that Zach had told him this before. They were discussing the Oklahoma City bombing. Timothy McVeigh had been caught because a police officer had pulled him over for not having a license plate the morning of the bombing. Zach had said, "It's always the dumb shit that gets you."

The Son of Sam had been caught because he'd gotten a parking ticket on the night of a killing. Richard Kint murdered young prostitutes in Toronto in the late '70s and was only caught because of a flat tire. While attempting to flee a canal he'd dumped his latest victim in, the tire went out, and he had to pull to the side of the road and turn on his hazards. Completely by chance, a police officer was heading home after a shift and pulled over to help him and noticed the droplets of blood all over Kint's clothes.

"The first two scenes," Solomon said, more to himself than Zach, "the first two scenes he wasn't in a rush to dump them, but he was probably in a rush to get away."

"Not probably. There's a few laws of human nature, Sol, and one of them is when you've done something bad, your first instinct is to run."

Solomon nodded. "On a subconscious level he would want to get away as fast as he could. He might've made some mistakes."

Zach smiled and held up his beer. "To dumb shit."

Solomon grinned and pushed off his cane. "I gotta go."

"I know."

"I'll come by after this is all done. Maybe we can go fishing again?"

"Thought you hated fishing."

He shrugged. "I just liked being out there with you, old man."

Solomon reached out and gently placed his hand on Zach's shoulder, keeping it there for a moment. He thought he noticed Zach's eyes glistening with tears, but the old man looked away too quickly, and Solomon couldn't be sure.

Solomon slowly made his way toward the front door. Zach didn't follow, but he called out from behind him. "Sol?"

Solomon turned around to face the old man. "Yeah?" he replied.

Zach looked at him with a sense of urgency in his eyes. "Do this old man a favor and watch out for his little girl," he said.

"I'm pretty sure I'm the one she watches out for, but I will," Solomon assured him, his voice gentle. He paused, his mind racing with thoughts and emotions he couldn't put into words. As soon as he said, "Zach," in a soft voice, the old man cut him off with a simple "I know. No need to say it."

Solomon nodded before he left and shut the door behind him, knowing that this might be the last time they would ever see each other.

45

Solomon took the steps and approached the front door later that night.

He knocked, then rang the doorbell, then pounded on the door, then shouted, and even resorted to calling and texting, but to no avail. He persisted for a good ten minutes before Einstein finally responded through the intercom on his porch, his voice laced with annoyance. "Go away," he grumbled.

"Open the door, Brian," Solomon said in his most serious tone.

"No way. I've done enough. And I still don't have any Twinkies or Dew to show for it."

"I'll get you double what I promised if you help me."

"No way."

Solomon hated bringing things like this up, but there was no way around it now. "Remember when your dad got arrested for visiting an escort agency, Brian? What did I do?"

There was a long, uncomfortable silence, and then finally the door opened. Einstein stood there with a look of disgust etched on his face, letting his glasses practically fall off his nose as he folded his arms over his MIT hoodie.

"I can't believe you brought that up. You didn't say that was a favor. You just said you would help him."

"Everything's a favor. Just a matter of when the favor gets called in."

Einstein stood there, arms folded and scowling. "I don't have to help you, you know. Even if you did do that."

"Then I'll call your dad and get him down here. I'll tell him that I took care of him when he needed it and you won't even help me find the man who killed the district attorney and kidnapped a police officer."

Einstein let out a deep sigh, his irritation apparent in his demeanor. "I hate you," he grumbled under his breath.

Solomon responded with a simple "I know," before Einstein relented and opened the door all the way, letting him inside.

Just as Solomon was about to step in, a pair of headlights circled around the house and parked out front. Billie emerged from her truck and made her way toward the porch, causing Einstein to shake his head in irritation.

Solomon turned to Billie as she approached the porch. "Einstein's agreed to help us. In exchange, I promised him that we won't pretend he tried to assault you, and shoot him in the kneecaps."

Einstein stared at both of them. "You wouldn't really do that, right?"

Solomon held his gaze and replied in a firm tone, "You have no idea how far I'd go to find this man."

Einstein groaned and started making his way down to his basement, with Solomon and Billie following closely behind. Once they reached the basement, he walked over to a plush leather chair with a pair of gaming headphones slung over them and sat down.

Solomon turned to Billie and said, "Thanks for coming."

"Sounded urgent."

"It is."

They went over to the rig, the screens blinking blues and greens. Solomon leaned on his cane and said, "I've been focusing on the cleverness of this man. How he's able to plan and cover. What I should have been focusing on is the dumb shit."

Einstein looked at him with a puzzled expression and said, "The what?"

"You can't plan for the dumb shit. That's where I should've been looking. Son of Sam was busted because he got a parking ticket. Richard Kint because of a flat tire. People like this fantasize about their crimes for years, sometimes decades, before they carry them out, but the fantasy doesn't include the dumb shit. It doesn't include, 'What if I get a parking ticket or my tire goes flat?'"

Billie immediately said, "Moving violations."

"Exactly."

Billie turned to Einstein and said, "Get the two addresses of the first victims and look for moving violations that occurred within a dozen miles of each location on those days."

Einstein went to work, his fingers moving with an expert speed that Solomon could only admire. He had the choice between taking an extra gym class or typing in high school, and he took gym and now he couldn't type. One of life's small decisions that becomes a big decision.

"Okay," Einstein said. "Now what?"

Billie said, "Narrow it down to within a couple of hours of the estimated times of death of each victim."

Solomon added, "Especially focusing on my house. It's out in the middle of nowhere, but there's a speed trap on the freeway on-ramp. It's like shooting fish in a barrel for the patrol guys."

Einstein adeptly navigated through various databases, with the ease and dexterity of someone who had done it a thousand times before. As he searched, Solomon couldn't help but reflect on how technology had completely transformed law enforcement. The next generation of officers and prosecutors would have no familiarity with the feel of paper files or the scent of fresh ink from a judge's signature on a hard-won motion.

"Sorry for just taking off at the station," he said to Billie, snapping out of his thoughts.

"Why did you leave without telling me?"

"I just had to get out of there. I knew it wasn't him. Was he pissed?"

"Yes, and so was the AG. I'll smooth it over, though."

Einstein said, "All right, here's your dumb shit. Rolling stop signs, jumping lights, not using turn signals, yada yada."

"Gotta love the dumb shit."

Billie said, "You sound like my father."

Solomon grinned.

"Look for speeding tickets near my house."

Einstein punched some keys and said, "On the day Roger died, there were eleven speeding tickets given in a ten-mile radius of your house. Man, that really is a speed trap, huh?"

"Now eliminate any motorcycles because he would need room to get the body to my house."

"Ten left."

"Now get rid of all the people over sixty."

A few more key taps and he said, "Seven left. What else?"

Billie said, "Eliminate all the female drivers." Solomon glanced at her, and she said, "We both know which sex is responsible for all the wars in history. It's a good bet we're after a man."

"Three left."

Billie folded her arms and said, "Pull them up."

Three driver's licenses came up on one of the screens.

"That one, Chad Wilson, he's got a disability on his license. What is it?"

"Um . . . code 217. What is that?"

Billie said, "Amputation or loss of limbs."

Solomon said, "Yeesh. You'd figure the officers would cut him a break. Our guy would be able bodied. Lose Wilson . . . so we got Steven Hall and Aziz Darwish. Pull up their criminal histories."

"A please would be nice."

"Pretty please. With sugar on top."

Einstein pulled up criminal histories on Steven Hall and Aziz Darwish as though he were googling their names.

"So," Einstein said, "your guy Aziz immigrated to the United States three years ago, no criminal history."

Einstein hit a few more keys.

"Huh," he said.

Solomon took a step closer to the rig and leaned down over his shoulder to be able to see the screen clearly. "What?"

"The other guy, Steven Hall, he's got a criminal history going back to 1985, but I'm looking at this guy's picture and there's no way. He would've been like five probably."

"A forgery," Billie said. "A good one, too."

Solomon couldn't make out much in the driver's license photo. "Can you make the photo larger?"

"Yeah. It's a DMV photo and they kinda suck, but . . . there."

The driver's license came up on one of the other screens. Blown up in high definition.

Solomon stared blankly at the screen. He felt a warmth dribbling down his body from his head, covering his limbs, making his muscles burn and his bones ache. Then he felt nothing. Numb and stunned. He took a deep breath to steady himself, but it didn't help, and he nearly lost his footing as his leg gave out.

Billie grabbed his arm, preventing him from falling, and said, "Solomon, are you all right?"

He pulled away from her and said, "I need to go."

"Where?" Billie said.

As Solomon rushed out the door, the cold winter air hit him, causing his head to spin. His stomach churned, and he felt hot bile rising in his throat. He stumbled down the porch, barely holding on to the railings, and doubled over and vomited. He heaved and gagged. His eyes watered, and his body convulsed as he emptied the contents of his stomach onto the ground. Finally, as the last of it came up, he wiped his mouth with the back of his hand, feeling the chill of the winter air against his damp skin.

He took out the Nokia phone and turned it on. Billie was outside now, approaching him, and he hurriedly texted one line:

I know who you are

A moment later, the text came back:

Good. Then we can meet

46

Solomon washed his mouth out with Scope in Einstein's bathroom. After he splashed water on his face, he looked down into the sink, only to see the clear water slowly getting darker and darker until it turned into a thick black liquid that splashed up out of the sink. Blood.

The sight of the blood made him freeze, and his heart raced. He closed his eyes and took a deep breath, trying to calm his nerves. When he opened his eyes again, the blood was gone, and the water in the sink was clear again.

Solomon turned off the faucet and wiped his face with a towel. As he reached for the doorknob, he hesitated, feeling a prickling sensation on the back of his neck. He looked back at the sink, half expecting the water to have turned to blood again. The air felt thick and oppressive, and the bathroom seemed darker than before. Suddenly, he heard a faint whisper, like a voice on the edge of his hearing. He spun around, heart pounding, but the bathroom was empty.

Solomon walked into the hallway leading to the living room, his hands still trembling. He leaned against the wall and closed his eyes.

When he opened his eyes, his vision was spinning, and he had to grab the wall to steady himself. He took a step forward and stumbled, his head feeling heavy and his vision blurry. He made his way to the living room, feeling like he was moving in slow motion. The smell of fresh coffee filled the room, and he could hear the soft hum of music coming from a nearby speaker. He collapsed onto the couch, feeling drained and weak, and closed his eyes for a moment to regain his composure.

Einstein lounged on a recliner, with one leg casually draped over the armrest, while the other anxiously tapped against the carpet in a flurry of restless energy. Billie had gone into the kitchen. She came out and handed Solomon a coffee and said, "No tea here."

"Tea's for the British," Einstein said. "We drink coffee in America."

"Thanks," Solomon said to her.

"I think we should have someone look at you."

He grinned. Instead of asking him what caused his reaction, she had first asked if he was okay.

"I'm fine now, thanks."

Solomon winced in pain, the brightness of the light worsening his already pounding migraine.

"I know who he is."

"Who is he?" she said calmly.

"I can't tell you."

"What?" Billie's voice carried an incredulous tone, the disbelief evident in the way her eyebrows furrowed and her mouth twisted in a mixture of shock and anger. She leaned in toward Solomon. "I know you can't be serious."

Einstein, on his phone and seemingly not paying attention, blurted out, "He's serious."

"You have to trust me on this one, Billie."

"I don't have to do anything. Do you know what this sounds like?"

"I do, and I'm sorry, but I have to do this myself."

She sighed and looked away, and he softly said, "I hate this. I wish I could fix it all with a snap of my fingers, but I can't. I can only do what I think is best."

She let a breath out and said, "All right. I'll trust you."

"Okay, then I need to go somewhere, and I need you not to follow me. Can you do that?"

"Solomon, what is going on?"

"Just tell me you won't follow me. Promise me. Let me handle this. I'll call you as soon as I'm able and tell you where I am."

They held each other's gaze a moment and then she said, "If that's what you think is best. I'll be waiting with tactical ready to go when you give the word."

"Tactical?" Einstein said, turning his head now. "Is that like the SWAT team? I wanna see the SWAT team."

Solomon looked at her, his expression one of both regret and sorrow. "Promise me you'll let me handle this my way."

She hesitated but then nodded.

As the car drove on, a vast field opened up before Solomon in the dark night, and he gazed out from the back seat at the horses and cows. In the moonlight, he could only make out their silhouettes, but the flash of the headlights occasionally revealed their features. Many animals froze when headlights hit them, an instinctual response to potential danger. Humans had a similar reaction.

"There's nothing up here," the Uber driver said. "These houses are all empty. I don't think anybody's lived up here for years."

Solomon kept his gaze out the window. "There's a small road coming up on the right. Please take it."

The driver's car bounced and jolted as they traveled down the old road with its cracked pavement. This neighborhood had seen better days, back when it was filled with middle-class families. Now, the abandoned homes and empty storefronts painted a picture of decline and neglect.

Solomon peered out the window, taking in the boarded-up buildings and empty lots where gardens and playgrounds used to be. He could see the faint outlines of where signs and awnings used to hang, faded remnants of a time when this was a bustling little town center.

As the car turned onto a cul-de-sac, Solomon's heart started racing, and his stomach twisted into knots. The headlights illuminated the beige house, its shape a hauntingly familiar sight. The windows were dark and ominous, causing a chill that sent shivers down Solomon's spine.

As the car came to a stop in front of the house, Solomon gazed at it in disbelief, his childhood memories flooding back to him. It was the same house his parents had brought him to when he was born, the same house where he had grown up, the same house where his mother had died.

Solomon stepped out of the car in silence, the wind whipping around him as he approached the front door of his childhood home. The door was blocked with red tape in an X shape, the word "Caution" printed in bold letters along its length. A torn and weathered notice of demolition was pasted onto the front door. Without a word, Solomon pulled the tape off and tried the door. It let out a creak as he pushed it open.

As Solomon stepped inside, the silence was deafening. The musty air made it hard to breathe. The cobwebs clung to his face and hair, making him feel like he was trapped in a spider's web. The darkness was suffocating, and he fumbled for a light switch, his hand shaking. When he finally found it, the flickering light only added to the sense of unease. He took a step forward, but his foot hit something and he stumbled, nearly falling to the floor. He quickly grabbed onto a nearby table, trying to steady himself. The sound echoed throughout the house, making him feel as if he wasn't alone.

Solomon froze, his body locked in place as a wave of memories washed over him, threatening to overwhelm his senses. The pain was all consuming, every inch of his being screaming with it. He closed his eyes, trying to calm himself down, but the memories continued to assault him. The peeling wallpaper, the creaking floors, the sounds of his parents screaming at each other late into the night. The sound of his father's fists hitting her, the feel of a belt against his face and chest and arms . . . the stickiness of his mother's blood all over his hands.

He felt trapped in this place. It was as if the walls were strangling him. The pain wasn't just physical but spiritual, a deep ache that he couldn't fight.

In the living room, there were only a few items left, all from previous tenants who had lived in the house after it was sold. Solomon's parents had died with no heirs of legal age since he and his brother were minors. The Court sold the house in probate, and after fees and taxes, there was barely any money left in the trust. But he didn't mind: he was going to give all the money to charity anyway. He didn't want anything from this place.

The old wooden floors beneath Solomon's feet groaned with every step. He made his way to the kitchen, the linoleum creaking and crackling under his weight. As he entered the room, a sudden image flashed in his mind—a young boy rounding the corner and catching a glimpse of his mother at the sink. He remembered how beautiful she looked, the sunlight streaming through the window and illuminating her face. But that image quickly morphed into a horrifying memory of her corpse, pale and lifeless with milky-white eyes. The thought sent a chill down his spine, making him shudder.

Solomon found an old wooden table pushed against the wall. The surface was scratched and stained, and the chairs surrounding it were worn and creaky. As he sat down, a drumbeat sounded in his chest, and he struggled to catch his breath. He focused on the table, tracing the grooves and knots in the wood with his fingers, trying to ground himself in the present moment. He started to breathe deeply, inhaling through his nose and exhaling through his mouth, willing his nervous system to calm down and his body to relax. He repeated the process until he felt his heart rate slow and his mind clear.

Solomon rose and went to the master bedroom. His parents' bedroom.

He approached the door, and his heart pounded so hard against his ribs he thought he might pass out. As he turned the knob, the door creaked open slowly, revealing the dark, musty room inside. The air was thick with dust, and the furniture was covered in white sheets, giving the impression that no one had been there in a long time. Though lots of tenants had lived here since, he thought the room was frozen in time, just as it had been the day his mother died.

Solomon stepped inside and took a deep breath, trying to steady himself. The memories flooded back, overwhelming him. The sight of his mother's lifeless body lying on the bed, the sound of his own screams echoing in his ears, the smell of death lingering in the air. He closed his eyes, fighting back tears, and then opened them again to face the room.

As he stood there in the doorway, Solomon's breathing grew shallow.

For a moment, a part of him had expected to see his mother still lying there, lifeless and pale.

But the room was empty, and the only sound was the faint creaking of the old floor beneath his feet. There was no furniture here.

He went back to the kitchen table, sat down, and waited.

47

Billie left Einstein's shortly after Solomon.

As she waited at a stoplight, Billie stared out the windshield, her mind racing with all the ways she could track down Solomon. But she didn't act on any of them. She had promised to let him handle it, and as she thought about it more, she realized it was for the best. Solomon clearly knew who they were looking for, and if she was right about who it was, she understood why Solomon hadn't said anything.

As she entered the station, a wave of discomfort came over her, and the thought of interacting with anyone made her stomach churn. But she needed her coat and firearm, so she pressed on. The first people she saw were two deputies who acknowledged her with a nod but didn't greet her. Billie returned the gesture and hurried on. She wondered how her work with internal affairs, investigating these people's comrades and colleagues, would affect her relationships with fellow officers.

Internal Affairs departments weren't like other departments within a law enforcement agency. They policed the police, so there was some natural resentment from rank-and-file officers. The problem was when IAD investigators identified more with the rank and file than the public. That was when bad shootings became good shootings through vague reports, or officers that were accused of horrible things were quietly transferred to other divisions.

The power of investigation that was held by IAD was transferred by the legislature to the county attorney in the same county where the law enforcement agency was located. The idea was to reduce bias, but it didn't really help. Most prosecution agencies worked closely with the police and saw them as part of their team. If prosecutors couldn't be trusted to uphold the law equally, even for one of their own, the system would break down and not work.

As Billie approached her desk, she noticed a Post-it Note from her assistant informing her of a delivery of documents that had been locked away in her bottom drawer. She retrieved her keys and unlocked the drawer to find a manila folder containing the commissioner's ruling in Dax's stalking case. The commissioner had determined that there was insufficient evidence to suggest that she was an immediate danger to him, and thus had denied his request for a protective order. She grinned to herself as she tossed the papers onto her desk and gathered her things before she left.

Billie parked her truck in her driveway and took a moment to breathe in the cold air. She gazed up at the full moon with its yellowish tint and shivered as a gust of wind swept over her. Once she had locked up her truck, she made her way inside.

After she turned off the house alarm, Billie switched on the foyer light. The floor was mostly covered by a rug that had been passed down from her grandmother to her mother, and then to her. Though Billie didn't like the rug, and found it to be ugly, she couldn't bring herself to get rid of it. It was the only thing she had that reminded her of her grandmother.

As she walked to the kitchen, Billie felt her phone vibrate in her pocket. She took it out, annoyed at the interruption. But when she answered, the voice on the other end was unfamiliar. Before she could say anything else, her eyes caught a glimpse of something in her peripheral vision. Something wet and red in the center of the kitchen floor. Her heart leaped in her chest as she slowly turned her head to look.

Dax.

Lying face down in a thick pool of blood that surrounded his body like a macabre halo.

Billie's phone slipped from her hand and clattered loudly against the floor. She let out a gasp, her mind racing with a mix of horror and disbelief.

"Elizabeth," a male voice said from behind her. "It is so nice to finally meet you."

48

Solomon's eyes fluttered open, and he was disoriented for a moment, not sure where he was. As he tried to move, he felt a sharp pain in his neck and realized he had fallen asleep in a chair. Slowly, he straightened his back and stretched his muscles. He looked around the room, taking in the familiar surroundings of his childhood home.

As he came to his senses, he realized a sound had woken him up: it was the engine of a car that had since stopped running. He rubbed his face and stretched before making his way to the front door with the help of his cane. When he stood a few feet away from the door, his heart thumped loudly, and he felt acutely aware of the sound of his own blood flowing through him.

Solomon heard crunching snow and the approaching footsteps, growing louder and louder until they reached the porch. He heard the boots stomp on the wooden surface, and a muffled sound followed as if the person was wiping snow off. Then, the door creaked open, and a man came in, his form silhouetted by the dim moonlight that filtered in through the windows. Flakes of snow clung to his hair and coat, and his shoulders were damp from the wetness outside.

Ethan Shepard's face lit up with a wide smile, revealing his perfectly straight, white teeth. His curly brown hair, damp with snow, framed his chiseled features, and his athletic frame filled the doorway. Unlike Solomon, who had always been slight and sickly, his brother had developed a strong and muscular build during his teenage years. Solomon always felt a twinge of envy at his brother's robust physique, and he became suddenly very aware of his cane.

"Hi" was all Solomon managed to say.

"Hi."

Solomon and Ethan stood in a heavy silence, each waiting for the other to break it.

Solomon couldn't tell if Ethan was at a loss for words or just didn't want to speak first. He studied Ethan's face, searching for any clues in his expression.

"You actually didn't bring anybody else here," Ethan said. "I'm both impressed and shocked."

Solomon put his hands over his cane. "Why are you doing this?"

Ethan looked around as he inhaled a deep breath. "When was the last time you were back here?"

Solomon's eyes were fixed on Ethan's face, which had now lost its youthful sheen. Lines etched across his forehead, and there were faint creases around his mouth that suggested a lot of smiles and a lot of frowns. Not the face he remembered from youth.

"I haven't been back here. I want you to leave, Ethan."

"Leave? You mean you're not arresting me? I thought you were a lawman? Out to get his bad guy? Only in this case, the bad guy turned out to be you, didn't it?"

Another silence passed.

"I knew you'd be here, Solomon, but I don't really like it here. I want to take you somewhere else."

"Where?"

"I'll show you. Come on."

Ethan left, and Solomon was alone, standing in the doorway. He felt like he was disconnected from his body, and his thoughts were floating aimlessly, like they belonged to someone else.

From outside, Ethan said, "Come on, baby bro. We got things to do."

Solomon hesitated and then followed him out.

The black car blended in with the darkness of the night. Solomon cautiously climbed into the passenger seat and scanned the interior before settling in. As Ethan started the engine and fastened his seat belt, he gestured toward Solomon's seat belt and said, "Safety first."

Solomon was in a daze, his mind elsewhere. He didn't move, and Ethan noticed, so he reached over and grabbed the seat belt, pulled it over Solomon's chest, and buckled it securely. Solomon barely registered the movement, his mind still lost in his thoughts.

"Where we going?" Solomon asked.

Ethan backed up and then flipped around. "I'm not going to hurt you, if that's what you're asking."

"It's not."

"Why not?"

"If you wanted to, you would have by now."

He nodded. "Sound reasoning." Ethan looked at him again. "You look really thin. And pale. Are you sick?"

Solomon didn't respond as he stared out the window.

"Sorry for chasing you in the car, baby bro. I just wanted to have a little bit of fun. Keep you on your toes."

Solomon didn't move his gaze from the window. "Where are we going, Ethan?"

"Relax. You'll like it."

Solomon had never seen the bar before. It was small and tucked away behind a restaurant, surrounded by tall trees, with no signage to indicate its presence. The place had a certain grime to it and had seen better days.

"What is this place?"

"A bar."

"I don't want to go to a bar, Ethan."

"Oh, come on. Don't be a Grumpy Gus. We haven't seen each other in, what, thirty years? I've been dreaming about having a beer with my long-lost baby bro forever, Solomon."

Solomon didn't say anything and didn't look at him.

"Okay," Ethan said, "well, I'm going in and having some expensive foreign beer to celebrate. I'm sure you have a lot of questions, so if you want them answered, I'll be inside."

Solomon hesitated as Ethan got out of the car and walked into the small unmarked bar. He pulled out his phone but paused before calling Billie. What would happen if the police arrived before he had a chance to talk to Ethan? He couldn't bear the thought of his own brother facing the death penalty. Instead, Solomon considered talking to Ethan and trying to convince him to turn himself in. If he could persuade the interim DA to take the death penalty off the table and avoid a federal case, there might be a chance to save Ethan's life.

He opened the door and got out.

As Ethan disappeared into the bar, Solomon took a deep breath and followed him inside.

The interior was poorly lit, but the warm glow of neon beer signs and several televisions flickering with various sports made up for it. The air was thick with the smell of alcohol and sweat, but there was also a faint scent of wood that mingled with it. Solomon assumed it was from the open windows that allowed the night air to seep in. Despite it being a weekday night, the place was surprisingly packed, and Solomon felt uneasy as he scanned the crowd.

Ethan was sitting at a booth with two beers in front of him. As Solomon approached the booth, he could hear Ethan humming along to the pop-country song that was playing. The booth was in the back of the bar, and the dim lighting and the crowded atmosphere made it feel like a secret place. Ethan's grin was inviting, and Solomon felt a sense of familiarity in his brother's expression.

The table was sticky with spilled drinks. Solomon's eyes darted around the bar, and he saw a few men in the corner playing pool.

Ethan said, "You look like you're about to have a panic attack. Do I really scare you that much?"

Solomon wasn't about to tell him it had nothing to do with him, but more to do with the fact that he was in a crowded bar. He hadn't been around this many people crowded into a tight space in half a decade, and he had no idea that his reaction would be so severe.

"I can't be in here," he said, rising.

"Easy," Ethan said, grabbing his arm as he wobbled. "It's the crowd, right? They have a patio with heaters. Come on."

Ethan led him to a table directly under a heater, and they both sat down. He placed two bottles of beer on the table and slid one over to Solomon.

"You look like you could use it."

Solomon's throat felt like he'd swallowed sandpaper, and despite wanting to turn down anything Ethan offered him, he took a few sips of the beer.

"It's good, right?"

Solomon felt his heart calming, the acid in his stomach dissipating. He took a breath before saying, "What makes you think I didn't just call the police?"

"Because if you wanted to see me with a needle in my arm, you would've told Billie where you were going."

Hearing Billie's name from Ethan's mouth sent revulsion through Solomon, and of all the emotions he was able to keep in check, revulsion was the one that he couldn't. His face must've twisted in an odd way because Ethan laughed and said, "Don't like that I know about how close you two are, huh? Are you in love with her?"

Solomon ignored his question and said, "Did you take that girl?"

"Yes."

"Where is she?"

289

Ethan looked down to his beer as he played with the lip of the bottle. "Do you know that Harold died?"

"Dad's brother?"

He nodded. "He was the last one, Solomon. The Shepard line is now officially you and me. It lives or dies with us."

"Maybe it wouldn't have been that way if Mom hadn't died," Solomon said with a subtle meaning that only his brother could have picked up.

He scoffed, "Yeah. That. Do you know what it's like, Solomon, to be fourteen years old, to have lost both your parents, and to sit in a cold room with two male detectives grilling you for twenty hours?" He looked up from his beer. "Twenty hours, because my little brother decided to tell them that I had something to do with her death."

"Did you?"

"I think if you really believed that, you would have brought the police with you."

Solomon shifted his gaze toward the waitress approaching their table. He nodded in response to her question and requested a glass of water, his throat parched. Ethan tapped the nearly empty bottle of beer and gestured for another. The waitress jotted down their orders and walked away, leaving them in a brief moment of silence.

"So, I saw you never married," Ethan said, "but are there any little Solomons running around?"

"No. But you already knew that. I'm guessing you know everything about me."

He nodded as he took a drink. "Good guess. This has been a long time in the making. I'm still a little shocked it's happening right now. That you're actually sitting here in front of me."

Solomon just managed to swallow down the taste of bile. The fake civility he was showing made him uncomfortable. All he remembered about Ethan was cruelty and little else.

"Why? Why would you kill innocent people to get my attention?"

"What was I supposed to do? Walk up to your house and say, 'Hey, it's the brother who grew up in a mental institution that you accused of killing our mother. Wanna grab a beer?'"

"Yes, Ethan. That's exactly what a normal person would have done."

He grinned a wicked grin. "We're anything but normal, you and I." Ethan drank down some more beer and sent a mischievous smile to a woman at another table who smiled at him. "We both know it would have to be something grand to get your attention. I wasn't expecting a thank-you, but a little gratitude would be nice."

"Gratitude? For what? Killing my friends?"

He laughed. "Friends? Mayor Yang and Roger were your friends, huh? I went back and looked at the video from the attack in court that day. You know what I saw?"

Solomon's guts turned to ice. All the courtrooms in that building were equipped with sound and video, and court proceedings, unless changed by some policy or court ruling, were available to the public . . . but he had never gone back and watched the video of his attack. Never even thought to.

Ethan leaned closer and said in a softer voice, "I saw a killer. A lawyer that knew his client was going down and told him to do something crazy. And then you get stabbed. You think that man was your friend?"

"He couldn't have known his client would attack me."

"Maybe. He at least could've shouted, there was enough time. He just sat there . . . interesting. Roger's the same. How many times did he try to get you fired or would write up infractions against you, or try to get you arrested? At least a dozen from what I saw."

"Those records are work product of the DA's office. How'd you see those?"

"Oh, I have ways. Not sure if you've ever tried to look up anything about me, but I was a cop. When I turned eighteen, I ran out of that institution as fast as I could and into the arms of Uncle Sam. USMC, oorah!" He took a sip of beer. "Joined the MPs and did my time, and then bounced around from department to department. Police work is really the most exciting type of work, don't you agree? Living in the underbelly of the city you're supposed to protect . . . there's something kinda romantic about it."

"So, you left police work and decided deranged serial killer was a nice profession to go into?"

He laughed. "They weren't the first to die."

"Who was? Our mother?"

He lowered his beer and held Solomon's gaze.

"I'll ask you again," Solomon said, his voice stern. "What do you want?"

Ethan sighed. "We're not just bonded by blood, you know. You don't go through the types of childhoods like we went through and not develop some . . . let's call them traits."

Solomon ignored his comments. "Dennis Yang had two children. Did you know that? His daughter's pregnant with her first child, his first grandchild. You took that from both of them."

"Who gives a shit?" he said with a wave of his hand.

"I give a shit," Solomon said angrily.

Ethan clicked his tongue against the roof of his mouth. "That is a shame. I really had hoped you would appreciate the artistry of it."

"That's not art. It's just chaos."

He nodded with a smile. "Order and chaos. You still remember Dad's little lectures, huh? I mean, when he wasn't drunk and beating the shit outta us. You really did dodge a bullet by being Mom's favorite. She would at least try to protect you from him, but not me. He had to beat somebody, and I was always there. She never protected me."

"Do you know what it must've been like to raise you? You were doing nothing but hurting other kids and animals, stealing, starting fires . . . that woman did everything she could for you."

Anger burst out of Ethan, and his eyes darkened again. "She didn't do shit!"

It lasted only a moment but didn't fade away like other people's anger. It was like he chose to stop feeling it, and instantly the anger went away. His ability to suddenly gain control was as scary as his ability to instantly lose it.

"Did you ever wonder why she hated me?"

Solomon opened his mouth to defend his mother, but the look in Ethan's eyes told him that any words in her defense would fall on deaf ears. The truth was that his mother had done everything she could for Ethan. Solomon could still hear his mother's sobs as she cried herself to sleep at night, knowing that Ethan had been arrested again, or when someone's pet disappeared and the neighbors came over to accuse her, or when a store was burglarized and the police showed up at their door to question Ethan.

Solomon had watched as it slowly wore down his mother until she could barely get out of bed.

"I," Ethan said, "was not our father's child. Did you ever figure that out?"

Solomon hesitated.

"Oh, so you did know."

"Not at the time. When I became a prosecutor, I had certain resources, and I used them to look into their lives. You were adopted."

"Not just adopted, I was the product of our mother's inability to keep her panties on. I think my father was just a one-night stand for her. I sometimes wonder what he was like. Probably a piece of garbage, like her. Maybe that's why our dear old dad hated me so much. I was a constant reminder of her betrayal."

Solomon felt his lip curl slightly and quickly smoothed it, but Ethan leaned forward, his eyes open, taking in everything, and he observed the reaction and smiled.

"Don't like to hear that, Sally?"

Solomon felt his body tense up as the name Sally reached his ears, sending a sharp jolt of fear and anger through him. It was a name that had been used to torment and humiliate him in his youth, and hearing it now made him feel small and vulnerable, like a scared child all over again.

His jaw muscles clenched, and Ethan chuckled. "See? I knew that was in there somewhere." He took a sip of beer but without taking his eyes off Solomon. "What else did you learn? Anything about who my father was?"

He shook his head. "There's no information on him. I did learn that my father was a professor of literature in the '70s."

He laughed. "I always thought he was just an unemployed bum. But he was smart, I'll give him that." He glanced at the waitress who brought a fresh beer and Solomon's water. "Did you ever try to find me?"

Solomon shook his head. "No."

"Why not?"

"By the time I had the ability to find you, I'd done a lot of healing. I couldn't go back there. Not to any of the places or the people."

Ethan kept his eyes down and then looked up when he said, "Did you read about what happened to me after?"

Solomon nodded. "Lakeview."

"Not just Lakeview, it's called the Sanctuary at Lakeview. You gotta get the full name, because none of the staff called it Lakeview. They called it the Sanctuary to convince us that it was someplace safe. What do you think, Solomon? What do you think happens to a strapping young man of fourteen in a psychiatric facility filled with boys that stick bunnies in microwaves and stab their parents?"

"That wasn't my fault."

"No, it wasn't. It was our mother's fault. She didn't care enough to list a single family member or friend we could've gone to if anything happened to both of them."

"You wanna blame them, fine. But I remember things differently, Ethan. Our parents went bankrupt trying to help you. They ruined their marriage, their health, and finally they both lost their minds. One to alcohol and the other to—"

"Suicide? Or murder?"

"I was going to say to madness. That woman broke mentally and physically trying to save you."

Calmly, as though pointing out something obvious, he said, "That woman died how she deserved."

"How is that? With you cutting her femoral arteries and convincing everyone it was suicide?"

"Believe whatever you want, Solomon," he said, glancing at a woman's butt as she walked by, "but I didn't come here to play the blame game. I came because you're the only family I got left, and I'm the only family you got left."

"You murdered two innocent men."

"Don't you have a soul, Solomon? Can you truly not appreciate the beauty of it? I dedicated two men's lives, two men that had harmed you, to you. I paid homage to our mother, who is the reason we're both where we are. Me, a wandering nomad jumping in and out of psychiatric facilities my whole life, and you locked away like a hermit in some cave you inherited. To be honest, I kinda hoped you swindled her out of the house. It would've at least made you more interesting."

"Interesting?"

"That's all life is, little brother. Interesting and uninteresting."

Solomon leaned forward, his voice softening. "Do you see what you're doing? Interesting and uninteresting. That's trauma talking. Black-and-white thinking. That's not life."

"Trauma . . . do you really know trauma, Solomon? Hmm? You went into foster care, where at least you had someone from Social Services coming and checking up on you. You know who I had? I had the Fridge."

"The Fridge?"

He nodded. "He was one of the orderlies at Lakeview. The most senior one. They called him Fridge because he was a square giant. Shoulders like four feet across, big poofy hair . . . sometimes he would wear fancy coats with scarves, trying to look like a mob boss. He was always quoting Mafia movies. Thought he was a real tough guy. He used to make us hold up buckets of water as a punishment, one in each hand held out horizontally. Whoever dropped their arms first went into the hole. It wasn't really a hole, of course, it was a closet. A little space the Fridge had made to keep troublemakers in line."

Ethan zoned out, his eyes glazing over as he went back to someplace else. "I can't tell you how many days I would spend in the dark in that little closet. I froze the first time I was there and wet my pants." He let out a breath. "How sad that must've been. A little boy shaking in the dark with piss running down his leg."

Solomon swallowed. "What did you do to Fridge?"

Ethan's eyes came up and met his. "When I was out, I waited a bit, and then I got the sharpest box cutter I could find, snuck into his house while he was sleeping . . . and slit his throat. Solomon," he said, shaking his head as though a shot of pleasure had gone through him, "he opened his eyes and looked at me before he died. He knew it was me that did that to him . . . and it was the greatest feeling in my life."

"You have to see what that means that the best moment of your life has been slitting a sleeping man's throat. You're sick, Ethan. It's a type of sickness they can't treat, but they can put you someplace where the symptoms won't dominate your life."

"Someplace like Lakeview?"

Solomon had nothing to say to that. His mind was a mess of swirling thoughts and buried emotions. Why was he trying to save this man? Scouring his memory, he wasn't able to come up with a single instance where Ethan was kind to him or showed compassion. Of his many tormentors, Ethan was one of the worst.

"They had a library in Lakeview. It was where I spent most of my time. You know my favorite book they had there? *Civilization and Its Discontents*, by Freud. I think we abandoned Freud a little too quickly, don't you?" He motioned to the waitress for another beer. "The point of the book is that civilization is necessary to control humanity's darker impulses, like murder, but by controlling them, we create unhappiness in ourselves with the restrictions. We're animals with invisible chains on us wherever we go." He leaned in close, a glint in his eyes. "But we don't have to be, Solomon. We can break free. Murder frees us from the confines of civilization, from the misery of discontent."

"I didn't come here to debate civilization."

"What did you come here for then?"

"I came here to ask you to turn yourself in," Solomon said. "You killed the district attorney. There's going to be a lot of cops with itchy trigger fingers. They'll be looking for an excuse to pull those triggers. If you turn yourself in, we can save your life."

He sat back and sighed. "I've been down this road before. Many times before. The problem is that I'm not legally competent to stand trial, so they can only hold me in a hospital. And though I'm maybe not legally competent, I am cognizant enough to be able to tell that I'm not legally competent. It's an odd little section of the law, don't you think?"

"The law's inadequately equipped to handle mental health issues."

"I agree completely. It's terrible at dealing with mental health. Which is funny because as far as my experience goes, everyone's insane. Maybe the ones outside the institutions can just hide it a little better."

Solomon swallowed and looked down to his glass of water. "You took two lives just to get my attention. You have to realize how sick you are."

"I do. But here's the thing, I don't care." He held out his arms. "I'm happy."

"Nobody who's happy kills for fun."

He looked around at some of the women nearby. "This isn't exactly how I wanted our family reunion to play out."

"What did you expect? Barbecues and baseball games?"

"Would it be so bad to have someone to do those things with?"

"No. But not if that person kills two innocent men—"

"There's that word again. Innocent. In the words of Inigo Montoya, I do not think that means what you think it means."

"Okay, not innocent. Dennis and Roger were two horrible people, who under normal circumstances it would take a lot for me to feel any sadness over. But to think they died because you thought it'd be fun to mess with me makes me feel sick, Ethan. It's not a tribute to me. You hated me. I saw nothing but cruelty from you. You killed those men because you knew it would terrify me, and because it would be fun."

He chuckled, but there was no joy in it. "You really were the smartest of the two of us, weren't you? I mean, your dad would always tell me that, but our mom never did, so it was hard for me to tell if it was true. But here you are, two master's degrees and a doctorate in law. To come from the background we came from and achieve that, Solomon, is truly amazing. You should be proud." He finished his fresh bottle of beer in a few gulps and then belched.

"Let's go. I have something to show you. You're gonna like it."

"Somehow I doubt that."

49

Solomon felt suffocated by the city as he sat in the car's passenger seat. Despite rolling down the windows and letting the frigid wind hit his face, he still couldn't shake the sensation that he was trapped in a shrinking box.

They had been on the freeway for over an hour, and the only thing that broke the silence was the occasional pebble flying up and hitting the car.

"How about some music?" Ethan said. "What are you into?"

"You wouldn't like it."

Ethan glanced at him. "It doesn't have to be this way between us, you know. I actually did come here to offer you something."

"What?"

"A choice. See, I'm free, Solomon. The world is my oyster. Whatever the hell that means. But I've connected with myself, with who I am and where I came from, and by doing that, I freed myself. But I couldn't do it by myself, I had to have someone show me. He was another inmate at Lakeview. An older boy who knew more about the world, I swear, than any ten men I've ever met. Pain can do that, can't it? People who grow up without any pain are helpless in the world."

"Is that what you think you do? Deliver pain to better the world?"

"No. I mean, granted, most of the people I've killed in my life deserved it, like your dear mayor and district attorney, or Fridge, so in a way, yes, I am making the world a better place. But that's not why I do it." He held up a finger. "And I think you know that. I think you know exactly why I do it because you have it inside you, too, don't you? I mean, not enough to go out and kill, I suppose, but it's in there. Isn't it?"

"We all have a shadow."

"Yeah, but most people's shadows don't tell them to kill and have the person follow through. It's more than a fragment of our psyche, it's who we are."

Solomon felt nauseated hearing him talk but had to keep him occupied. It was clear he wasn't going to turn himself in—there was too much damage done throughout his life—but maybe Solomon could still save his life if he could get Billie out here first, before tactical or trigger-happy deputies.

He had purposely avoided the subject of Mazie as much as possible, hoping to make his brother more comfortable first.

"Where's Mazie, Ethan?"

He grinned. "Why? You banging her?"

"Ethan," he said softly, "please. Where is she?"

His jaw muscles clenched and unclenched. "I can't wait for you to see what I have planned. Really. I think you're just going to love it."

As Ethan continued to ramble on for another hour, Solomon felt relief when they finally arrived at the top of a hill with a stunning view overlooking the Salt Lake Valley. In the distance, a lone figure, a young woman, made her way up the well-lit hillside of a nearby cemetery, capturing Solomon's attention.

Beside the cemetery, a striking old building caught his eye. It appeared to be a hospital from the 1950s or '60s, likely a place where affluent families would send their children or siblings who suffered from unidentified disorders. Solomon knew it was more of a way for families to hide their perceived shame than for any true therapeutic reasons.

A wrought iron sign with the words "The Sanctuary at Lakeview" hung above the entrance to the property.

Ethan drove into the front lot and parked. The headlights lit up the worn-down facade of the hospital.

The building had once been white but faded to a urine-colored dull yellow. Some pillars were on the front porch, but they were chipped and nearly paintless now. Most of the windows were removed, and the ones that hadn't been were broken out.

Nature had begun to overtake the building with ivy, moss, and ferns growing over the walls. Solomon had read once that if humanity were to suddenly disappear, either by disease or nuclear self-destruction, those would be the three plants that would most thrive in an urban environment without people.

Solomon had dreams for weeks afterward of entire cities littered with skeletons, plants intertwining between the sun-bleached bones.

"Tears on a river," Ethan said.

"What?"

"Something Fridge used to say whenever somebody cried when he was inflicting one of his punishments. Tears on a river. I hadn't thought about that in twenty years before today."

"Ethan, whatever you think's going to happen in there, it won't go down like you think. Listen to me, please . . . you are sick. This is all in your head. It's your trauma response and your mental illness convincing you this is a rational course of behavior. It is not."

"Do you ever get sick of listening to yourself talk?"

Solomon held his gaze, but there was nothing there. They were like a doll's eyes, black and glossy.

"I'm not moving until I know Mazie is safe."

"Really? So you'll just sit in the car all night? I don't think so. This night has been years in the making, Sally. You want to see what I have planned for you as much as I do."

"What you have planned for the little brother you think snitched you to the cops and got you locked up in this place? I think I'd like to skip that part."

He laughed. "I learned a long time ago that grudges are a waste of energy. It's all energy, Sally. And you only got a finite amount, so you gotta be careful what you spend it on. I don't hate you for what you did. In fact, this night, believe it or not, is for you."

Solomon wanted to explain to him the difference between illusion and reality, and how it was almost impossible to tell the difference. That ever since Solomon could remember, Ethan had been hearing things that weren't there, misinterpreting social situations and responding with violence, even sometimes claiming to see people no one else saw. If someone had gotten to him young, maybe a difference could've been made, but not anymore.

He got out of the car.

"See," Ethan said, "you can be reasonable when you want to be. I am really excited for this, Sally. It's really gonna be something."

Solomon trailed behind Ethan as they pushed open the massive double doors and stepped inside the atrium of the asylum. The scene before them was one of complete chaos, with discarded papers and debris all over the floor. The remaining pieces of furniture were in shambles, either broken down or rusted, and covered in a thick layer of dust that had accumulated over time.

As Solomon took a deep breath, he was hit by the overpowering stench of damp earth, giving the impression that the place had been untouched for decades.

"What are we doing here?" Solomon said.

"It's no fun to ruin a surprise."

After a few moments, Solomon cautiously pulled out his phone, quickly typed out a text message to Billie to let her know where they were, and then just as quickly slipped the phone back into his pocket.

As Solomon turned the corner, a reception desk came into view, adorned with a thick transparent plastic barrier that had small openings at the bottom for passing items back and forth. On the other side of the wall, a colossal rusted steel door loomed, its intimidating presence taking over the room.

Ethan stepped forward and placed his palm gently on the cold metal surface, his mind seemingly lost in thought and memory as he ran his fingers over the rusted steel before pulling away and grabbing the door handle to open it.

"Memory lane?" Solomon said.

"Yeah, and not the good kind. This door represented freedom to everybody here. If you could get out of this door, you had a real chance to get away."

He inhaled through his nose and opened the door. "After you."

As they ventured farther into the building, the hallway stretched out before them, seeming to extend infinitely into the depths of the asylum. The few windows that were present offered little to no light, leaving Solomon to rely on his cane to avoid tripping on any unseen obstacles.

Ethan was manic. He was skipping and kicked a box, shouted just to hear his echo. It was as if the outside world didn't exist to him, the circumstances didn't matter.

"This isn't good for you, Ethan. Your mind's not ready to process this kind of trauma from being here. You have to ease into it over time."

"Oh, I've already been here once today. Didn't I tell you? Yeah, I already took the tour, defecated on the Fridge's desk, and took a little nap in my old cell. They didn't call them cells, but that's what they were." He held out his arms. "You're looking at my childhood, Solomon."

"This wasn't your childhood. This was the place you went after your childhood. Your childhood before this was—"

"Whatever psychobabble you're about to say, don't. I've heard it all. Psychiatrists, counselors, neurologists, behavioral experts, you name it, I've been through it. This place was nothing if not thorough."

"You made it sound like nobody in this place gave a crap about you. Sounds like a lot of people did."

It was the first time he saw a look of . . . not quite surprise but more like hesitation on Ethan's face. A thought had made a connection that he didn't want, and Solomon could almost see his mind begin to shut down the thinking process of where it would lead.

"Ethan, do you know why I just made you uncomfortable? Because your mind was about to have a realization that your body already knows. This place wasn't out to get you. Nobody was. These people were here to help you." He took a step toward him so they were closer. "There is a disorder called depersonalization-derealization disorder. People that suffer from it are completely detached from their surroundings. It's like the real world isn't real and that things that are happening are not really happening."

He took another step toward him. Ethan was staring wide eyed, unmoving, unblinking.

"You feel like you're observing all this in a dream, don't you? Like none of it is real."

"How do you know?"

Solomon hesitated. "Because I have it too."

Ethan's brow furrowed a moment, but only a moment. Then it softened, and he smiled and pointed his finger playfully and said, "You're trying to stall me because you texted someone back there, didn't you? Well, it's not gonna help, Sally. Because I'm pretty sure the person you texted isn't coming."

He opened a door to his right and said, "Because she's already here."

Solomon's heart sank as he rushed toward the door and peered inside. The sight before him made his blood run cold. Billie was tied to a metal gurney with straps securing her ankles and wrists, rendering her completely immobile. Next to her, Mazie lay in a similar position, bound by the same restraints, her clothes dirty and bloodstained from a wound on her head that had since dried.

The only source of light in the room was a lamp lying on the floor between them, casting a haunting glow. The corners of the room remained cloaked in darkness.

Mazie was struggling and trying to scream against the duct tape over her mouth, but Billie looked unconscious.

"What is this?" Solomon said breathless.

"This," he said with his arms out, "is your birth. The real me was born here, right in my cell. This is the place that made me. With beatings and torture, it created who I am. So I figured where better for you to be born into this life with me than here?"

"Born with you?"

"Mm-hmm. We're all we got left. Neither one of us are going to have kids, so the Shepard line dies with us. So hell, if our genetic lineage is about to be extinguished, let's go out with a bang." He put his hands on Solomon's shoulders. "I've studied your life. You might as well already be dead. You sit in that giant house, protected by fences and guns, thinking you can keep the world away. But the world never stays away, Solomon. It'll creep back in. So don't fight it. Come with me. We'll travel around the world doing whatever we want. No restrictions, no slave morality of the masses to hold us back. No discontent. True freedom."

The thought wasn't unpleasant. Solomon pictured long drinking sessions in bars in Madrid and gondola tours in Venice. Away from a dark, empty house. Away from everyone who wanted to hurt or use him. But then he looked at Billie and knew that Ethan saw something in his expression.

Ethan's next words cut through Solomon like a knife, seemingly reading his thoughts with unerring accuracy.

"She used you," he said, his voice heavy with accusation. "The first time she came to you, she knew exactly what it would do to you. And she knew it this time, too, but she still came to you, didn't she?"

Solomon felt a surge of anger, but he couldn't deny it was true. Billie should have known the emotional toll her actions would take on him. She should have understood that he wasn't psychologically prepared to handle investigating crimes anymore.

Solomon looked at her on the metal gurney. Her face was mostly hidden in shadow, but she looked peaceful. Her brow wasn't furrowed in concentration, no muscles were contracted, her posture wasn't perfect. It was only seeing her like this that he realized how intense a mask she had to put on just to survive in the environment she was in.

Solomon shook his head. "Let them go."

Ethan leaned against the door and folded his arms. "No. But I will make you a deal. You kill one of them, and I'll let the other one live. Then we fly to Brazil tonight and spend the next year in a haze of drugs and booze."

Solomon, the fear and rage inside of him barely letting him move, touched Ethan's arm to make sure his attention was focused solely on him, and spoke calmly as he said, "I know this feels like a show to you, but it's real, Ethan. You're about to murder real people. You're not watching this from somewhere else. You are right here, and you're the one doing this."

Ethan looked confused a moment, but the moment passed.

In a quick movement, he picked up a thick knife that was lying next to Billie's leg on the gurney. Solomon felt an icy fear slither its way up his spine. But Ethan flipped the knife over, holding the blade, and held it out for Solomon.

"Actually, you're the one doing this. So choose."

"No."

"You have to. If you don't," he said as he pulled out a handgun from his waistband, "I'm going to shoot both of them in the face."

"Ethan—"

"No!" he shouted. "No more talking. Choose."

Solomon's gaze fell onto the knife, taking note of the blood that had crusted into a small crevice between the handle and the blade. Tentatively, he reached up and grasped the handle, feeling the smooth wood in his palm. The knife was heavy.

Ethan had a smile of anticipation that faded when Solomon lowered the knife.

"I'm not going to kill them, Ethan. No matter what you say or do."

"Then I'll do it," he said, lifting the firearm and pointing it at Billie.

"Don't, Ethan. Not her."

"The other one, then?"

Solomon watched him, the glee in his eyes. The pleasure he got from this was immeasurable. Solomon pictured him lying in this cell, daydreaming about what this reunion would be like. In truth, Solomon hadn't thought much about his brother for thirty years. He'd convinced himself that cutting out Ethan was intentional, but as memories now flooded back, he questioned if his brain had just locked them away.

Knife in hand and leaning on his cane, Solomon approached the bound women on the gurneys. He stopped at Mazie, her wide, tear-streaked eyes reflecting terror. Her muffled screams, restrained by duct tape, filled the air with haunting echoes. Despite her bindings, she thrashed in raw desperation.

Solomon looked over at Billie, and the thought of her dying filled him with a sadness so deep it felt like it would cause him to pass out. Then he looked back at Mazie.

Solomon's grip on the blade was viselike, his fingers so tightly wound around the hilt that they were turning white. He could see the glint of the blade in the dim light of the lamp, casting a sinister shadow across the room.

"Do it," Ethan said, coming up behind him and whispering in his ear. "It will free you. You were covered in blood the first time you were born and will be covered in it again. Birth is a violent, destructive process. For one thing to live, another has to die. You want your freedom, you want to break the chains that civilization has put on you, all you have to do is thrust down with that knife and you'll have it. One movement, one second, and your life will change forever."

Solomon's hand began to shake. "I can't do it."

"Yes, you can. It's inside of you, it always has been."

The knife lowered a few inches, its sharp edge glinting, but Solomon's hand was trembling so badly that his arm seemed to be unresponsive. His fingers, which were still clenching the knife's hilt, were shaking with such intensity that the blade itself began to wobble in his grip.

Ethan gingerly placed the gun on the gurney, its cold metal clanging against the hard surface, as he approached Solomon. With a tender touch, he placed his hand over Solomon's trembling fist, as if trying to soothe the fear that had taken hold of him. The contrast between the two hands was striking—Ethan's was steady and warm, while Solomon's was cold and trembling. The touch had a calming effect on Solomon, as his hand gradually stopped shaking, and his arm relaxed under Ethan's reassuring grip. The two men remained locked in that position for a few moments.

"We can do it together. Are you ready?"

Solomon swallowed. "Yes."

Solomon drew in a deep breath, his chest expanding as he filled his lungs with air. With a nod of understanding from Ethan, the two men gathered their strength and slowly began to push the knife downward, the blade slicing through the air with a chilling whisper.

With a sudden surge, Solomon swung the knife back with all his strength, his arm guided by Ethan's unsuspecting grip on the hilt. The blade sliced through the air with a wicked hiss before plunging deep into Ethan's thigh, eliciting a bloodcurdling scream.

As Ethan writhed in agony, Solomon let go of the knife and snatched up the gun, his mind already racing with his next move. But before he could even raise the weapon, Ethan was on him with a fierce rage.

Ethan was wiry and strong, and he hurled Solomon back into the wall with so much force that the thump could probably be heard outside.

Solomon clung onto Ethan's shirt with one hand and the gun with the other, the fabric of the shirt tearing, revealing a massive tattoo of a skull on his chest. The intricate design seemed to pulse with an eerie life of its own, as if it were alive and writhing under the dim light.

Solomon's breath got knocked out of him in a wheeze of pain. But even as he gasped for air, his fingers never left the grip of the gun, his knuckles white with the effort. With a cold calculation, he raised the weapon, the barrel trained on Ethan's head.

Ethan snarled and lunged at Solomon. The two men grappled, their muscles straining. They fought with a ferocity that seemed to transcend reason, with every movement a blur of motion and violence.

The two men finally broke apart, their bodies heaving with exhaustion. Ethan stumbled back a few steps, his movements labored and uneven as blood continued to gush from the wound in his thigh.

Despite the pain, Ethan's eyes still glinted with a violent determination, his gaze locked onto Solomon's.

The silence was broken only by the sound of ragged breathing and the rhythmic drip of blood hitting the floor. For a moment, it seemed as if time had stood still, as if the entire world had frozen.

"Just put the gun away, Sally. You're not going to kill me."

"I wouldn't kill you," he said, looking down at the gun, "but you killed my mom."

As Solomon lifted the gun, Ethan's eyes widened with fear, and he jolted forward in a desperate attempt to disarm him. The two men grappled for control of the weapon, their fingers knotted around the cold metal. Ethan slammed him like a linebacker, sending the gun flying from his hand.

The impact was bone jarring, and Solomon felt the breath leave his body in a whoosh of pain. He struggled to regain his footing, but Ethan was relentless, pinning him to the wall with a force that seemed almost superhuman. With a snarl of fury, he swung a hook at Solomon's face, the blow connecting with a sickening thud. For a moment, Solomon's vision blurred, and his body went limp, almost collapsing to the ground. But through sheer force of will, he managed to stay on his feet, swaying unsteadily as he fought to remain conscious.

Ethan was in a boxing stance but eased up when he saw the blood dribbling out of Solomon's mouth.

"It doesn't need to be this way," he said, breathing heavily. "There is no one on this planet that you can be more open with than me. You can be yourself. No one will connect with you like I can. We're exactly the same, Solomon. Going through this world alone and thinking we're the crazy ones. We're not. *They* are. The ones driving to jobs they hate in their tin coffins and thinking that's life. It's not life. You know that, because you're just like me."

"He's nothing like you."

Ethan turned, only to meet the full force of Billie's swing as she slammed the metal filing cabinet drawer into his face. Dazed and disoriented, Ethan staggered back, his world spinning as his senses reeled from the crushing impact.

Solomon quickly grabbed his brother by the neck and pulled him close to his own body. He locked his grip around Ethan's throat.

Billie darted across the room, her eyes on the gun as she picked it up off the floor. Blood dripped down her wrists, leaving a trail of crimson behind her, and Solomon wondered if she had resorted to self-mutilation to escape her binds.

The room was silent except for the sound of their labored breathing.

"You gonna let her kill me, Sally?" he gasped with Solomon's arm around his throat.

With her chest heaving and sweat beading on her forehead, Billie stood there, panting as she held the gun steady, pointed right at Ethan's head. Every muscle in her body was taut with tension, and she looked disoriented.

Suddenly, she took a few quick steps back and ripped the binds off Mazie's wrists and mouth. As Mazie sat up, gasping for breath and clawing at the tight bindings on her ankles, she let out a wild scream.

"Get them off me! Get them off me!" she shouted, her voice rising to a fever pitch as she struggled to free herself from the restraints.

With a viselike grip around his brother's throat, Solomon felt a sudden, violent movement. He struggled to maintain his hold as his brother's hand darted toward his mouth, and a look of horror crossed his face as he realized what was happening.

His brother was swallowing a pill.

In a moment of panic, Solomon tried to pry his brother's jaws open, to force the pill out of his mouth, but it was too late.

"He swallowed something!"

Ethan's body went limp in his arms and Solomon struggled to hold on to him.

Ethan's eyes were wide, bloodshot, and wet. The foam was increasing now, bubbling as whatever poison he'd just swallowed worked its way through his system.

"No," Solomon said, "Ethan, no!"

With shaking hands, he reached into Ethan's mouth, fingers clawing at whatever remnants of the poison he could find.

But it was too late. The pill had already done its work, and Ethan was slipping away from him, the light of consciousness fading from his eyes. With a shuddering gasp, Ethan lapsed into a deep, wracking unconsciousness, his body writhing and thrashing in a last, futile attempt to fight off the effects of the poison.

Solomon could only stand by helplessly, watching as his brother's body continued to convulse and spasm. His fingers were coated in a slick, sticky film of foam and saliva, the remnants of Ethan's final struggle for life.

Solomon's gaze flicked up toward Billie and Mazie, who were already making their way toward the door, but he couldn't move. Couldn't even breathe.

He just held his brother.

50

Solomon sat outside the Lakeview building, his body tense and his mind reeling as he recounted the events of the past few hours to Detective Parsons. The world around him seemed to spin in a dizzying haze, his thoughts consumed by the feeling of his brother in his arms, slowly dying.

The entire sheriff's office had descended upon the scene, their presence lending an air of urgency and tension to the already fraught situation. Solomon could feel their eyes on him, could sense the unspoken questions and accusations.

As he spoke, his words falling out in a jumbled, disjointed rush, he wanted nothing more than to leave.

"Where's my brother?"

"They're taking him to the University Hospital."

Solomon nodded. Parsons waited there a moment, thinking of something to say, and finally he touched Solomon's shoulder and said, "I'm sorry."

Solomon watched him leave and was glad he was gone. Not that he was a bad guy, but because Solomon couldn't tell what he was saying or doing right now. It felt like he was floating, drifting, not even making new memories. As he was telling Parsons what happened, he was shocked that bits of his memory were already gone. He was dissociated to the point that he could barely speak.

Through the haze of grief and confusion, Solomon's eyes fell on Billie, who stood there with a fierce determination, commanding the attention of the people around her. He watched as she barked out orders, her eyes blazing with intensity, her wrists bound in tight, blood-stained bandages.

As several men approached her, their faces marked with concern, Solomon could see that Billie wasn't processing what had just happened to her. She was lost in her own world, driven by a need to control the chaos that surrounded her.

Solomon made his way over to her, using his cane to support himself as he approached.

"I need you to get me out of here, Billie."

She stared at him, and he could see the conflict within her.

"I know you want to stay and run things, but that's only because if you don't, you're going to have to feel everything you just went through. I'm sorry, but it's going to happen anyway." He leaned in closer so the paramedics, who were standing by waiting for the sheriff to come to her senses and let them fully check her out, wouldn't hear what he said.

"I'm about to lose it, Billie. Please."

She swallowed and then looked to Dobbs, the assistant sheriff, who was standing by in jeans and a sweatshirt, and said, "Tom, take over, please. I'll be at the hospital."

She took Solomon's arm and led him away from everything.

As they climbed into the truck, the silence between them was deep, heavy with the weight of everything they'd just gone through. Billie sat in stony silence, her eyes fixed firmly on the road ahead, her breathing deep and measured. But Solomon was different. His breath came in shallow gasps, and he felt . . . nothing.

They drove in silence a long time, and then suddenly, Billie spoke.

"It was cyanide," she said, her voice barely above a whisper. "He had it sewn into his jacket."

Solomon nodded, his gaze fixed on the road ahead. He had suspected as much, but hearing the words spoken aloud only served to deepen the despair he was feeling.

"Are you all right?" she asked, her eyes fixed on him.

Solomon looked at her, his face etched with pain. "Super," he replied.

They both knew there was nothing to laugh about, nothing to find humor in. The events of the day had left them both raw and wounded.

As they drove on, the canyons slowly gave way to a bleak and desolate wasteland, a tundra of dust, salt, and volcanic rocks that stretched out in every direction. It was an ancient landscape, a place where the earth seemed to have been torn apart by the struggles of countless species throughout the ages.

Solomon imagined the terrible battles that must have taken place here, the countless fights for survival that had raged across ages.

"He killed Dax," she said flatly.

Solomon looked at her. "What?"

"He killed Dax," Billie repeated, her voice hollow and lifeless.

Billie's eyes had glossed over; she was barely there, too.

"Pull over," he said quietly, his voice scarcely carrying over the hum of the engine.

As they came to a stop, Solomon rolled down his window, taking in the scent of sage and watching the sand kicking up in front of the headlights.

"How?" Solomon said.

"He was probably there in my house waiting for me, and Ethan found him before I did." She hesitated a moment. "His protective order was denied."

Solomon had to take a couple of breaths before he could speak. "How do you feel about it?"

She swallowed. "I don't know how I feel right now. Just . . . empty." She looked at him. "Were you really going to shoot him?"

315

He shook his head. "I don't know."

He rubbed his lip, which had been cut during the struggle. "I didn't know it at the time, but he showed signs of his disorder early on. He had the luck of being both a sociopath and having a disorder that didn't allow him to see reality as real. If nothing's real, other people's suffering isn't real."

She was silent a moment. "That sounds like justification."

"It's not. It's understanding."

"No one can understand men like him."

Solomon softly tapped his cane on the floor of the truck. "They can if they have the same disorder."

Billie waited a beat, and then took Solomon's hand in hers, her fingers clasping tightly around his.

The two of them sat in silence, watching as the desert landscape stretched out before them, the snow-capped dunes rippling and shifting in the soft breeze. The air was still thick with the scent of sage, and the moon cast a pale glow over everything, illuminating the landscape with an otherworldly light.

51

Solomon made his way down the hospital hallway, the sound of his cane echoing loudly against the cold linoleum floors. His visit to the University Hospital in Salt Lake City had been granted by Billie and the interim DA, after four days of pleading and negotiation. He was now standing outside his brother's room, waiting to be let in.

Solomon was met by one of Billie's deputies, who opened the door for him after checking his ID. The room was small, with only a single bed and a window on the far wall that allowed the afternoon sun to pour in, casting an orange hue across the room. Ethan lay on the bed, hooked up to various machines and monitors, but his breathing was steady, a sign that he no longer needed help to breathe.

Solomon took a seat in the recliner in the corner of the room and watched his brother closely. Ethan's face looked so different from what Solomon remembered of him from their youth. Every scratch and scar an emblem of a life lived, a life that had taken its toll on Ethan.

"I wondered for a long time if it was true," Solomon began, speaking to his unconscious brother. "If you really did kill her. I believed it, but . . . I'm not so sure now. Maybe you were just a screwed-up kid who never had a chance, or maybe you were wicked from the moment you were born. I don't know. I don't know what the truth is. But if I was wrong, if you really didn't hurt her, then I am so sorry. More sorry than you can ever imagine. All we had was each other, and I completely abandoned you."

He hesitated.

"But if I was right, and you did kill her, then you belong here . . ."

Solomon trailed off, running his hands through his hair in frustration. He had no idea what he was expecting from this visit.

Standing up from the chair, Solomon used his cane to make his way over to the bed. He stared down at Ethan's serene face for a few moments before tapping his cane on the floor twice and leaving the room.

52

As the sun beat down on her skin, Billie basked in its warmth. It had been a harsh winter, the kind that seemed to stretch on endlessly, the kind where every night was a battle to balance the need to save on bills with the need to stay warm.

But now, as the winter slowly gave way to spring, Billie could feel the weight of the season lifting from her shoulders. She breathed in the fresh air, reveling in the scent of new growth and life that was beginning to stir all around her.

The truck was filled with the sound of Johnny Cash's music. Billie sang along softly to the lyrics, her voice low and husky as she drove along the winding roads of Coalville County. Solomon just stared out the window.

It had been a long time since she had been out to this part of the state, and as she drove through the dense pine forests and looming mountains, she felt a sense of wonder at the natural beauty that surrounded her.

Despite its name, Coalville was anything but dark and bleak. The mountains rose up in lush green peaks, their snow-capped summits shimmering in the sun like giant vanilla ice cream cones. As a child, Billie had always thought of them that way, and even now, as an adult, the sight never failed to fill her with a sense of childlike wonder.

Her gaze went to Solomon, his face a mask of stoicism that belied the turmoil brewing beneath. His brother had been transferred to a long-term care facility, but the prognosis was bleak. The doctors had all but given up hope, and a decision loomed on the horizon—one that would require Solomon to make a choice that no one should ever have to make.

Her heart ached for him, knowing the weight of the burden he carried. She wanted to reach out, to comfort him in some way, but she knew that his pain was his alone to bear. The enormity of the situation weighed heavily on her, and she struggled to find the right words.

"I haven't been out here since I was a kid," Billie said.

"I've never been out here. Isn't that weird? People travel from all over the world to come to Park City, and I've lived in the state my entire life and never been here."

"People rarely do the tourist attractions in their own states."

As the truck rumbled down the road, a new song came on the radio, its beat pulsing through the speakers. Billie turned up the volume, the sound filling the cab of the truck and drowning out the noise of the road.

The melody was familiar, and as Billie listened to the words, a memory rose up within her, vivid and powerful. She remembered her father, long ago, coming to pick her up from school early one day. He had taken her out for snow cones, the two of them laughing and joking as they sat in the sunshine.

And then, as they drove home, this song had come on the radio. Her father had hummed along to the melody, his deep voice filling the car with a warmth and joy that Billie had carried with her ever since. As a child, it had been her favorite sound in the world, the sound of her father's voice.

When the song was over, she turned down the volume.

"I spoke with the interim DA. They've contacted the FBI and gotten Blackbird federal witness protection. He's going to be testifying against Bigfoot Tommy, Comanche, everybody. I don't think Tommy's going to get out as easily from this one."

Solomon nodded as he stared at the passing landscape.

"How's Mazie?" he finally said.

"She's doing well. I have her on the DUI squad doing patrol. She enjoys it. I'm surprised she stayed on, actually."

"She's got strength, she just doesn't know it."

"I agree. She was initially resistant to seeing the department counselor, but the reports I'm getting are good. She just needs to control that temper and she'll be a great cop."

"Like her mentor."

Billie grinned but said nothing.

As they drove along the winding road, the landscape suddenly shifted, revealing a charming building perched on a hilltop in the distance. The building was surrounded by lush greenery, the trees and bushes stretching up toward the sky in a riot of color and life.

The details of the building came into focus as they got closer. The architecture was elegant and refined, the white stone walls and red-tiled roof standing out against the deep blue of the sky. A series of steps led up to the entrance, flanked by colorful flower beds and manicured hedges.

When Billie pulled into the parking lot, she could see that the building was bustling with activity, the sound of laughter and conversation drifting out into the warm spring air.

Pleasant Valley was a haven for those struggling with mental health and substance abuse issues, a place of refuge and healing for some of the most high-profile individuals in the state. Celebrities and public figures would come here for respite, seeking the kind of world-class care and support that only a facility like this could provide. They had even briefly filmed a reality series here about celebrities in rehab.

Billie parked her car in front of the building, which resembled a luxurious resort. The elegant architecture and lush landscaping added to the ambience. The building had a restaurant and several boutique shops, like bookstores and coffee shops, that were all within easy walking distance.

"As far as loony bins go," Solomon said, "I could've done a lot worse."

"I hope you can keep that sense of humor with morning cardio kickboxing and nightly Pilates classes." Solomon gave her a quizzical look. "I may have seen your schedule."

"You are your father's daughter." He seemed to be hesitant about something and then took out a couple of tickets from his jacket pocket and held them out for her.

She took them and said, "What's this?"

"Two tickets I booked to Aruba. Gotta be honest, would never have guessed it's off the coast of Venezuela."

She smiled. "You got us tickets to Aruba?"

"Yeah, but for sixty days from now, when I get outta here. You hang on to 'em. It'll give me something to look forward to."

As she looked down at the tickets, she struggled to contain her emotions but managed to say, "I'm proud of you for doing this."

"Yeah . . . well, better go before they send out some goons to take me in. I'm already an hour late."

As he opened the door to leave, she reached out and grasped his hand, making him turn back toward her. She said, "I'll be here waiting for you when you get out."

He leaned in, placed a gentle kiss on her cheek, and replied, "I know."

After exiting the truck, he made his way into the building. Billie watched him go before turning her attention to the tickets in her hand. She carefully placed them in the glove box.

Suddenly, her attention was drawn to Solomon, who was speaking with the intake nurse. She couldn't hear what they were saying, but the nurse was laughing at something Solomon had said. Billie felt a wave of happiness as she watched them interact.

Taking one last look at the building where Solomon was, Billie pulled away, her mind buzzing with anticipation for sixty days from now, when she would get to see him again.

ABOUT THE AUTHOR

At the age of thirteen, when his best friend was interrogated by the police for over eight hours and confessed to a crime he didn't commit, Victor Methos knew he would one day become a lawyer. After graduating from law school at the University of Utah, Methos cut his teeth as a prosecutor for Salt Lake City before founding what would become the most successful criminal defense firm in Utah.

In ten years, Methos conducted more than one hundred trials. One particular case stuck with him, and it eventually became the basis for his first major bestseller, *The Neon Lawyer*. Since that time, Methos has focused his work on legal thrillers and mysteries, winning the Harper Lee Prize for *The Hallows* and an Edgar Award for Best Novel nomination for his title *A Gambler's Jury*. He currently splits his time between southern Utah and Las Vegas.